I O You Ranch

By Warren Dunlap

Bob

Enjoy the read. hope
to cross trails again

Vaya con Dios

W——

6-22-'17 "

Cover illustration by
Gary Gillum

www.chugwatercowboy.com
ISBN 978-0-692-38305-6

First Edition
2014

DEDICATION

To Gerald Anderson of Wallace and Sherman Counties, Kansas. His enjoyment of ranch life and cowboy life inspired many.

His words of encouragement spurred me to work diligently on this book. He always makes me feel as if I were a family member. I and others desire to spend more time with him, but God has other plans.

"H. B. arrived in Colorado to meet people that were great mentors and who became good friends. He learned about ranching, life and living. Most of all he learned who he was."
Gerald Anderson – cowboy, rodeo man, rancher

ACKNOWLEDGMENTS

I first want to give God the thanks for giving me the type of mind I have. When I was young, I was called a "day dreamer." What I realize now, it is those dreams, mixed with my experiences which allows me to write western stories.

I am humbled and thankful to RW Hampton, for his generosity in taking away from his busy schedule and time with his family to write a foreword to this book.

To Pastor Scott Hunt whose understanding of God's word and his ability to communicate it to others stimulated me to make this book more than just a western novel. He showed me how we are to be messengers for Jesus.

I want to thank RaNaye for patiently waiting while I worked on this book. Somehow I will make up all that lost time we could have spent together. I am in your debt.

I also want to thank Joan Smith and Dru Dunlap for their efforts and time spent in editing my ramblings. I know they both had better things to do with their time.

To my cowboy friends, Kevin Adams, Gerald Anderson, Gary Gillum, Juan Gonzales, Joe Mingus, Dale Painter, Jack Shivers and Gary Woods. They showed me, corrected me, encouraged me, accepted me and talked with me. I cherish their friendships and admire their abilities. I tip my hat with a big thank you to all my pards.

FOREWORD

Well, don't s'ppose it would do any good to say "Just take my word for it, it's great!" Didn't think so, and honestly this modern-day tale of the West deserves a whole heck of a lot more than that. The problem is Warren Dunlap's IO You Ranch is so durn good on so many levels it's hard to know just where to start.

So let's start here. Where would a person go to find a "read" that has such skillfully developed characters and a storyline that you become a willing participant in the story? No, not an outsider looking in. You become swept up in such a way that you lose all sense of time and space around you and the pages seem to turn themselves. As I "lived" IO You Ranch, Warren Dunlap's story seemed more real to me than the actual goin's on around me. And there in lies the magic.

When the four principals were bone tired, so was I. When they laughed, so did I. When they grieved, I was right there along with them! Now add to that a gritty accurate depiction of modern day ranch life with a built-in guide on basic cowboy skills. Then to top it off, stir in romance, intrigue, twists and turns, and a message that put a lump in this cowboy's throat and conviction in his heart! A big beautiful story as big and beautiful as the West we know and love.

Somehow Warren Dunlap delivers all this and more because as the reader you are drawn in and become part of the crew.

Are you with me now? I figured so. Now swing up, take a deep seat and ride with the IO outfit. If you're not moved by this powerful Western tale, then pardner, ya better check your pulse.

RW Hampton – cowboy singer/western entertainer, song writer, cowboy/rancher

FOREWORD

Author Warren Dunlap has a unique way of presenting a story. IO You Ranch is a blend of cowboy culture, descriptive details about ranching and old west life, along with well-developed characters. Having grown up in the West myself, and hiking, hunting, and exploring many of the areas described in the book, I was drawn into this story of living out among the animals, breathing crisp fresh air, and looking up into the vast starlit sky. The characters give us a glimpse of what life looks like when lived far from the cities. As well as showing how different people deal with the situations they find themselves in while living in remote places. As with all good stories, we might find ourselves reflecting on how we would or should deal with similar situations. And much like real life, this story is sometimes slow and methodical, other times fast paced and exciting, still other times we are challenged to ponder some of the deeper truths that all of us must face at some point. Not only did I learn more than a few things about cowboys and ranching, I was encouraged to examine my own life. Slow down – simplify – pay attention to the details. These are things I found myself thinking. Dunlap is an honest, straightforward cowboy in real life. He is also a man of deep faith and sincere concern for others. IO You Ranch is a reflection of these things and a story very much worth reading.

Pastor Scott Hunt – Los Alamos, New Mexico

JIGGS' POEM

I purchased a 1923 copy of "Cowboy Songs" by John A. Lomax. On the inside front fly leaf was a handwritten poem. In the book, I refer to it as Jiggs' Poem. It was signed "Jamie," dated Christmas 1925.

CHAPTER ONE

Hugh Boyington Sullivan gazed out of his bedroom window at his folks' house, pondering his next move. He had graduated from a private college in upstate New York almost a year ago. Through a contact of his mother, he was able to obtain an interview with one of the Feature Editors at *The Saturday Evening Post* prior to graduating. After graduation he was hired as a staff writer for community interests and as a reviewer of local events and activities. The telephone call he received this morning from Mr. Wiseman, Special Feature Editor, at the magazine, may change his status to Feature Writer. Mr. Wiseman wanted H. B., that's what they called him, to investigate ads that have been appearing in *The New York Times, Boston Globe,* and various other New England newspapers. Offering adventures on a western ranch for a certain sum of money. Mr. Wiseman wanted to know if these ads were legitimate or some scam. H. B. was to respond to one of these ads and upon returning from this adventure, write a story about the legitimacy or expose what type of scam is being pulled off. The magazine was looking to bring back some type of nostalgic article to its readers, and this was Mr. Wiseman's choice. Mr. Wiseman was known to give assignments to aspiring writers to determine if they really can write. The secondary reason for choosing H.B. Mr. Wiseman explained, "He was chosen because he was the only person in their organization that had horseback riding as a hobby on his employment application."

Standing there at the window, he felt uneasy about doing this type of writing, he wasn't even sure the writing he currently was doing was any good. He was pretty sure he had gotten the job because of his mother. Here he was 22 years old and less than a year into a profession, having graduated the summer of 1979. At the time of his graduation, the economy was tanking and he never thought he would be lucky enough to land a writing job. He wasn't even sure with his less than sterling grade point average he would be able to get any job and thought his prospects looked slim.

He was standing there waiting for his folks to arrive home from their jobs so he could give them the news. His parents were both successful professionals, who offered starting positions for him at their places of employment. His father was a vice president with a national insurance company and his mother held an upper level management position with an international printing company. Not wanting to take the jobs his parents offered he continued searching on his own.

With both parents working, the only time they resembled a family was on their vacations. They spent more time with nannies or in boarding schools than with their parents. They weren't spoiled, but did enjoy more of the nicer things in life. Their parents were disciplinarians and expected their children to behave and obey. He and his younger sister had great opportunities to attend some of the best schools in New England. All they had to do was apply themselves in their school work and opportunities would come. H. B. just didn't seem to apply himself, while his sister on the other hand, seemed to excel in school.

Being anxious to begin research on these ads, he quickly grabbed his portfolio, which contained his tablets and note cards, and headed downstairs. Passing through the kitchen he snatched an apple from the fruit bowl and went outside.

Firing up his Chevy Nova which he had parked next to the garage, he backed out of the long driveway heading to the Danbury Library. His position as a Community Interest writer offered him lots of flexibility, including keeping unusual hours. Some days he may not go to the office at all, and this was going to be one of those days.

At the library he came across ads for dude ranches, dairies, grain farms and hog farms, mostly in southern states. Those ads which offered excitement in the west on a ranch all had local blind post office boxes for replies. It was near six o'clock when he came across Friday's edition of *The Wall Street Journal*. There in large bold print, read:

"Western Adventure, Unique Opportunity." Experience working on a cattle ranch. Need to be available for six months. Cost is $3,000, half due upon acceptance, the balance due thirty days after arrival. Send inquiries to: J. O'Bryn, Manager, P. O. Drawer 7, Wages, Colorado 80001."

H. B. smiled to himself. Was this a business investment or was it a job posting? Either way it was of interest to him. He copied the ad and went home.

When he arrived back at his parents' house they hadn't yet returned from work. Rushing up to his room he picked up the telephone, hoping to catch Mr. Wiseman, the Feature Editor for this new story, still at his desk. After four rings, a voice answered sharply. H. B. identified himself and gave him a report on the ads he found at the library, including reading the one he copied. Mr. Wiseman said he should make submission to that ad but use his home address. Thinking quickly, especially since H.B. didn't have an extra $3,000 lying around, he asked.

"Would the magazine advance me the $3,000 dollars mentioned in the ad?"

There was silence on the telephone. H. B. began thinking it may have been foolish for him to ask, and was about ready to say "forget it," when a reply came back.

"Look, you are going to be riding around or checking this place out on company time, so we will advance you three months of your salary to cover this or any other expense you may have in getting to that ranch. Keep track of all these expenses and we will reimburse you when you get back. Stop by my office tomorrow morning and we will lay out the details. I will call your present boss to fill him in. See you in the morning!"

With that, the telephone went silent. H. B. just looked at the handset and smiled, thinking this really was a big deal. Hearing the back door close, he hurried toward the kitchen to greet his mother. The printing company she worked for was on the

outskirts of New York City. His father's office was further in the city and he took the commuter train. His commute took an additional thirty minutes, so his mother always arrived home first. She had just placed a small sack of groceries on the counter as H. B. came into the kitchen wearing a big grin.

"I got an assignment today for a story. Not some small community article, but a chance to write a real story. I began my research today."

His mother was looking at him excitedly when she asked, "What is this story supposed to be about?"

H. B. replied eagerly. "It seems there are a lot of ads in Boston and New York papers asking people to come out west and experience ranch life. There is a fee associated with these ads but most only give a local blind post office box. However, I found one using an address in Wages, Colorado."

His mother had stopped putting groceries into the cupboards and was intently listening. "Does this mean you're going there, so you can write what your find out?"

"Yup!"

His mother continued with questions. "When will you be leaving? How long will this assignment take?"

Remembering what the ad said, H. B. responded. "I need to make application and if they like what I say, I will be accepted. The ad did say I would have to make a commitment for six months."

His mother, looking surprised, repeated "Six months! That's a long time from now."

H. B. hadn't even considered the length of time he needed to commit to this, hopefully Mr. Wiseman thought about it. After a brief pause H. B. responded, "I can always write you. I'm sure this will be like a dude ranch and I will have free time in the evenings to write letters and take notes for my report."

Just as he finished his last sentence, his father walked into the kitchen, leaning toward his wife to give her a kiss he said.

"What reports are you doing now?"

H. B. started all over and explained his day along with locating the ad at the library. When his mother made the comment about being away so long, his father replied.

"You were away at college about the same length of time."

They all smiled and turn their attention to preparing their meal.

The next day H. B. rode the commuter train into the city, then took a cab to *The Saturday Evening Post* offices. He first checked in with his current Feature Editor and then the two of them went to the office of Mr. Wiseman who was heading up this project.

He was given instruction to investigate whether this was a scam or genuine, what kind of experience requires someone to pay first? Why are they running these ads in the New England papers and not papers out West? Lastly, what are these people like that are placing these ads? He was also told that he would continue writing/reviewing local community events until such time that he left on this assignment. They all walked to the floor where the accounting offices were located. All three of them met with the executive in charge of payroll. Instructing her to cut him a check for three month wages, explaining in general terms his assignment and why these funds were need up front.

The Feature Editors returned to their offices and left H. B. to wait for a check. When he was handed his check, it wasn't as big as he thought. Lots of taxes were taken out along with the other deductions, but still more than sufficient to pay the required fee and air fare along with any purchase required for the trip. He quickly headed back to Danbury, Connecticut so he could prepare his answer to the ad. On the return back, he stopped at his bank where he deposited his check and purchased $3,000 in Travelers Checks.

At home, he hand wrote his response to the ad, expressing his interest in the west. He also mentioned his desire to experience western culture and hoped to gain experience which may assist him in developing a career. He signed it H. B. Sullivan. He then drove to the drug store and made copies of his letter and the Traveler Checks he was enclosing. From there he went to the Post Office and sent his application Air Mail to: J. O'Bryn, Manager, P. O. Drawer 7, Wages, Colorado 80001.

In mid-March he received a small package from J. O'Bryn. He ripped off the end and shook the contents onto the table. Inside was his original Travelers Checks with his letter and a typed reply on plain white paper. The reply stated that it is indeed a job opening but they are looking for someone with experience and not a tenderfoot. "Please reply if you have experience with cattle and horses by April 10th." It went on to say that the $1,500.00 fee would be collected upon arrival. We would also appreciate some personal information such as: date of birth, education, military service, organization memberships, i.e. 4H, FFA or vocational ag training. He read the response over a few times.

That evening he discussed the reply with his parents. He explained how excited he was about this opportunity and wondered if they had any suggestions for him as to what he could say to make his application more attractive. They reminded him how they went horseback riding in Hawaii during a couple of vacations, and that for two summers he rode horses at a summer camp he attended. The second year they even went on an overnight ride. One summer he stayed with his grandfather who ran a dairy heard and helped him feed and move the cattle to the barn and pasture. He returned to his father's den and with a little embellishment he could establish some experience and maybe qualify for the job.

It was close to the end of the month by the time he mailed his qualifications and personal information for the job. He continued searching ads but nothing else provided out of state address as this particular ad. He anxiously awaited a reply. Towards the end of April another letter arrived from J. O'Bryn. The letter said he was one of the finalists under consideration and there were a few more questions: Would he be able to commit to the entire six months? Does he have any physical disabilities which would prevent him from working with cattle or riding horses for a long period? Does he have his own saddle, bridle or other tack? The letter also provided a list of items that should be brought along if H. B. was selected for the position. Some of the items were very obvious while others he wondered about. He understood the riding boots, gloves, hat, sleeping bag, and personal items including laundry soap. But he wasn't sure why they asked about long underwear, raincoat, rolls of gauze, aspirins, tape, sun burn lotion, slave or ointment for blisters or abrasions and foot powder. He quickly wrote a thank you for considering him up to this point. He answered the questions and said he could leave on little notice but would appreciate any advance time they could provide. Again he sent off his reply air mail. He spent a day gathering and going over everything he wanted to take along so he would be ready on short notice. He accumulated or purchased the items named on the list and clothes they requested. He packed a suitcase with all the items and anything else he thought would be needed. Everything fit except his new sleeping bag.

On the 18th of May, a letter arrived from J. O'Bryn.

> "Congratulations Mr. Sullivan, We cordially invite you to experience what it means to work on our cattle ranch. You will learn and hopefully come to appreciate what is involved in ranching. When it is over sometime in mid-November, we truly hope you will treasure this experience.
>
> I will meet you near the information booth in the main part of the Albuquerque, New Mexico, air terminal on May 31st at 2:00 p.m. sharp. Best Regards, J. O'Bryn"

CHAPTER TWO

H. B. scheduled his trip so he would arrive early, even if there were to be delays. His trip required him to change planes in Denver, Colorado, but he still had time to go from one concourse to another. May 31st was on a Thursday and he needed an early start. He had called for a limo to take him to the airport and told them what time he was to be picked up. He said his goodbyes to his parents and had called his sister at school the day before to say goodbye.

The trip went without any complications and he arrived in Albuquerque with plenty of time. He gathered his suitcase and sleeping bag and went to the main lobby of the terminal. It was a good thirty minutes before he was to meet J. O'Bryn. Taking a seat, which allowed him to see the information desk and keep an eye on the front entrance, he relaxed and began observing people. He watched each man that came through the front door or approached the information desk, especially those wearing western hats. A majority of men were wearing those type of hats. The closer it got to two o'clock the more his head seemed to swivel between the two locations. A striking looking woman who looked Indian or Mexican, with long black hair walked in the front door. The combination of her natural beauty and the striking appearance of her clothes caught his eye. She wore a long pleated red skirt with a white blouse and a beautiful black beaded vest. Her hair was gathered into a pony tail. He noticed how others were also following her or at least turning their heads as she walked past. He quickly turned his gaze back to the front entrance hoping he didn't miss anyone. He then turned his attention back to the information counter. By now the attractive lady was talking to the man working at the counter. He again looked back at the front entrance, then back to the counter. This time the lady was holding a sign which said "Mr. Sullivan." Was this for real, was this the rancher's daughter or Mr. J. O'Bryn's representative? He got up and quickly walked over to the counter.

"Hello, I'm Mr. Sullivan, H. B. Sullivan."

The lady then said "Hello, I'm Johanna Cepione Brindisi O'Bryn, but I go by the name of Jo."

H. B. paused to let that sink in and then realized this was J. O'Bryn. With that, their introduction was over and H. B. retrieved his suitcase and sleeping bag. She led him to a 1964 Thunderbird parked next to the curb. She opened the trunk and H. B. placed his suitcase and sleeping bag inside. She retrieved a small suitcase and asked him if he wouldn't mind waiting in the car for a few minutes.

"Not at all. I'll just sit here and take in some of the local color."

He was still a little shocked that this woman had anything to do with a ranch. If she was back East people would think she was some magazine model. He then remembered about the $1,500 fee and he took out the envelope with the Travelers Checks from his shirt pocket. The trunk quickly opened and closed, and just as quick Jo opened the door and sat down. She had exchanged her dress for a pair of jeans,

"I feel more comfortable in these," she said as she started the car. Pulling away from the curb, H. B. placed the envelope on the center console.

"Here is the $1,500. These are same Travelers Checks I mailed previously."

They both chuckled.

"I'm going to stop and fill up with gas and have the oil checked. You may want to pick up some refreshments or something to snack on. It's over two hours to the ranch." Jo stated, as she pulled into the filling station.

Driving away from the filling station, H. B. asked how long she lived in Wages. She replied that she was born there and grew up there. He then asked how long her parents lived there. She replied that they moved there at the end of World War II, but looked quizzically at H. B..

16

"Is that when he bought the ranch?" H.B. asked.

Jo started to laugh, "You think my dad owns the ranch?"

"Yeah, since you're the manager, I assumed he owned it."

"No, no. The ranch was started by my husband's father," she explained.

"I see. How big is this ranch?" H. B. asked.

"Mr. Sullivan," she said formally, "out here we don't ask the size of one's holdings. It's impolite. It would be the same if I asked you how much your father is worth. Maybe that is not a good analogy but suffice it to say, it's something we don't ask or discuss. A lot of folks think that is rude."

"I'm sorry I did not realize that," H. B. said apologetically.

"I know but I wanted to correct you in a polite manner before someone else may do so, only not so politely," Jo replied.

H. B sat quietly and observed the scenery as they passed through Santa Fe. Thinking to himself, he realized that people out West do think differently and aren't bashful about setting one straight. Breaking the silence, H. B. asked "will we be going through Taos?" "No," Jo replied, "we will be northwest of it. It's still a ways to the ranch and you might want to take a little nap between the time change and elevation. You must be tired? There is a pillow in the back seat, you could prop it up against the window and rest."

He reached into the back seat and sandwiched the pillow between the seat and window. Before dozing off he asked her to wake him prior to their arrival at the ranch. She agreed that she would. It seemed like he had just fallen asleep when he heard "Mr. Sullivan, Mr. Sullivan! Wake up! We are approaching the ranch."

He sat up straight and noticed that the sun was almost touching the tops of the mountains. She informed him that they had crossed into Colorado and the ranch was about fifteen or twenty minutes away. She explained how she always tries to get home before dark because the wildlife start to move about after dark and sometimes it's difficult to avoid hitting them. The mountains did look dark and purple. The sun's rays streaked into the evening sky. Jo and H. B. came down a mountain and there on the gentle slope of the side of the mountain was a cabin tucked near the edge of a meadow. A long sloping roof of a barn was also visible. They had been traveling on a gravel road but he didn't know when it transitioned from hard surface to gravel. Turning off the gravel road onto the driveway to the ranch was a small sign hanging from a cross member. On the sign were the letters IO.

"What does the IO stand for?" H. B. asked hesitantly.

"That's stands for Ivan O'Bryn who was my father-in-law. He died in 1968," Jo responded. As they drove closer he could see a garage with two swinging doors and a side wing. Under the wing was a bench which ran along the side of the garage, and parked under the roof of the wing was an old pick up truck. Jo stopped the car in front of the garage, she instructed H. B. to grab his bags as she pushed a button for the trunk. H. B. followed behind her in the long evening shadows over a ridge to a small cabin amidst some trees. The small trail they were on ended at this cabin. Below and beyond the cabin was a screened-in building and past that, on the same level, was what looked like an outhouse.

She opened the door to the cabin, or as she called it, "the bunkhouse." It was neat and clean. There was a bed along one wall. On the opposite wall were two windows and straight ahead a small pot belly stove. Next to the stove was a coal bucket with kindling and a few larger pieces of wood. A small table stood between the windows and a chair was in the corner between the bed and the doorway. There were two shelves, one above the bed with a couple of books and another by the chair with a stack of newspapers on it. Under the bed was a foot locker, which he could use to store his things. She said he could check out the shower and facility on his own. There were towels and soap down there for his use. She told him to rest for a while and unpack. Supper would be at 7:00. It was about 5:00 p.m., H. B. checked his watch and moved his watch to the local time. Jo left and headed back towards the house, disappearing over the ridge. He laid his suitcase on the bed and pulled out the foot locker, he commenced to unpack. He laid the items he planned to wear in the morning on the chair. He put his jeans, shirts, sweatshirt and long underwear in the foot locker. The rest he left in the suitcase along with his cash. He hung his laundry bag at the bottom of the bed. He stuffed his suitcase and foot locker back under the bed.

He picked up his shaving kit and walked down the hill and past the bunkhouse about eighty feet. There, he saw a four-sided structure built on stilts. On top of the structure was a large steel tank. A pipe ran to the top of the tank from a point higher up the mountain. It must be the line used to fill the tank with water he thought. One side of the structure was shorter, thus acting as an opening. Inside was a cement floor with a drain that ran the water outside onto the ground. Inside was a shower head with a chain attached to it. Attached to the short wall was a shelf with a small basin, a mirror, and a cabinet attached to the wall which held towels and soap. The floor in this area was also cemented. He left his shaving kit on the shelf and walked to the privy, which had the aroma of gas, but learned later it was diesel fuel.

He came back to the bunkhouse and sat on the bed looking out the windows, through a small grove of aspens. Further in the distance was a valley and beyond that were more mountains. He still had the excitement about this job and felt that this may be a once in a life time opportunity. There on the table was an oil lamp with a box of matches next to it. A small tin can was fashioned into an ash tray for disposal of matches or ashes as needed. He struck a match and lifted the globe off the wick of the lamp. After lighting the lamp he set the globe securely back, then adjusted the flame. He smiled to himself having learned how this was done from the movies. He had never actually seen one of these. The lamp gave a soft warm glow to the inside of the bunkhouse.

Checking his watch, he saw that it was almost 7:00 p.m., so he blew out the lamp and followed the path back to the main area in the light of dusk.

A half dozen steps led up to the screen porch of the main house. As he began his ascent, Jo appeared at the door. "Were you able to get any rest?"

"No," replied H. B., "I just unpacked and checked out the plumbing facilities."

Jo was smiling as she said, "Come on in. Let me introduce you to the rest of the crew."

H. B. saw two forms over her shoulder, standing just outside the entrance to the house. The taller man was completely in the shadows and his features could not be determined. The other had the light from the house on part of his face. He had dark skin with braided hair. He was wearing a light shirt with a vest and jeans.

Jo held out her hand palm up "Mr. H. B. Sullivan, this is Ike O'Bryn, my husband."

The slightly taller figure standing in the shadows stepped forward with his out stretched hand. H. B. noticed he had a flat top haircut, with a large scar on the side of his face.

"Pleased to meet you, Mr. O'Bryn," H. B. said as he extended his hand for a hand shake. As they shook hands H. B. thought it was as if he grabbed a large piece of iron. His hand seemed to melt.

"Welcome to the ranch." Ike O'Bryn stated.

Jo continued the introduction, "This is our hired man and dear friend Jiggs Jaqua. Jiggs this is H. B. Sullivan."

Again H. B. extended his hand thinking it would again be crushed. "Nice to meet you."

"Howdy" Jiggs replied, without shaking his hand.

H. B. realized he had never shook hands with an Indian or Mexican before. Maybe they don't have that custom. Jo interrupted this awkward moment,

"Lets go in and eat before the food gets cold."

Ike gently reached out and grabbing H. B.'s bicep he pulled him aside to allow Jo to enter the kitchen first. It was a subtle way to remind him that it's ladies before men. Still holding his arm, Jiggs went through the door next, another subtle reminder age before youth. He quickly released his grip as Jiggs went through the doorway. H. B. followed Jiggs, his attention went to the sound of the little silver bells attached to Jiggs' spurs and their melodic sound. Ike assisted Jo with her chair and the rest then sat down. Ike said a prayer and Jo got up and placed the meal on the table. Each plate she set on the table came with the warning that it was hot. The food looked great and each platter received lots of "Ohs and Ahs," and rightfully so, since the taste was wonderful. The kitchen was fairly large with the table in the middle. The appliances weren't modern, but everything was neat and clean. Everything seemed to be utilitarian with no frills. There was little conversation except for the acclaims of flavor and the cooking prowess of Jo. The plates were being emptied but the coffee was just getting started as the porcelain pot was passed around. H. B. enjoyed a cup only once in a while, usually in the winter, so he passed the coffee and stayed with water.

At first, the conversation was casual, focusing on topics such as the weather and cattle prices. Things that H. B. only listened to. Jo suggested the men retire to the porch while she cleared the table and prepared dessert. Everyone thanked her for such a delicious meal as they headed to the porch. Ike lit an oil lamp, while Jiggs busied himself by taking out a small leather bag from one vest pocket and a packet of papers from another. He then commenced to roll himself a cigarette, and offered the makings to H. B. saying

"Care for one?"

H. B. just watched and said "No thanks."

Ike began explaining that they are a family ranch and run a cow calf operation, which runs cattle on federal leases and some of their land and their neighbor's lands. Working with their neighbors is important and Ike expected him to assist in that endeavor.

"Right now the herd is in the high country and the calving is about over, and in about a month we will brand and vaccinate. That is when you will come up to assist. Currently, there is work here at the headquarters which needs attention. That will be your immediate task."

H. B. was excited to hear how they had plans for him to assist in the operation of the ranch. After going through the general operation of the ranch he looked straight at H. B. and said

"As in any outfit there are rules which are not to be ignored. Number one rule: never complain about the cooking or the cook. Rule number two: you are not allowed in the house when Jo is here by herself. Rule number three: no alcohol on the ranch. The other rules you will learn as you go. If you break something fix it, or at least let us know. For now you will report to Jo. Any questions?"

The only word that came out of H. B.'s mouth was "No."

For the second time that evening, Jo interrupted an awkward moment by requesting they come back in for dessert. After coffee and some more light conversation, Jiggs stated

"I want to get back to the camp, but before I take my leave, we've got to get something settled."

H. B. thought more rules were forthcoming. Jiggs continued,

"I don't know about you all, but I'm not going to call this kid," flipping a thumb in the direction of H. B., "Mr. and I will never remember if it is C. B., J. B. or H. D.. So I'm going to call him," again pointing that thumb in the direction of H. B., "Boston.

He comes from back East and we all know that's where that first famous horseman Paul Revere hailed from. I don't care if you agree or not, I just want everyone to know what I think."

Jiggs had sat there most of the night and hadn't said that much until this point. Ike looked around the table and then at H. B. and asked

"How does that suit you?"

"I kind of like it" H. B. said.

"Well then Boston, and everyone else, good night." Jiggs got up and walked out the door. Boston said "I think I will say good night as well. Thank you for the wonderful meal and for inviting me to your ranch." He left with a big smile on his face. He had often heard of cowboy nick names and now he has one, which really delighted him. As he made his way in the dark towards the bunkhouse he wondered how a person on a horse can see where they are going. His walk was more stumbling and tripping than anything else. Once he arrived at the bunkhouse he was glad he knew where the matches and lamp were located. Striking the match he lit the lamp. Again the entire inside of the place had a soft glow about it. Prior to undressing he headed toward the outhouse. The light through the bunk house windows gave off enough light. He was able to see the path there and back. Returning to the bunkhouse he stripped for bed, opened one of the windows a couple inches and blew out the lamp. When he slipped between the sheets he realized the bottom sheet was flannel. He had never slept on a flannel sheet before. He lay there listening to the gentle rustling of the aspen leaves. Sleep came quickly.

CHAPTER THREE

When he opened his eyes the birds were singing and the sun was over the tops of the mountains in the East. He went to the outhouse and then quickly got dressed and headed to the house, known as the headquarters. He realized he needed to know and use the terms they use. It would be useful for any article. He passed the barn where there were three horses in the corral. He hadn't noticed how many there were when he went to dinner. Oops, he corrected his thoughts, they call it "supper." Smiling to himself he continued on just looking around. From the base of the stairs he hollered out "Good morning." Within a few seconds Jo appeared in the door way and said

"Good morning. We kind of figured that you would sleep in after such a long day of travel. Come in and sit down." As she pulled a chair out from the table on the porch. "Do you drink coffee in the morning?" she asked walking away toward the kitchen doorway. Thinking quickly Boston replied "Yes." Knowing that he normally didn't, but he thought it might be nice.

"Do you take anything in it? Everyone here drinks it strong."

Boston replied "If it's strong I'd better have a little milk or cream."

She laughed and said "No, by strong I mean black, although you may think its strong. Coffee with cream in we call light and then there is sweet coffee"

He laughed also, remembering rule number one, "I'm sure its fine. I'll just have it strong also." Boston made another mental note. "What time to you eat breakfast?" he asked.

She smiled "Normally around six o'clock, but I saved some bacon and I can fry you a couple of eggs."

"That would be fine." Boston said as he checked his watch which showed almost 8:30a.m. He sat there with his coffee, staring out listening only to silence, broken by the voice of a

Meadow Lark or Blue Bird singing. There weren't any other sounds. It seemed surreal not to have any type of background noise. He thought this was not a good start, being late the first day.

Jo came back out and told him that Ike thought he should go light the first couple of days because of the altitude. She said "After you have finished your breakfast and take care of any personal business, you can start working in the corrals." She would show him what needed to be done on a daily basis. Boston inhaled the bacon, eggs, toast and potatoes. Jo had also brought him a glass of water and explained the need to keep hydrated especially at high altitudes. He excused himself and said he would get his gloves and meet her at the corral. He quickly trotted off to the bunkhouse and retrieved his gloves and returned at a trot to the corral before Jo arrived. Jo showed him how to feed the horses and afterwards how to clean up the stalls and corrals. Dumping the manure on the pile at the back of the barn. She then showed him the different tools needed to do fencing and where they were stored, along with the spools of wire and stack of fence posts. Some posts were wood others were called "T" posts. She instructed Boston to bring a stretcher, fence pliers and fill his pockets with staples and she would meet him at the pick-up truck and drive out to where they would start fencing. He saw this barb wire fence everywhere so it must not be that difficult to do. As he stepped out from under the wing of the garage to wait for her return, he saw Jo coming down the steps. She was wearing a large straw hat, and a pistol stuck in a holster, carrying a two handled cooler. Boston put the tools on the truck and went to relieve her from the weight of the cooler. He wondered why she needed a pistol, so he asked. "What's with the gun?" "Well, you just never know when the Indians will rise up again." She responded. They both laughed but Boston was still curious. They got into the pick-up, after Boston put the cooler on the back and drove out to the main gate. She told him to grab the fencing pliers from the back. She was reaching under the seat and brought out another pair of fencing pliers. These pliers didn't look like any tool he had ever seen. Jo was explaining that the pasture they were going to fence was to hold the cattle during winter and it was necessary to make the fence secure. He thought it was strange that they were doing the work now instead of prior to the cattle arriving but he didn't say anything. The task was to make sure the wood post stood securely and that all the wires were stapled to the post. She demonstrated the technique on the first post by shaking the post and then tapping in any lose staples with the pliers. She then pointed to the next one as she leap frogged past him to the one after the next. They leap frogged past each other from post to post. Any post that was real wobbly had the staples removed, and the post was pulled out if possible or just left for later. As they continued down the fence line Boston thought that this fencing wasn't much work. They walked the half mile of fence back towards the headquarters. He learned that going around the "half section" meant they would be walking a total of three miles. Boston got the hang of it all pretty quick, but wondered why fencing pliers had such a small hammer head. It seemed to take a long time to hammer in each staple.

They had gotten to the last half mile, which headed them back to the pick-up. Boston had gotten into a pattern, where he would come up to a post and shake it first than check to see if all the staples were there and if they were tight. He had just started to reach for the post when Jo yelled "Stop!" Turning around he saw Jo coming at him with the pistol drawn and pointed directly at him. His eyes grew big and he wondered what she was thinking. She kept saying "Don't move!" She kept advancing with the pistol grasped firmly in her out stretched arm. Boston watched as she cocked the hammer back. He just stood there with his mouth and eyes wide open. A couple of steps away, she lowered her arm slightly and fired. Boston jumped as the impact from the bullet hit just behind him. She fired again. This time Boston grabbed the post. He looked where the bullets had hit and saw a snake. A rattlesnake.

"That was close" Jo sighed with relief.

Boston exclaimed "You scared the living day lights out of me!"

"I am sorry but there wasn't time to do anything else. The snake had curled up and was ready to strike." Jo apologetically explained. "A bite from one of those and you may not make it to a hospital in time. To get snake bite serum you would need to go to Trinidad, Colorado or Taos. By the time anyone got you there it may be too late." She explained, "I should have warned you to be on the lookout, around here we need to always be listening and looking for them. Not so much in the high country, but here in these meadows." As she was talking Boston just kept staring at the snake.

"Take you knife and cut off the rattles as a souvenir or reminder," she suggested.

Still a little shaken, he stated, "I don't have a knife." She handed him her folding knife. When he opened it the blade was about two inches long. She then placed her boot behind the snake's head and stretched out its torn up body.

"Hold onto those buttons and cut them off," she commanded.

He reached down trying not to act like a sissy and grabbed the buttons. Then with one heavy downward pull, the knife separated them from the snake.

"How many?" she asked.

He counted ten buttons. Then shook them in an effort to duplicate the sound.

"Oh they don't really rattle. Its a buzzing sound. Did you hear it?" Jo inquired.

"No" came his response.

"Let's get back to work," she said as she walked off. Needless to say Boston spent the rest of that day, and his entire time on the ranch watching and listening to what was moving around him.

When they arrived back at the truck it was just past noon. Jo needed to go to town so she gave instructions to remove all the loose posts, then replace them with new wooden ones that were on the truck after he had his lunch. She wanted to leave her pistol but Boston said he had never fired a pistol and thought it best she keep it. He did promise her that he would be very careful and move slowly and cautiously the rest of the day. Seeming reassured, she headed back to the headquarters on foot.

Boston had eaten a sandwich and was working on some chips with a pop, when Jo came back down the drive in her car. She stopped to inform him that she would be back around supper. Boston just smiled and waved as she drove off. He returned to the cooler to see what else could be eaten. A small piece of cobbler from the night before, and a thermos along with a jug of water. He unwrapped the cobbler and took a big bite. He unscrewed the thermos top and inside was cold milk. He took a couple swallows, then the rest of the cobbler and sipped on the milk as he sat on the back of the flat bed admiring the view and enjoying the surrounding beauty.

He checked his watch which showed 12:50, he counted the posts that were stacked on the truck. There were eighteen, he didn't think there was that many bad posts out there. He started to wonder what he would do with the rest of the day, as he stuffed the pliers into his back pocket and carried a post out to the first location. It dawned on him that he would need a shovel and the jack. Walking back to the truck he picked these two items up and headed out to the first rotted post. Jo had described how the "jacking out" of a post worked, as he remembered the directions he realized he had forgotten the chain he would need. Again back to the truck he went. This time before he left the truck, he paused, going over the process in his mind that Jo had explained. Now he was thinking ahead, so he grabbed another post and walked back to where he was going to start. He was now ready to begin the process of "jacking out" a post. He had never seen a Handy Man jack before, but his grandfather had a similar jack in the trunk of his old car. He attempted chaining the post to the jack and after a number of attempts he finally gained success of extracting the old post from the ground. The hole that it left wasn't quite big enough for the new post, so he dug it out until the new post fit into the hole. He then back filled the hole and packed the dirt in with the handle. As he started off to the second rotten post which was about fifty yards away, he realized that he could not carry all this equipment in one load. He then decided to get the truck and that way he would have everything he needed on wheels. So once again he walked back to the truck.

He guessed the truck was a late 1960s model Ford which had four wheel drive. As he climbed into the truck and started reaching for the key, he first noticed there were three pedals on the floor, with two gear shifts on the floor, one short and one long. The white knob on the short gear stick said 4X Hi, 4X, N, 4X Lo, obviously for the four wheel drive. Not having driven a vehicle with a standard transmission before, he studied the shift pattern on the longer gear stick, it had an H pattern with the numbers 1, 2, 3, and 4 at each end and then up on the upper right was an "R". The third pedal and long gear stick were the only things he hadn't previously seen in a vehicle. He figured they went together. He stepped on the far left pedal and pushed the gear stick into where he thought the number 1 gear was. He then turned the key. The truck chugged forward in small jogs. He quickly turned the key to the off position. He placed his foot on the brake pedal and holding on to the steering wheel turned the key again. This time the truck kind of jerked in place but did not start. He then pressed the third pedal and turned the key. The engine fired. He released the pressure on the third pedal and the truck took a big leap forward and died. He did the process again, this time releasing the third pedal a little slower. The truck was moving slowly as long as he didn't remove his foot. He finally released his foot when he thought the truck had enough speed. But again, after two or three violent jerks it quit running. The next time he attempted it he kept his foot on the third pedal and drove to where he left the fencing tools. He turned the key off and released the pedal. The truck back fired and lurched to a stop. Boston was now thinking this could take a lot longer than he thought. He was just glad nobody was around to see his driving skills. Loading up the tools he got back into the truck and restarted it. This time he revved up the engine before releasing the pedal slightly. The truck again moved slowly to the next rotten post location. After unloading the shovel and jack he started the process of taking out the post and then enlarging the hole to accommodate the new post. He wanted to make sure the post matched in height to the others in the fence line, so he would lay the old and new side by side and determine how much deeper the hole needed to be in order to keep the post at all the same height. Now that he figured out how everything worked, replacing the post seemed to go relatively smooth. It took him almost as long to drive to the location as it did to remove the post. Boston again loaded all the equipment onto the truck, then he got back inside. He looked at the gear stick and wasn't sure if he was in the number 1 position or the number 3 position. He pulled the gear stick back and then pressed the pedal down which he figured allowed him to move to another gear, so he pulled the stick down and slightly over to the number 2 position. The gear stick seemed to slide into this position fairly easy. Still holding the pedal to the floor he started the truck. Revving the engine up, he slowly let the pedal up. This time the truck moved faster and he was mentally giving himself a pat on the back when he looked out the window as he past the next rotten post. He quickly stepped on the brake with his left foot. The truck slowed and then began jerking to a stop. When it stopped jerking he turned off the key. He repeated the process of post replacement and after loading the tools climbed back into the truck. He scanned the fence line and then realized the next post brought another challenge. He would need to turn off the drive way and through a gate opening into the pasture. If he hit the gate posts or fence, he could tear them out and smash the truck. He had to figure out how to control the truck without causing it to quit or jerk to a stop. His skills needed to improve immediately. Once he got the truck up to speed he thought he would step on the third pedal and see what the truck did. Again he started by revving up the engine and slowly releasing the third pedal keeping his foot on it until the truck gained momentum.

He then pressed the third pedal to the floor and the truck continued to move evenly but the engine raced. By now he was approaching the gate opening. He took his foot off the accelerator and the revving ceased. He then placed that foot on the brake and slowed the truck down to make a controlled turn through the gate and into the pasture. All the tools and posts bounced on the bed of the truck, but nothing fell off. He kept his foot on the third pedal and the brake until the truck stopped. He turned off the key and when the engine quit running he removed his foot from the third pedal. A big smile came across his face as he got out to work on the next post.

His skills at removing and replacing posts were far superior to those of his driving but he knew he could make progress on his driving as he went from one rotten post to another. At some point during his time in the pasture Jo had returned home. He glanced at his watch and then at the sun which was approaching the mountain tops. He had been out there over three hours and still had four or five post yet to work on. When he had completed all the posts, the shadows of the mountain stretched past most of the pasture he was in. Loading up the tools he headed back toward the gate where he entered. The truck bounced onto the drive way and then headed towards the headquarters at a slow rate of speed.

Ike was standing outside the horse corral when he saw Boston coming down the drive. He wanted to be sure to tell Boston to put all the tools away and park the truck under the wing, along with putting the old post near the fire pit. It appeared that Boston was driving very cautiously. The engine started to rev and then it ceased and the truck glided up next to Ike. He relayed his message and walked over to the house when he heard the engine rev as the truck moved slowly. He smiled as he kept walking knowing that Boston was slip clutching the truck.

After storing the tools and parking the truck, Boston trotted towards the bunkhouse to clean up before supper. While washing his hands and face, he noticed his soft white hands were scratched, cut and blistered. He thought it wasn't much of a reward for all the hard work. But at least he was proud that he had accomplished some work he had never done before. He walked back up to the house for supper.

Somehow Jo had prepared a wonderful meal in the short time she had returned. Ike asked how Boston's day went. Of course the snake incident came up which Ike was genuinely concerned about for both of them. Boston said how he felt when he saw Jo pointing the pistol in his direction, but now he thought he must have looked pretty scared.

Jo said " No, I think I was the one that looked scared."

They both laughed and Ike looked relieved.

Ike asked "Have you ever driven a vehicle with a standard transmission before?"

Boston knew that he needed to tell the truth, "No."

"I never realized. I should have asked you," Jo exclaimed.

Ike just smiled as he said "Looks like you and the truck got along OK."

"Yes sir." Boston said.

Ike told Boston a few pointers to help him with driving the truck especially about when to shift and how and when to down shift. The meal discussion was primarily about driving and being careful as well as watching out for snakes. Boston asked to be excused, but before he left Ike said one more thing. "All cowboys carry a knife. It is a tool of the trade. Some are straight blades, like Jiggs carries. Most are folding knifes. Get one first chance you can. You'll find it handy."

"Yes sir. First chance I can. Good night!" Boston replied and went back towards the bunkhouse.

Boston took the lantern down to the shower. The water felt warm from soaking up the rays of the sun all day. Remembering that there was only a limited amount of water, that didn't afford him the luxury of relaxing as the water ran over his body. Instead, he headed back to the bunk house, doused the light and crawled into bed. He was reflecting on the happening of the day when sleep landed.

CHAPTER FOUR

He awoke at what he thought was the middle of the night. He lit the lantern and looked at his watch. It was just after five o'clock. Looking out the windows there was only a line of grey light outlining the eastern mountain tops. Thinking that he can't be late for breakfast he got out of bed, then made his morning rounds before getting dressed. He headed over the ridge and as soon as he cleared the barn a booming voice said "Good morning Boston!" He flinched and looked toward the direction of the corral, where he saw Ike brushing his horse.

"Good morning!" he stammered. "You startled me," replied Boston.

"Sorry about that, next time I'll growl," Ike said with laughter in his voice. "Let's go in for coffee and breakfast." The two walked toward the house. Jo was busy making the breakfast as she said, "Good morning," over her shoulder. Ike poured the two of them a cup of coffee, and began to lay out what work he had lined up for Boston that day. "The first order of business," he began, "is to make sure everything from the previous day was complete. Then re-supply the truck with new posts. Make sure you take plenty of staples and clips for the "T" posts. You will probably need the rock bar." Now that term Boston was unfamiliar with.

"Rock bar?" he questioned.

"Jo will show you what it is. The two of you soon will become best friends." And then Ike chuckled.

"Enough." Jo said as she set a large plate of ham and a bowl of scrambled eggs on the table. Ike said a prayer and they commenced to eat. Boston was surprised by how hungry he was, especially after eating a big meal the night before.

Ike and Boston left the house together walking toward the truck. "Let's take a drive to the county road. Maybe I can show you a couple of things. You drive! "Ike said.

Boston got in and Ike immediately explained about the reverse gear and letting out on the clutch, the third pedal. His explanation on how the clutch worked and it's purpose helped Boston to understand how the transmission worked with the engine and vise versa. He also told him that when the truck had a heavy load, start off in first gear.

"If you stop the truck on a hill, leave the truck in gear to help hold it there."

Boston turned around at the county road and headed back to headquarters. Other than a few jerky moments when he shifted gears, he thought it went well.

"You'll get the hang of it eventually" Ike said as he walked to the corral.

Boston drove over to the fire pit to unload the old posts and watched enviously as Ike rode off into the trees. After piling up the old post he drove the truck to the stack of new posts and loaded forty posts and plenty of staples, which he put in an old can laying on the work bench. He found a bag of clips which Ike told him about, then piled all the other fencing tools onto the truck. He was about ready to turn to head to the house when Jo's voice said "That's the rock bar standing in the corner." Boston turned his head and noticed an iron bar about seven feet long, pointed on one end and flat on the other. He grabbed for it with one hand and then realized this object had some weight to it.

"It's used for prying or breaking rocks and for packing the dirt around a post," Jo instructed.

She had already carried the cooler out to the truck and placed it on the seat between she and Boston. She asked "Are you ready to go?"

"Yes ma'am," he replied.

He started the truck and they headed back down the drive way. At the county road he was instructed to take a right. He drove for a couple of miles when he was told to turn left into another pasture stopping at an old gate. Jo got out and opened it. She then got back into the truck.

"Just leave the gate open while you are working in here. You will need to build a new gate anyway. Turn right."

This maneuver put the fence between the truck and the county road. He drove slowly as she pointed out that this fence was installed by the county a couple of years ago and wouldn't need any work. It was a "T" post fence with the wire strung tight, five strands high. This pasture was much bigger than the one he was in yesterday. He must have driven another mile. She instructed Boston to stop at a tall stump of a tree, just inside the county fence line.

"That is the section corner post," as Jo pointed to the tall stump about two feet in diameter. "Turn left here and drive up the hill. I will show you the other corner," she instructed.

"Where's the fence?" Boston asked.

"You are going to build it," she replied.

As they drove away from the county road the ground went up hill. Boston told her,

"I'm not sure I can start the truck on this hill if it quits."

"Just pick up your speed a little. You will be fine" she encouraged him.

The hill wasn't that long and it leveled out some at the top. Over to the left was a windmill standing on the edge of the slope going downhill.

Jo said "Drive to the large dead pine tree in the distance."

He complied as they continued the drive. As they arrived at a small grove of trees she told him to stop.

"Leave it in gear and put the hill brake on." Jo commanded.

He was pretty sure the hill brake was the same as parking brake, must be another western term, he thought. We walked over towards the dead tree until we came to a rock about the size of a basketball. Pointing to the rock she said,

"See that rock,? That's the other section corner. See it's marked with a large cross." Boston looked down at the rock. Sure enough there was a large looking cross chiseled out.

"The early surveyors used trees or rocks to mark the section corners. This rock actually marks the corner of four sections. Where the two lines on the rock cross is the common corner to four section."

"I see" said Boston as he examined the rock. He had learned a historical fact, he thought would be useful information to possibly use for an article.

"You'll be placing your corner post next to this rock, but under no circumstances move the rock." She instructed.

Boston replied, "I understand."

Jo continued, "This line runs towards the west. Jump in. I'll drive to the next section corner."

They got into the truck and she drove off slowly down the gently sloping hills towards the west. She had driven around a steep ravine, as she explained how to fence that particular area, and reminded him to ask questions if he didn't understand or needed guidance on anything. Again she stopped in an open area near a partial fence running north and south. They got out and walked toward the fence. She again pointed to another large rock having a cross chiseled into it.

"You will need to build corner posts here. I'll show you an example of them later," she stated.

"What about this old fence? Should I repair it?" Boston asked.

"No. It will need to be ripped out and all new posts and wire put up. All the old wire will get rolled up. I'll show you where it's stored." Jo responded.

They walked back to the truck and she turned the truck toward the south, heading toward the gate off the county road that they used to enter this pasture. Boston watched as she put the truck in first gear and took her foot off the gas pedal and let the truck take them down the hill. Boston noticed that the old fence quit after a couple of hundred feet, so he didn't think that would be such a big job to remove it. At the county road she stopped and the two of them got out and walked across the road. There, she showed Boston what a corner post looked like. It consisted of three larger posts, forming a ninety degree angle, with two smaller posts running between the larger posts. They drove a little further down the road and stopped again. Crossing the road she showed him an "H" post, which is placed within the fence line. She explained these were put in everywhere the terrain changed or, on fairly level ground, every quarter or half mile. Boston looked at it closely and noticed that there were notches in the larger post where the cross member of the "H" rested.

"How did they put the notches in these posts, or do they come that way?

"I don't think they do. You will need to use a saw and chisel to make the notch." She informed him. "The "H" and corner posts are used to pull or stretch the fence tight and keep it under tension." She added. "Ike says to get the most effect from these, the cross member should be about six feet." Jo concluded.

"How come you know so much about fencing?" Boston inquired.

"In order to make this ranch work, it takes a team effort. We all need to pitch in and do what is necessary. I've done my share of fencing, Ike and Jiggs taught me what and how to do it." Jo explained as she returned to the truck.

They drove back to the headquarters, since Jo had other duties she needed to handle. As she stopped the truck she suggested Boston locate a saw, hammer and chisel. Then meet her at the house. Boston searched the work bench and the wall where the tools were hanging up, located these items placing them inside the truck, then headed towards the stairs of the house. Jo came back outside carrying a tablet. She then sketched a square and made some other lines and marks. When she had finished she put an N for North, and E and W for East and West and an S for South. She had drawn out a rough map of the pasture they had just come out from including the wind mill, ravine, and stock tank locations. She put "H's" on the lines from the tree trunk to the stone where she thought they needed to go, and then from the line from one stone to the other. She put "H's" on either side of the ravine, and large single posts on either side of the ravine at the bottom. At the location of the corner stones she drew three circles and connecting lines to indicate the location of corner posts. She even made a profile of the hill and showed how and where she thought an "H" post would be needed.

Then on the back of the paper she wrote 1) Pick up old post and wire. 2) Standing with your back to the old tree trunk post, hold up the compass and pick a point at the bottom of the hill which is due north from the tree trunk post. Pound a stake or "T" post at that point. Go back and check to make sure it is within the compass's site line. Then do the same from that point to a point at the crest of the hill. Put in a stake or "T" post and double check. From the crest position to the first stone corner marker should then be within the site line of the compass. She demonstrated this method by using two objects nearby. Explaining that is how he will line out where the fence is to go from each section corner. However when going from east to west he would need to move the Lubber Line so it points to the 270 degree mark on the compass or true west. To make sure the posts all line up he should run a string line. She continued to write, 3) Dig holes for "H" posts. 4) Set "H" post and run string line. 5) Pound in "T" post every fifteen feet. 6) After all post are in, string wire, top to bottom.

When she had finished writing she said, "If there is something you don't understand or are having trouble with, we will help. If there is something you can't figure out ask for help."

"This sounds like a big task," replied Boston.

"It most certainly is." Jo agreed.

She then went to the truck to see what equipment was already loaded. She motioned for Boston to follow her into the lean to. She pointed to the post pounder and the wire stretcher but added

"You won't need these right now but you will when you're putting in the "T" posts. There are some smaller wooden stakes." Pointing under the work bench to a shelf. "Use them to mark the fence line with so you don't need to lug "T" posts all over. I've got to run. I packed a lunch for you, if it's not big enough let me know and I'll do better tomorrow." She turned and headed toward the house. Boston climbed back into the truck and drove back to the pasture he was to work in.

After going into the pasture he unloaded the wooden post near the old wood tree post, and then headed up the hill to tear out that section of fence. He liked being given a task and sent off on his own to accomplish it. He first pulled out what staples remained and began rolling up the wire. Again he learned on this first attempt and his second attempt went smoother. He decided he was getting hungry so he went to the truck to get something to eat. There were two sandwiches, fruit, half dozen cookies, a carrot and a jug of iced sweet tea along with a can of pop. He wolfed down everything except the jug of sweet tea and a few cookies. He again sat on the back of the truck and admired the view from on top of this hill. The quiet was refreshing to him. He listened to the sounds of the birds and wind which seemed to come from all directions. He hopped off the truck and tackled the third and fourth strand of wire. There wasn't much left of the fifth or top wire. When he had all the rolls of wire stacked on the truck he started to jack out the posts. He wanted to complete this task before he headed back to the headquarters. He struggled with the few which were broken off. He ended up digging them out. By the time he had loaded all of them onto the truck, the sun was just about on top of the mountain. As he climbed into the truck he realized his back ached from all the bending and pulling he had been doing. He started the truck. Pushing the gear stick into first, he let the truck take him down the hill. While steering down the hill he realized he had scratched his arms in a few places. He was sure he would be more careful with more experience.

At supper there were comments about the wire biting back and wearing a long sleeve shirt goes a long way in protecting the arms. He said he didn't bring any long sleeve shirts and it was too hot to wear a jacket or sweatshirt. Jo mentioned that she would pick one or two up if he would tell her his size. Besides, on Sunday they all could go to town since they attended church that day and then went to the café afterwards. But none of the stores are open. He was invited along to attend church and join them for dinner.

Ike explained, "We only do our chores, go to church, come back and relax the rest of the day. That's kind of a day off for you. Until you get up to the cow camp. Enjoy the day and do as you please. But you are welcome to join us."

"Thanks, I might join you. My shirt size is 16 and 33, if you could pick me up a couple. I'll pay you back." Boston promised.

"I will see what I can do." Jo said.

CHAPTER FIVE

The next morning Boston and Ike were in the corral and barn cleaning. Ike suggested "You might want to take your laundry to town. The wash house is open. Unless you don't need to do any laundry."

"These are the cleanest clothes I have. Hope they are good enough for church."

"I'll guarantee you Boston, nobody there is going to care what your clothes look like. Besides, this is a worship service, not a fashion show!" Ike exclaimed. "We'll be heading out in about thirty minutes if you want to put your dirty clothes together."

"I'll be ready and waiting by the truck." Boston replied.

Ike was grinning, "We're taking the car today."

After Boston had emptied the wheel barrow and put the shovel and rake away, he headed for the bunkhouse.

At the bunkhouse he searched for all his dirty clothes. It seemed he had changed his jeans and shirt every day. His laundry bag was stuffed full. After cleaning up, he grabbed his laundry bag and headed toward the garage. Ike was walking toward the garage when Boston noticed Ike was wearing a different hat. It wasn't all dirty and soiled. He called out "nice hat!"

"Thanks Boston. It's my Sunday and meeting hat." Then disappeared into the garage. Soon he had the car backed out and left the motor running as he went around by the passenger side. Jo appeared on the steps and hollered "Let's get a shake on or we will be late." Ike opened the passenger door and Jo got in. Boston pulled the driver's seat forward so he could get in the back where he had thrown his laundry bag. The drive didn't take that long and the car soon pulled up in front of Wages Bible Church. The three went inside and found a place up near the front. Boston felt a little squeamish sitting so close to the front. They no more than sat down and the piano started playing. They sang songs, some talking, another song and then the sermon and collection. This was followed by more singing and then announcements and finally they were dismissed. As they tried to get to the exit folks kept coming up and introducing themselves wanting to know who Boston was. Ike and Jo said his name is Boston and he is helping them this summer. There was no way Boston was going to remember any body's name. He was relieved when they got to the car. He still felt out of place wearing the dirty stained shirt and jeans he had on. That reminded him. "Where is this wash house you spoke of Ike?"

"We'll drop you off on the way to the café and when you got your machines started join us there for dinner." Ike replied.

The wash house wasn't but a few blocks from the church. Boston squeezed out from behind Ike and pulled his laundry bag with him. "See you later!" as he turned and went into the wash house. That's exactly what it was, a house. They just put a few washing machines and a couple of dryers in. Near the front windows was a table with a couple of chairs. Against the opposite wall were a few vending machines, one for soap, one for pop, and one for candy. On the back wall was a change machine. He put down his bag of dirty clothes and took out a few dollars to run through the change machine to get the desired quarters the machines required. He decided to use two of the wash machines and soon had them both filled. He went to the soap vending machine and purchased two small boxes of soap. Emptying the soap into the machines he then plied them with the required number of quarters. He closed the lids and pushed in the slides holding the coins at the same time. He stood there and listened until he heard water running and then thought it's time to eat.

The café was on the opposite side of the street a few building down. The whole street was parked with cars and trucks, all parked at an angle. The café was packed and it took Boston a minute until he saw where Ike and Jo were seated. As he approached he noticed an elderly woman was seated with them.

Boston felt less conspicuous in the café since there were others wearing work clothes. Ike did the introductions and said the lady's name was Adeline, and she used to own the big pasture he is fencing now. She was very polite and explained how her father had homesteaded that land and fenced it sometime around the turn of the century. She said it actually was a larger piece of ground but the north end is mostly trees. Food was brought to the table as they visited.

"I took the liberty of ordering a luncheon special." Jo said looking at Boston.

"Wonderful. I like fried chicken especially with the dark gravy." Boston replied.

Their conversation ranged from church activities, community news and Shylo. Boston sat listening not really caring about most of it, but he paid more attention when he realized that Shylo was the name of a girl living in another town. Boston looked at his watch and realized he had been there thirty or forty minutes. He asked to be excused so he could put his clothes into the dryer, he would return to get his dessert which came with the special. He quickly went out and walked to the wash house. It took him less than five minutes to place his wash into the dryer and then he was walking back into the cafe. Adeline had left the table and Jo and Ike were sitting drinking coffee. Boston informed them that it would be at least an hour before his clothes would be dry, at least that is what he set the dryer for. Their desserts arrived and the waitress poured each a fresh cup of coffee.

"Did you separate the colors from the whites?" Jo asked.

"No. I put everything into one dryer. Are you suppose to dry clothes that way?" Boston inquired.

"No. It's just that sometimes the colored clothes will bleed into the whites. You did wash the colored clothes separate from the whites?" Jo asked with a quizzical expression.

"No. I just threw about the same amount of clothes into each wash machine to make sure they got clean," was Boston's response.

"Oh I'm sure they will be clean, but you may have different colored clothes now." Jo said smiling.

They all kind of laughed. Ike and Jo were going to go to the grocery store before it closed, and they would come by the wash house on the way out of town to pick him up.

Boston paid for his dinner and went back to the wash house. He checked the dryer which had stopped. Some of the smaller items were dry but his jeans and a shirt were still wet. He took out the dry clothes and placed them into his laundry bag and then put another quarter into the dryer. He walked to the table and checked over the reading material. One item was a small newspaper about the size of an insert in one of the papers back home. He sat and began reading to pass the time. The paper consisted of three folded sheets or six pages. He scanned most of the headlines and once in a while read an article. Near the last page was a section titled "Peaks of the Past." The segment was divided into various sections of history, each part had a paragraph or two. There was a section entitled 100 years, 75 years, 50 years, 10 years, and finally last year. He started reading at the 100 year and was working his way toward the column titled last year. However, the history at the ten year section seemed to freeze his mind. He stopped and read it again. The words seemed to leap off the page at him. "Local man, Ike O'Bryn convicted of train robbery, sentenced to prison at Canon City." His mind still couldn't make sense of it. Was this the same Ike O'Bryn he was working for? Again he read it. This time his thoughts wondered who would rob a train in this day and age? What train? Where? Ten years ago would make it 1970. Could that be he robbed a train in 1970? His mind kept pumping out questions. He quickly folded the newspaper and stuffed it into his laundry bag. By now the dryer had stopped and he checked his clothes. The waist of the jeans was still damp but he didn't want to wait any longer. His attention kept returning to the article he read.

Stuffing the remaining clothes into the laundry bag he stepped outside to wait for Ike and Jo. He stood there next to his laundry bag just observing the town. He didn't see any people and only once in awhile a vehicle drove by. This really was a small town. He stood there thinking as he looked around. Does this story change his opinion of Ike and Jo? What should I do with this information? Like a flash the light came on. He came here to experience the West and maybe find material for a story. Well this would certainly make for a good story. How would he find anything out about this? Should he ask about this or would this cause a problem? His thoughts were interrupted when Ike and Jo drove up in the Thunderbird. The trunk opened and Boston put his laundry bag in, then went to the driver's side where Ike had stepped out and folded the front seat down to allow Boston to climb in the back. It was a pleasant drive back to the ranch with Ike and Jo asking Boston how his family spent the week-end. He told them sometimes they went to a mall or shopping in another town. Once in a while they would drive to the ocean.

Upon reaching the ranch, Jo said "I'll get you some sandwiches, chips and a pop to hold you over until breakfast."

"Thanks that would be great." Boston exclaimed.

"Get yourself some rest. The next couple of weeks will be hard. You've got a lot of fencing to do." Ike encouraged.

Jo came out with a large sack and handed it to Boston who was standing there with his laundry bag.

"See you tomorrow!" he yelled, then headed off in the direction of the bunkhouse.

Arriving at the bunkhouse he began placing his clothes back into the foot locker or suitcase, then grabbed the lunch sack knowing that Jo would put some sort of snack in it. Sure enough there was an apple. He took it out and unfolded the newspaper to read over the article again in case he might have missed something. He laid back on the bed and bit into the apple as he went over the article again. Then he realized there were old newspapers here in the bunkhouse. Possibly one of them may have something. He spent the rest of the day going through the stack of old newspapers on the shelf. He had almost gotten to the last one when he spotted a small article with a heading "Local man released from prison." His focus went to it like a bee to honey. The article went on to say how Ike was released early because of his exemplary behavior. It again mentioned that he was sentenced to a ten year prison term for robbing the Cumbres-Toltec train in October of 1969. He was originally scheduled to be released in February of 1980. Boston read and re-read the article trying to gain another small morsel of detail or information. He turned to the front page and saw the date May 1977. He placed the two papers which contained the article on Ike on the bottom of the stack of papers and then placed the stack back on the shelve. The days light was starting to fade as he lit the lantern. He sat at the table eating the remaining food Jo had prepared, wondering how he could write this into a story. As darkness set in so did the reality that tomorrow was going to be a tough day. His thoughts turned to the fencing which lay ahead of him. Mentally he went through what order would work best in accomplishing this task. Stretched out in the bed he focused on the day. Sundays out here really did seem like a special day.

CHAPTER SIX

For the next 3 - 4 weeks Boston dug post holes, compacted the dirt around new posts, and pounded in "T" posts. He learned how to use the fence stretchers and come-along. He also knew how to make fence clips out of pieces of wire. When he had finished running wire to the first "H" post, Ike came out to inspect. He showed him how to tighten the wire. It was to be like the strings of a banjo, tight and even. Boston had kept the posts in line which Ike complimented him on. Ike stayed long enough to help him tighten the first wire, and left. Once again Boston was back working by himself. Being alone didn't seem to bother him. He just enjoyed the beauty and the occasional sighting of wildlife. Once while digging post he came upon a bear. He stood still and watched as it climbed the hill and disappeared in front of him.

Each portion of the fence didn't become easier, but the results of his efforts showed improvements. Boston had blisters on top of blisters. His gloves had worn through at his finger tips and his shirts and jeans all had rips in them. He thought everything he had was wearing out.

The work day was longer than anything he had experienced previously. He started his chores before sun up and then got back to the headquarters after the sun went behind the mountains. He was starting to see that this ranch or cowboy life was pretty hard. On Sundays, he caught up on his sleep and did laundry. He wasn't attending church with them anymore. He just felt other things were more important and he just didn't see any reason to go. He was always on the lookout for old newspapers. When he found any he read them, front to back, looking for any additional information on Ike. These local papers only had article about local events or activities, there wasn't any national news. Once in a while an article about a town in New Mexico appeared since they were so close to that state. He would send a short note to the feature editor but would mail it to his parents address. Expressing to him that this is turning out to be more work than anyone would imagine. But he did not say anything about the newspaper articles he had read.

After weeks of doing nothing but fence building, Boston began wondering if this was a good idea. It seemed to Boston that he paid Jo and Ike so he could work for them. He wasn't enjoying this experience at all. Except for the newspaper article, it seemed to him he was getting all the crappy jobs and Ike and Jiggs were out riding horses and looking after the cows. He didn't say anything to anyone, but one morning before he left for work Jo caught him.

"They are testing you. They want to see what kind of metal you are made of."

"OK" was Boston's response.

Jo continued "Every job on the ranch is important. Even washing dishes. If the fence in the pastures is weak, down or non-existent we won't have a place to put the cattle this winter. Some jobs aren't as glamorous or don't appear that way, but fencing is very important on any ranch and not everyone can do it well. They want to be sure you can handle a hard work load. Believe me, the real hard work is still ahead. If you take your work serious and show pride in it, they will take you serious."

He did not respond, but got in the truck and went out to the pasture. Fencing gives a person a lot of time to think. Since there is nobody to talk to, you work things out thinking them through. Taking pride in fencing means to make it straight, tight and strong. He wasn't in a hurry with the fence anymore since he had been at it so long. He now focused on making it the best he knew how, keeping it straight and making sure each post stood at the same height. He wanted to be proud of the fence he built. After all it may stand fifty or sixty years, maybe longer. He now looked at it more as building a monument which would reflect on him. He would pull the wire as tight as possible with the stretcher. He was giving the stretcher a couple extra ratchets, when the wire broke.

He had been looking at the wire as he was tightening it, when the wire snapped. Before his reflexes could kick in, the barbs on the wire cut across his face. The wire settled in coils at his feet. His face was stinging with the fresh cuts on his forehead and checks. He quickly untangled himself and went to the truck. Examining the cuts, using the mirror on the side of the pick-up. He poured water on a napkin and dabbed away the blood. Holding the wet napkin on the cuts, the bleeding eventually stopped. He went back to his fencing.

When he returned to headquarters, Jo and Ike examined him and determined that no stitches would be needed. Both commented how lucky he was not to have been hit in the eyes.

Boston had been at the ranch almost a month and outside of going to town for laundry on Sundays he never really checked out Wages. Boston was on the last leg of the fence, the portion heading south towards the county road. That evening while dessert and coffee were being passed around, Ike informed Boston, "Tomorrow, Saturday, is a special day," and they would all be going to town.

Boston asked "Why?"

Ike continued, "It's county fair week and everyone goes to town sometime during the week. We are going on Saturday. Besides, that is when the rodeo is going to take place. We'll enjoy freedom day at the ranch on Monday."

Boston looked puzzled.

Ike explained, "That's what I call July Fourth."

That night after cleaning up he went through his clothes and found a pair of jeans with just one small hole. He laid it aside and went searching for a shirt. He did find a dirty shirt with a short tear under the fore arm, and decided it would have to do. Maybe he could buy some clothes before they went to the rodeo. He reached under the bed and pulled out his suitcase. He had stashed the remaining money he owed Ike and Jo along with a couple of hundred dollars cash. He took out the Travelers Checks and a hundred dollars to buy clothes. Hoping he could purchase two pairs of jeans and two shirts. Sticking the money in the jeans he laid out his clothes on the chair. He found himself getting excited about going to town. He couldn't remember when or why he had felt this excited. He had never been or seen a rodeo before. The closest he got was walking past Madison Square Garden when a rodeo was in New York. He laid in bed making mental notes on what he needed to buy. At the top was a pocket knife, two pairs of gloves because they wear out fast. Jeans and shirts seemed to be the next priority. Then personal items if he can find them, such as razors, shaving soap, and toothpaste. Back home, anytime he needed something he just went to a mall or some store. He didn't think ahead what he needed. He didn't even know what kind of stores or how many the town had. The simpler things seemed to take on more significances, more thought and preparation. His body didn't ache like it had the first week, oh yeah! Aspirins, as his mind jump back to the mental list. The long physical days brought sleep quickly as it did this night.

CHAPTER SEVEN

Saturday came with the usual routine beginning with breakfast then chores. The breakfast wasn't as big as previous days. He quickly went out and started the barn and corral chores. Ike walked by "When you're finished, would you help me clean up the truck?" "I'll be right there when I finish" Boston cheerfully replied. Ike had backed the truck up to the lean to and was unloading the tools and fencing material when Boston arrived. "You work on the inside and I'll finish the outside." Ike instructed. Boston picked all the paper trash up that was on the floor and then began sweeping it out with a whiskbroom. When he finished that he took a rag and wiped the dashboard and dash. Ike brought out a small blanket and draped it over the back of the seat, allowing enough to cover the seat itself. Boston quickly went to the bunkhouse and cleaned his face and hands then returned to the house. Ike was waiting at the bottom of the stairs when Boston arrived. Jo opened the screen door on the porch and started down the stairs at the same time. This time Boston opened the door and Jo slid across the seat next to Ike. Boston got in and shut the door. As they drove to town Jo and Ike pointed out landmarks along the route. Names such as Humboldt Peak, Eagle Summit and Gunsite Peak. There were rock outcroppings called Spires Point and The Kraig. Boston looking at them easily related why they had those names.

Coming to a fork in the road, Jo mentioned that by going straight they would eventually arrive at Santa Fe, New Mexico. The winding valley road followed a small creek, then made a sharp right turn climbing and turning up to a tree covered hill. On the other side began a long gentle decent to a wide curve. As the curve straightened out, the small town could be seen a half mile ahead. Boston noticed a sign alongside of the road which stated elevation 7,763 feet and nothing else. He asked why it didn't give the population.

"I guess because that doesn't change." Ike stated.

"What's the elevation at the ranch?" Boston asked.

But before an answer was given, Jo said "Welcome to Wages, Colorado. The population at the last census was 420 people. There are just over 1,000 people in the entire county."

"Is the elevation at the ranch higher or lower than Wages?" Boston asked again.

"It's about the same at the headquarters. It's about 9,000 feet at the cow camp. You will notice the difference when you work up there." Ike responded.

Boston wondered if that meant he would start going up there soon. He still remembered how tired he got his first week at the ranch. Would it be different at the cow camp? Even though he had been here to do his laundry, he really hadn't taken a good look at the town itself. The business portion was about three blocks long with a few businesses on the side streets. The remaining part of the town was made up of single story homes which had big yards. The yards weren't manicured as they were where his parents lived. Instead it appeared to look like the same grass in the pasture he was fencing. The business structures were single story buildings except for a two story building which was the hotel. As Ike drove down the main street, Jo pointed out where they set up a Christmas tree each year and lots of people showed up when they lit it up on December 1st. Upon hearing that Boston commented,

"That sounds like a real old fashioned Christmas."

Ike angled the truck to park in front of the General Store.

"I'm going to the feed store just down the street," Ike continued, "Boston, come join me when you have finished shopping at the General Store."

Boston wasn't even thinking about going into the General Store, let alone shopping. "Come on Boston let's go in." Jo said encouragingly.

The store was a combination of a grocery store, hardware and clothing store all in one. Everyone they met greeted them with smiles and conversation. Jo introduced Boston as their hired man who came out to experience ranch life for the summer. A few made comments about how much a person could learn from Jo and Ike. Jo showed Boston the clothing section

"You might be able to pick up a nice pair of jeans and a dress shirt here. But I'll send you to another place that has a better selection and better prices."

He found a pair of jeans and shirt that fit and was bringing them to the counter when he encountered a display of pocket knives. A young girl was behind the counter where the knives were displayed and she brought out any knife Boston wanted to see. He had never bought one before but did notice that Jo's knife was pretty good size. He found one with two blades having a nice wood grained body. The girl was very helpful answering his questions. He asked how long she has been working there. She commented ever since her folks bought it from Jo when she was little. Boston didn't inquire further, he just stored that information away, wondering what else doesn't he know. After he checked out he put the sack of clothes in the truck and headed down to the feed store.

The feed store not only sold feed, but fencing materials, salt and minerals, lumber, bigger hardware items and jackets, coats and boots. Ike was in the corner where there the saddles and clothes were displayed.

"You're going to be riding soon and you will need a pair of riding boots." Ike stated to Boston. "Those things you have on your feet now are great working boots but you will need something with a heel to prevent your foot from slipping through the stirrups. Sit down here and let's try and find a pair for you."

Boston's quick response seemed defiant "I have ridden in these boots before."

"Not on my ranch, you're not" came Ike's quick reply.

"Ike, I didn't bring enough money with me to buy a pair of boots." Boston confessed. "That's alright, we'll put it on the ranch account." Ike stated.

They didn't have a big selection, but they did have his size. He tried a pair on and liked walking in the taller heel. The boot came half way up his shin, which at first felt uncomfortable but not that it bothered him. He asked if he could wear them now and the man said "Sure." Boston put his old boots in the box and dropped it back at the truck. Just then Jo came out side of the General Store.

"Boston, go up the street two blocks and turn left. A few doors down you will find the second hand store. There will be all sorts of work clothes at very reasonable prices. We'll meet you at the fair grounds near the grand stands." Jo instructed.

"OK" Boston said, and walked up the street in his new boots, enjoying the feel of wearing cowboy boots. Finding the second hand store wasn't difficult. It seemed like finding anything in this small town wouldn't be difficult. When he opened the door he was meet by a familiar face.

"Good morning Boston, what can I help you find?"

It was Adeline, standing behind one of the many tables and racks neatly set up in the small store.

"Hello, Adeline. Do you work here?" Boston greeted her with a smile.

"Yes, This is my store. I wasn't ready to quit working so I opened a store that I thought the town needed. What can I help you find?" Adeline asked politely.

"I need some work shirts and jeans. Do have anything of those?" Boston asked.

"On the shelves in the back room you will find the mens pants and shirts are hanging on the clothes rack next to the shelf." Adeline replied.

Boston stepped through the door way to the back room. Against the wall was an old book case with tags on the shelves providing the sizes of the pants folded neatly on each shelf. He found his size and started checking them out. There were about six pairs, some with tears across the knees and others with paint or grease stains. He grabbed the two pair that had stains.

"How much are the pants?" he asked.

"They are five dollars apiece." Adeline replied.

He realized his remaining twenty seven dollars will go farther than he expected. He then turned his attention to the line of shirts hanging on hangers suspended from a pipe. They were sized Large, Medium and Small. He went to the Mediums and flipped through them. He figured style wasn't going to matter since nobody would see him. He skipped past all the short sleeve shirts and focused on the long sleeve ones. He found a colored plaid shirt and two white shirts that would work.

"How much for the shirts Adeline?" he asked.

"They are fifty cents apiece. If you're interested the men's jackets range from ten to twenty dollars. They are on the opposite wall," replied Adeline.

Upon hearing the price of shirts he went back to the rack and picked out two more shirts, figuring he would have one ruined before the end of next week. He then walked over to the pipe holding the coats and jackets. He began picking through them. He had brought a light coat but would need something a little heavier when early fall came. As Boston was browsing the coats, Adeline was telling him how special Jo was and that she had taught her grand-daughter to play the piano, and how she is always looking out for others. Boston was half listening as he checked each coat, most of which looked like something a rancher would wear. Not skiers or college kids. He found a lined jean jacket that he thought was really nice and it was in pretty good shape except for some wearing at the elbows. He checked the tag and it said eighteen dollars. He tried it on but it was slightly big. Adeline had been watching him when she said

"Come cold weather you'll be wearing long underwear and a heavy shirt so you will want some extra room."

He knew she was right and he took it to the front counter along with the rest of his purchase. Adeline added up the clothes one by one and then said

"Thirty dollars and fifty cents."

Boston was so impressed with the cheap prices he failed to keep track of his total purchase. Boston sheepishly said

"Adeline, I only have twenty seven dollars and I need to get into the rodeo and get dinner yet. I guess I didn't keep track of my money very well."

"Oh don't worry! Just give me twelve dollars and fifty cents for the pants and shirt and pay me later for the jacket."

"I couldn't do that Adeline. I'll come back for it later." Boston stated.

Adeline looked at the coat, "Let me put some patches on the elbows and I'll get it to you after I've finished and you can pay me."

"Well, that sounds OK. How much for the tailoring?" Boston asked.

"There's no charge for alterations." Boston couldn't believe this. He would have never been able to experience anything like this back in Connecticut or New York City. He settled up and said good bye, heading back to the truck with his purchases. Pleased that he now felt he had enough shirts and jeans to make it through to November. That is unless he would be fencing until then. Boston spotted the Post Office and went in, purchasing a couple of stamped envelopes and paper. He quickly jotted a note to his parents telling them he is fine and really enjoying his Western adventure. He wrote another note to the Feature Editor, Mr. Wiseman. "Still feel like I signed on as a laborer." He admitted to himself that he did have some doubts from time to time. However, he was learning new things and seeing country that he had never saw except in movies or pictures.

Boston found the truck sitting there with the windows down and his packages still on the seat. He placed the latest purchase inside the truck next to the others. He glanced over and noticed the keys were still in the ignition just like at the ranch. The town seemed busy with people walking here and there, cars and trucks with trailers going past, up and down the road. People were darting in and out between the parked cars. Walking on the side walks, and in the street. Ike was right. The fair brought out everyone. Wherever he looked people were looking into stores or standing around on the sidewalk visiting. Over at the feed store some men were leaning against a pick up visiting. Everybody seemed so friendly, he thought. It reminded him of a scene in a Norman Rockwell painting.

While he was so engaged in people watching, he failed to see Jo coming out of the General Store.

"Are you hungry?" she hollered.

Boston quickly turned toward the voice.

"Come on," as she motioned with her arm, "let's beat the rush to the café."

Boston quickly joined her as they walked down the side walk to the cafe.

"Will Ike be joining us at the café?" he inquired.

"No." she responded, "He's at the rodeo grounds with Jiggs."

"Jiggs is here?" Boston asked excitedly.

"Yup" replied Jo, "He's working the rodeo."

"How did he get that job?" Boston asked as they entered the café.

Chuckling Jo responded "It's not that you apply for it. Everything is volunteering, and I really don't know what type of work he's doing."

The special was a hamburger with a piece of apple cobbler, which is what they both ordered, hoping to get served quickly and start to the fairgrounds before everyone else. Their timing was perfect. They had just gotten their food when the café started to fill up. They quietly ate their meal and walked back to the truck. Boston was telling Jo about his purchases at the second hand store and that he still owed for the coat he bought. He told Jo he would give her the money and maybe she would be able to get it to Adeline. They agreed to that plan, as they arrived at the truck.

"Let's drive to the fairground parking area so we don't get so dusty." Jo suggested, "Are you up to driving?"

"Sure." Boston said confidently. They got in and Boston maneuvered the truck through the street to a pasture a half mile away which served as parking during the fair. As they walked to the gate, Jo told Boston that Ike suggested they find a seat in the grandstands where they could see the activity in the chutes. Boston wasn't sure what that meant but just kept walking. Jo had picked a place in the grandstands which she thought would be acceptable to Ike and the two of them spread themselves out so there would be enough room for Ike. Boston said

"I'll get some refreshments, what would you like?"

"A cup of sweet tea would be nice. Thank you!" Jo replied.

Boston headed to the refreshment stand and hurried back with two cups of sweetened tea. Country music was playing on the loud speakers. Boston hadn't really listened to that type of music before, but he noticed that Jo seemed to like it.

The crowd started to fill the grandstands and bleachers which were set up along the outside of the arena. The two of them searched the people arriving in hopes of finding Ike.

Jo started waving, "There he is," pointing to the far side of the grandstands.

Boston joined in and then hollered as he got closer. Ike spotted them and quickly climbed up to where they were sitting. He kissed Jo.

"Great seats," he stated.

"How's Jiggs doing? What is he doing? Where is he at?" Boston rattled off the questions. Ike said " He's just behind the chutes just smiling and laughing with the other cowboys. Look back over there" Ike said pointing towards the announcers' tower.

"What kind of work is he doing?" Boston asked.

"He's working the stripping chute."

"What's that?" Boston wanted to know.

"That is where the horses or bulls are run into after the riders get off them in the arena. The rigging each rider used needs to be removed and that is what Jiggs wanted to do." Boston had a lot more questions but his thoughts were interrupted with the announcement of the National Anthem. Everyone rose up and either placed their hat or hand over their heart and sang as a rider carried the American flag around the outside of the arena. Boston sensed a more patriotic feeling among this audience. He even felt a little more pride singing the National Anthem. The first event was the women's barrel racing. It was amazing how well they could ride and make those turns. Ike explained a little about each event that was to take place, it was very helpful for Boston. Steer wrestling was next, then came bare back riding, calf roping, and saddle bronc riding. At the end of the saddle bronc event the announcer came on to say they had a special treat. A birthday gift, and everyone in attendance will be able to participate. The audience will be helping this cowboy celebrate his sixtieth birthday. The audience yelled and clapped and hollered. The announcer came back on

"Please give a round of applause to Mr. Jiggs Jaqua, in chute number One."

The whole crowd's attention was focused on the number one chute. Boston was watching the figure on top of a large black horse. Suddenly his hat shook quickly, the gate opened, the horse jumped out and as the horse's feet touched the ground, a cloud of white dust-like powder came off the riders leggings. The crowed whooped and hollered even louder. Boston got caught up in the commotion yelling, "Ride 'em Jiggs."

The horse just bucked and snorted and jumped. Jiggs took off his hat and began slapping the horse's mane. Again the crowd yelled "ride em cowboy." The buzzer sounded and two mounted cowboys came up along each side as Jiggs grabbed one and slid off. When he touched the ground he turned and bowed to the crowd. First on one side and then turned around and bowed to the other side. By now the crowd was standing whistling and yelling and whooping. They kept it up until Jiggs left the arena. The announcer came on "Ladies and gentlemen, now that was a ride."

Jo and Ike were standing there clapping and smiling.

"He's something" Ike said aloud "he the last of the old timers."

"Let's catch up with him and treat him to ice cream!" Jo suggested.

The crowd was still buzzing about the ride as the rodeo crew prepared for the team roping. Jo and Boston walked to the truck, while Ike headed to the area behind the chutes to make sure Jiggs would meet them at the café. Boston drove the truck to where Ike said he would meet them and Ike got in.

"What was that white stuff, we saw at the beginning?" Boston asked.

"Cowboys always like a good show so I guess he put flour or baby powder in those woolly chaps he had on and let us see one." Ike responded smiling.

Boston angled the truck into a parking space on the corner just past the café. As they entered the two ladies who worked their said "Hello Jo" in unison. No one else was in the café. Jo waived as Ike pulled out a chair for her at a table that allowed them to see outside. They hadn't been there five minutes when a man on horseback came riding past the window. He rode to where the truck was park and tied his horse to the headache rack. Walking into the café the three of them stood up and clapped.

"Enough of this, I came to eat some cake and ice cream. Ladies bring it on." Jiggs bellowed.

We all sat down and the ladies served us cake, ice cream and coffee, with any extra scoop of ice cream for Jiggs.

"You cut a mighty dashing figure in the arena with your white shirt and vest." Jo exclaimed. "But where in the world did you find a pair of woolly chaps?" Jo inquired.

Jiggs began "Adeline had mentioned something about them a few years back, wondering if I would be interested in them. When she told me they belonged to her grandfather, I just couldn't buy them. So, yesterday I told her I wanted to wear them in the rodeo, if they fit. Well you could have folded me with a breeze when she agreed. She even gave me the idea of putting baby powder on them for effect. When I'm done celebrating, I plan on taking them back to her."

Boston couldn't relate to what he had done, he just knew it was hard to imagine that a sixty year old just rode a bronc. All Boston could say was "Happy Birthday Jiggs."

"Thanks Boston." Jiggs said as he sipped coffee. " I saw the fence your working on in the big pasture, it looks pretty good."

"Thanks for that compliment" said Boston.

Jiggs then said to Boston, "I know in the coming days your work is going to get harder but you will make it. Heck we all have made it through rough patches."

With that comment Boston wanted to know, "Will I be going to the cow camp soon?"

Ike looked at Jiggs who looked back while placing a spoonful of ice cream in his mouth. "Maybe in a week or so, but the fence needs to be finished first." Ike stated.

Boston just grinned. Ike then asked Jiggs

"Are you staying in town tonight for the dance?"

"Heck No." Jiggs stated. "None of those beauties wants to dance with an old saddle polisher like me."

"I'd be pleased if I could have a dance with you. We'll call it my birthday gift." said Jo. "Ike, would you select an appropriate song from the juke box."

Ike got up and strolled to the machine studying the selection for a minute. Put in a quarter and came back to the table where he gently pulled the chair away from the table allowing Jo to stand up. Jiggs was busy dusting the crumbs off his shirt and vest and he came around. Ike had selected the song "The Tennessee Waltz." The two of them glided around the tables as the music played. The waitresses and cook came out and joined the observance. When the music ended everybody applauded.

"There are two more songs, one for each of you ladies," said Ike.

The music started again and Jiggs gently lead one of the waitresses around the room. Before the ending of this song a few customers came in, prohibiting the second waitress from taking her turn. The four of them went out the door towards the truck and Jiggs' big horse. Jiggs thanked Jo for the dance and thanked Ike for putting him up in the hotel the night before.

"Happy birthday my friend" Ike said.

As soon as he thanked Adeline he was heading up to camp. He mounted up, turned his horse, waving his hand Jiggs said "Adios." Boston hollered back

"Happy birthday Jiggs. See you in a week."

"The rodeo is about over what should we do now?" Jo asked.

"Jo, we have the appointment with the tax man remember?" Ike replied.

"Oh, before I forget," Boston handed them the envelope with the remaining balance of the $3,000 that he owed them.

"Well thank you Boston, that was very nice of you to remember" Jo stated.

"Boston, why don't you go to the dance while Jo and I are at the accountant's office. It's at the saddle club building next to the fairgrounds. It will starts shortly after the rodeo." Ike suggested. "We'll even give you a ride over there." Ike continued.

"Hey, that sounds like fun, but first I think I'll walk around town and take in a few sites. What time would you pick me up?' Boston inquired.

"Look for us around seven o'clock" Ike stated.

They got into the truck and drove down one of the side streets. Boston crossed the street and walked back towards the fairgrounds. He figured he could find the building by the sound of the music. Walking through the town he was observing all the different details hoping to remember them should he use them in a story or article. He had seen small villages in New England, but in this town the buildings just seemed old and stark, in need of sprucing up. The paint didn't seem to last long. Possibly because of the intensity of the sun. He enjoyed talking to the people. They seemed genuine and not phony or trying to impress someone like so many people in the big cities seem to do. He knew more about a few of these people he just met than some of his neighbors back home. The main street through town was the only one paved. All the side streets were dirt. Some of the sidewalks were cement, some wooden and the rest just a foot path. The feed store looked like something left over from the turn of the century, especially from the outside. The people didn't seem to have much money. At least you couldn't tell by looking at them or their businesses. They worked hard, played hard and seemed content with their lives. They would take time to talk and actually listen to a stranger. It made him feel welcome.

It was quarter to six when he arrived at the saddle club building. They had a live band and there were lots of people inside. There were some cowboys standing outside talking and smoking, but didn't pay him any attention. He paid the cover charge and went inside. They were selling beer, so he purchased one and walked over to stand against the wall to observe. This is the most people he saw since he came to Wages. Some were junior high, and high school, but those with beers, he assumed, were about his age. He observed the guys and how they were dressed, as well as the girls. Everyone seemed to be wearing jeans, western shirts and hats. Not all of them were straw hats. A few were felt hats, like Ike's. He didn't really want to dance. He was having fun soaking up the sights of all the locals. While enjoying his view, a female voice said "You're not from around here are you?" Boston was a little startled and turned to his left to identify where the voice came from. There standing close to him was a blond haired, green eyed girl about four inches shorter then him.

"Hi. No. I'm not from this area, but how would you know that?" Boston asked.

"What's your name?" the girl asked.

He started to say H.B., but stopped himself and said "Boston. What's your name?"

"Shylo Meadow," came the reply. "You're the guy at Jo and Ike's place aren't you?" she concluded.

Boston had heard about how news traveled in a small town and wondered where she got her information from.

"Yeah, but how do you know that?" he hesitantly responded.

"My grandmother runs the second hand store and she told me you bought some things from her and was probably still in town." Shylo replied.

"Adeline is your grandmother?" Boston asked in disbelief. In an instant he remembered his manners and quickly pulled his hat off.

She just chuckled, "Yup, you're getting lessons from Ike. It shows. Don't get me wrong. I like it when a man, especially a young man, shows manners."

Had it not been for the dim lights she would have seen Boston blush.

"But you can put your hat back on now," she instructed.

They carried on a casual conversation about the town and the rodeo. Boston asked her to dance but checked his watch.

"I'm sorry. I won't be able to dance right now. My ride is probably waiting outside."

"Yeah, and you don't want to keep Ike waiting." She said in a reprimanding voice, then continued, "I'll walk out with you."

She began teasing him about getting out of a dance when Ike and Jo pulled up. When Boston opened the door, Shylo leaned in and said hello to Jo and Ike. They responded in kind. Boston got in and with the window already down, Shylo said in a loud voice,

"I'll take a rain check on that dance cowboy."

Boston said "Good night."

She just waived. The truck drove off. About the time Ike shifted gears, he said, "Shylo is a real shiner isn't she Boston?" Before any reply came back he continued. "Jo, maybe we shouldn't have exposed the town to Boston. He might be a real womanizer." They all laughed. Boston quickly changed the subject to the upcoming weeks work.

CHAPTER EIGHT

The morning chore of barn and corral cleaning allowed Boston to be around the horses. At first they were cautious, and now they accepted seeing him every day, and becoming more trusting of him. Every time Ike went to the cow camp he rode a different horse and trailed a second. It seemed he rotated at least one horse every day. One horse always remained behind called Peaches, which was Jo's horse. Peaches was the oldest horse and was privileged to have more down time from work. The horses ranged in age from four years to fifteen. There were seven horses plus Jiggs' horse. Two were kept at the cow camp at all times. At least one was changed out most every day if possible. If two riders were at the camp, then there were a total of four horses there. Even if there was only one person in camp there was still two extra horses. Ike had explained all of this to Boston on the first day. Ike told Boston their names and expected him to know them. Not just the names but what the horses looked like and what made them unique from each other. So, as Boston did his morning chores, he was also studying the horses. Admittedly, it took him a couple of weeks before he saw all of the horses and was able to recognize them so he knew which one was which.

The Tuesday following the rodeo, Ike told Boston Jiggs would be coming down to do some work with the horses and he was to assist him. Boston was excited that he was actually going to be riding and working from a horse. He was wondering what type of work they would be doing. Tuesday began as a beautiful warm July day like many previously, and lately rain showers would start in the afternoon and sometime go until evening. Boston was hoping that would not be the case today.

Jiggs arrived just before Jo rang the dinner bell. He dismounted and loosened his saddle, led his horse into the corral, threw an armful of hay to him before exiting the corral. Boston and Jiggs walked towards the house exchanging pleasantries. Jo had set a table on the porch, in order to catch some of the breeze and get herself out of the hot kitchen. "Smells good" Jiggs said as they climbed the stairs to the porch.

"Brisket, beans, corn bread and peaches for dessert." Jo exclaimed.

When they had sat down Jo said a prayer, then brought the food out. The portions were just the right size to fill you up but not to the point of being tired. Jiggs and Boston thanked Jo for her efforts and the food and returned to the corral.

"I need to leave for the camp around four o'clock so we need to get started." Jiggs explained.

Jiggs squatted on the ground next to the corral fence and took out his small leather pouch of tobacco and reached into another pocket and brought out his papers. He began methodically preparing a cigarette. His rough wrinkled hands deftly handled the task of making a perfectly round cigarette which he placed between his lips. Reaching into another vest pocket he brought out a wooden match which he struck against a fence post. It exploded into a small flame which he quickly used to light his cigarette. He squatted there staring straight ahead, as Boston just observed him.

"How ya gettin' along with Ike and Jo?" Jiggs asked.

"Fine," Boston began, "I talk easier with Jo than Ike, but maybe that's because I've been around her more than Ike. I kind of think Ike tolerates me more than anything."

Jiggs took a drag off his cigarette before responding,

"Well, maybe he wants to see how you are going to play the hand you've been dealt." Jiggs continued, "I don't know what kind of cock and bull story you told to get here, and I don't know what people are like where you come from. But out here we go by what a man says. Now we all know that you are not the person you said you were on paper. Since you have stumbled into two of the most gold hearted people in all of God's earth, you need to be givin' them your level best. They need a fella who can ride and rope to do the work comin' up. I'm not the kind of person to mince words so I want you to tell me straight what you can ride or have ridden? Sure as hell fire, I don't want to let these folks down and I'm here to make sure your not going to let them down when they need you. Now, that the air is cleared, tell me how much you ride. Oh yes, I don't abide with a liar. I'll know if you given it straight."

He then pushed his cigarette into the dirt, as if to punctuate his statement more than actually snuffing the cigarette out. Standing up he looked Boston straight in the eyes. Boston stood there red faced with one hand on the corral rail facing Jiggs. From the first time Boston saw this man he was, in his mind's eye, the quintessential cowboy, with his face like burnt leather, bowed legs and gravelly voice. Now, true to cowboy form, he called Boston's bluff.

"The truth is I have about twenty hours total in my life, riding horses at summer camp and riding a couple of times on a vacation." Boston confessed.

Jiggs rested one boot on a corral rail and stared out across the corral most of a minute, then turned back towards Boston.

"You really want to help these folks?" Jiggs asked.

"I do" Boston began, "I want to know what to do and why I'm doing it. I know I came here under false pretenses but I want to be able to carry my load. I'll give them the best I got. I really want to learn what to do."

There was a pause before Jiggs spoke again

"You got try which is a good start, you pay close attention to what I say. You will need to savvy fast, and keep your trap shut. Ask questions and do lots of practice. You will not know all you should but hopefully you know enough to help and get by. Now go bring Peaches out here."

Boston ran to the barn, got the lead rope and brought Peaches to the corral. The two of them went to the tack room and selected a bridle and saddle that would fit Boston which he carried out. Jiggs had grabbed a blanket and saddle pad carrying them to the corral. "Why do you use both a blanket and a pad. Isn't one enough? Boston asked.

"We want to protect the back on the horse, especially when riding in the mountains. There isn't much level ground. Between that and roping causes strain on the back of a horse. You need to treat them right so they will be there when you need em." Jiggs continued "When we get to the corral watch and listen, cause I'm only going to do this once."

He brought Peaches over and keeping the lead rope in the bend of his elbow he first put the bit and bridle on, then the blanket and pad and finally the saddle which he cinched down. Then he undid everything, starting with the back cinch. When he had everything stripped he said "Now it's your turn."

Boston had done this previously and was rusty at it. At first he tried to force the bit into Peaches mouth.

"Stop" Jiggs commanded, "This isn't a race and you need to take care how you put the bit into the mouth so as not to hurt em. You keep that up and they'll get bit shy. Here, put one hand up here at his head, spread you thumb out to behind his ear and your fore finger behind the other. They have a sensitive spot which you can use to aid you in holding the head still, but don't be knocking on their teeth. You don't like it when someone knocks on your teeth. Now try again."

Boston did as instructed and continued until he had finished, then turned to Jiggs.

"Now strip it." Jiggs ordered.

After Boston had completed that task he was told to repeat the process. This he did four consecutive times. When he had completed saddling Peaches for the fourth time, Jiggs said,

"Horses are like people. Some are calm in spirit, others nervous, some lazy, other spirited, some more so. Some good, some great and some outlaws and a few just mean. The horses here have been treated well and expect that treatment. Each person here can ride any one of the horses in this small string, including Jo. You need to practice every chance you can with whatever horse is available, to get your confidence. Now mount up and take Peaches around the corral."

The corral wasn't all that big, but before he finished his first circuit, Jiggs asked him to reverse his direction which Boston did and upon completing that circuit Boston stopped Peaches.

"Do that again without using the reins" Jiggs commanded.

Boston squeezed the horses side and Peaches walked off, but Boston was unable to turn her the opposite way.

"You need to use your legs to give directions and not so much with the reins. They don't like having their head pulled around. Practice that some I'll give you pointers as you go." For the next fifteen minutes Boston rode around following Jiggs' instructions and soon he was getting the hang of controlling the horse with his legs and not the reins. Jiggs then opened the corral gate and asked Boston to take Peaches down the drive to the county road at a trot. He first explained how to get Peaches to a trot. Boston complied and the two went down the drive way at a trot and returned. Boston was excited to be riding even if it was just down the driveway and back.

"Do you know how to post?" Jiggs asked.

"Yes" replied Boston smiling.

"Then do it again, only posting as you go." Jiggs instructed.

Again Peaches and Boston went at a trot to the county road and back. This time with Boston posting all the way. The third time Jiggs told Boston to stand up in the stirrups. When they return from the third trip, Jiggs walked over to the corral fence and started to build himself a cigarette.

"Should I dismount?" Boston asked.

"No stay in the saddle. You need to be able to ride, stand or post for long distances. Be able to stop and roll your horse back quickly. You'll need to spend as much time as possible riding and practicing these things."

Raising his arm and pointing towards the pasture in front of the house, "Go out there and find yourself a couple objects on the ground, sixty or seventy feet apart. Ride a figure eight pattern and then reverse your direction. Start at a walk and then go up to a trot and when you're confident and feel relaxed, go to a lope. But practice, practice. You still need to do your assigned tasks and chores, but make it a priority to ride. Do it early morning or at dusk whenever you can."

He took his last drag, dropped his cigarette on the ground and twisted it into the dirt with his boot.

"I'll be back in four or five days to see how you are doing."

He then held the gate for Boston and gathered in the reins to his horse leading it out of the corral. After tightening his cinch he mounted and rode off leaving Boston standing in the corral.

He was striping the saddle and bridle when he heard the sound of a truck coming down the drive. It was the first time any vehicle came down the drive other than those that belonged to the ranch. He stood in the corral holding the saddle as he watched this pick up drive up to the house. It was a slim person wearing western attire with a broad straw hat that stepped out of the truck. The person waved at Boston and then climbed the stairs to the porch. Boston turned to the tack room to store the equipment, his mind trying to remember everything Jiggs had said. It was a little early to do the evening chores, but since he was already there he watered and put out hay to the horses. He was just about through when a truck horn honked. He went outside the barn to see. All that was visible was an arm waving over the top of the truck as it sped down the drive. He looked towards the house but Jo was not outside. Being on a horse for a couple of hours made his legs sore. He was thinking to himself that he needed to find three hours a day to ride in. If he started early in the morning before chores, he could get in a hour and a half, possibly another hour and half at dusk. He had made up his mind that he wouldn't visit so much at meal time and spent that time practicing. He wanted to show everybody that he was serious and hoped they saw how much he really want to help. That night at supper Jo presented the jacket Boston had purchased, the one Adeline put patches on. She had sewn on leather patches at the elbows, which really gave a neat look to the jacket.

"Shylo brought it out." Jo said. "That's who was driving the truck that you saw earlier." "I'll have to thank her next time I see her." Boston responded. His mind still on going out to ride.

Four days had past since Jiggs was last there. Both he and Ike were now staying at the cow camp preparing for branding. Boston had done what Jiggs suggested, he was riding a different horse each time he went to ride. When Jiggs showed up again at dinner time, Boston was anxious to show him how he had improved. He demonstrated his riding in the pasture where he showed Jiggs how he had improved on his riding and how he was trotting and would lope once in a while. Not everything was smooth but Jiggs said "showing improvement." He continued to urge him to practice and mentioned Ike may be sending him up to camp in a few days. That was music to Boston's ears.

CHAPTER NINE

Ike informed Boston that he would be headed to the cow camp Sunday afternoon. He should have his gear ready to go by four o'clock. All morning and evening chores would need to be completed prior to leaving. Boston wasn't thinking about going to town on Sunday. He focused on his chores and then heading back to the bunkhouse to pack his things. He spent Saturday night gathering the clothes he would take. Ike had told him to bring whatever he would need for a two week stay. The clothes he planned to take along he stuffed in his laundry bag. Any dirty clothes he put into the pillow case he stripped off the pillow. He wanted to pack enough but then again he didn't want to bring along too much. He put in two pairs of jeans, three shirts, four or five socks and underwear. He brought along a sweatshirt in case it got cold. He got his shaving kit and a roll of toilet paper from the shower and outhouse.

Boston said he wasn't going to church but would be doing his laundry instead. They said he could take the truck and come back to pick them up at the café at one-thirty. That would allow plenty of time to get back to the ranch and have his things ready, as well as do any chores if necessary. After leaving them off at church, he went straight to the wash house. He had learned the washing his jeans and shirts separate from the other items kept the colors from fading but also seemed to allow the clothes to dry faster. He was taking his clothes back to the ranch in short time. With his laundry done, he had everything packed into the laundry bag which he stacked by the door of the bunkhouse. He headed back to town. With time to spare he went to the General Store and purchased some snack type foods for his lunch and then drove to the café.

Parking in front of the café, Ike had just come out holding the door for Adeline, Jo and Shylo. Boston quickly exited the truck and said "Good morning!"

"We missed you in church Boston." Adeline said.

"Well I, I…" Boston stammered, "needed to do my laundry."

"It's better to have a clean heart than clean clothes." Adeline chided.

There was a pause in the conversation when Shylo said "Bring your laundry to Adeline's house on Sunday and I'll do it. Then you can pick it up the following Sunday."

Boston was surprised by the offer but wasn't sure he wanted a stranger to be doing his laundry.

"I'll think about that." he replied.

The three of them climbed into the truck and waved good bye. Ike broke the silence, "Boston, before you head to the bunkhouse I want to give you something."

The remainder of the ride they commented about the surrounding beauty and again Boston noticed the various peaks Jo previously pointed out. Arriving at the ranch, Ike & Jo went inside, while Boston waited by the truck. Shortly Ike came back out carrying what looked like a pair of pants.

"Here, try these on. They're old but I think they will fit," as he tossed him a pair of chaps. "Old but still functional. I quit wearing them years ago."

Boston caught them and holding them up to his legs he said, "Thanks!"

Before Ike turned to leave he said, "The buckle goes in the back."

He then disappeared through the porch door.

At the bunkhouse Boston quickly put them on. Remembering what Ike had said he placed the buckle in the back, then buckled it. He then zipped the legs together. Staring down they looked to be about four inches short but Boston thought they looked cool. He walked around in them to get the feel. The first thing he realized that his legs felt warmer. He had seen Ike and Jiggs wearing these as they rode to or from headquarters. He went over in his mind what he had packed trying not to forget anything. At 3:30 he picked up his laundry bag and sleeping bag and wearing his chaps walked up to the barn. He began saddling the horse Ike told him to ride. When he had finished, he saddled Peaches for Jo. Before he finished with Peaches Ike came in and began saddling his horse. Looking over the top of his horse at Boston Ike said, "They look pretty good on you."

"Thanks again for the use of them." Boston replied.

Just then Jo came out dressed to ride and wearing her pistol.

"Do you think there will be snakes in the high country?" asked Boston.

"I've taken the snake shot out and loaded it with hollow points. There are bigger varmints up there." Jo responded as she checked and re-tightened Peaches cinch.

Ike had gone back to the house but reappeared carrying two medium sized cloth sacks that were tied together with a leather throng. He placed this across the base of a pack horses neck, in front of its withers. As Boston watched he noticed Ike take a hank of mane and tie it around the leather thong. All the horses were lead out of the corral. Ike instructed Boston to mount up and then he looped a lead rope from one of the pack horses to Boston's saddle horn. "Hold on to this but don't take it off the horn." Ike instructed. Joe and Peaches took the lead followed by Boston and a pack horse with Ike and another pack horse bring up the rear. It was a warm mid-July afternoon as they began the ascent to the cow camp. They were in pines as the trail zigged and zagged upward. At first there wasn't much to see because the trees were so dense. The pace was steady and slow. To Boston it seemed like a trail ride, but he knew this was going to be the beginning of something different. The trail widened and a wire gate appeared. Jo dismounted and opened the gate. The rest rode through, and then waited until she got the gate closed and remounted. Everyone else followed along in the same order they left at the headquarters. Boston followed the fence line with eyes as it disappeared into the trees. The riders stayed in the trees parallel to the fence, until the ground rose up quickly. The trail then broke back to the left as it became steeper with switch back turns. As they neared the top, Boston could look back and see that he was twenty feet above Ike and his pack horse. As they topped the hill the trees became fewer and a meadow started to come into sight. The trail began to level out. He realized that if he had tried to find this on his own he most certainly would have gotten lost. He heard water running and then he saw a small stream about three feet wide and maybe ten inches deep. Peaches walked right through it. Boston's horse jumped over it which caught him a little off guard. He regained his seat just in time to observe Ike's horse walk through the stream. Boston decided to make a mental note about the horse he was on. The clearing began on the other side of the stream. Boston estimated the meadow to be the length of three football fields and twice as wide as one. Toward the far end was a bare knoll sticking out from a grove of aspens. At the top of the knoll was a figure standing and waving. Jo returned his wave. Jo went just past the knoll to a small opening in the aspens. At the mouth of the opening she stopped and dismounted, Jiggs took Peaches into a make shift corral of poles from pine and aspen. The corral was rather large, allowing room for the horses to graze. Each horse was led into the corral where they were unsaddled or pack saddles removed. Each saddle, pad and blanket was hung on a rail. Boston watched Jiggs pull out his knife and cut the mane hair that was holding the two medium size sacks. When all the horses were unsaddled, Jiggs looked at Boston. "I'll show you where you can stow your gear and throw out your bed."

Quickly grabbing his laundry bag and sleeping bag he followed Jiggs. They walked to the top of the small knoll to a level area on top. This area at top was kind of "U" shaped. At the upper end were a number of larger aspens. Between two of the aspens was some sort of metal box about six feet tall and two feet wide. "This is our chuck box." Jiggs exclaimed, setting the two sacks down. Another twenty feet past this box was another metal box of similar size only wider, laying parallel to the ground on four stumps.

"What's this?" asked Boston.

"That's where Jo sleeps. We stash our bedrolls underneath to keep them out of the rain." Jiggs responded "Throw your bedroll and war bag down there." Jiggs pointed to the area below the metal box. Boston threw his bed roll and laundry bag down but it seemed dwarfed compared to the two canvas rolls already there. They turned back to join the others who were in the process of opening the chuck box. The lid was hinged about two thirds down from the top, which allowed the lid to fold out while at the same time metal legs came out to support the top of this table. The bottom third had a long hinge across to allow that door to be lifted up. Inside was a cold chest of insulated tin, called the meat locker. The top half, when opened, revealed shelves holding cooking utensils, pots, pans along with cans or bags of supplies.

"Do you like it?" asked Ike.

"It looks like one of those old chuck wagons without the wagon, and I do think it looks neat." replied Boston.

While the others restocked supplies from the two sacks and the pannier from the second pack saddle, Boston walked around the knoll. There was a fire pit ringed by rocks, that had two three foot metal stakes on either side, with another steel rod laid between the two across the fire pit. On one side were some "S" hooks and on the other side was a hook with a handle. Out past the fire pit were two large logs making a "V" shape. Then a little beyond that the knoll began dropping off to the meadow about twelve feet down. His walk around the camp was cut short when Ike called him. Everyone was still gathered around the chuck box as Boston came over. Ike stepped away and led Boston to the back of the chuck box.

"Each person here has responsibilities at camp. Yours will be to make sure there is plenty of wood," pointing to the stack, "as well as keeping the Lyster bag full of water." Ike then led him to the back side of the camp, "This is a Lyster bag." Pointing at a canvas bag with a pointed top suspended off the ground by three poles. Sitting on the ground next to the Lyster bag were four green metal cans, Ike picked up two of them and handed one to Boston. "You are always to keep at least two cans full so we don't run out of water. Every morning or night you will pour two cans into the Lyster bag. I'll show you where to get the water." They continued walking away from the camp going downhill about seventy-five yards, to a fast moving stream. Ike laid the can he carried on its side in the stream until it filled with water and Boston followed his example. The two of them turned around and walked back up the hill. Placing the cans down, Ike continued giving instructions," Put two of these chlorine tablets in each can you fill up. I'll show you where in the chuck box they are kept. It is very important you do this, or we'll all get sick."

"I understand." Boston nodded in agreement.

Ike then showed how to fill the Lyster bag and replace the top. "You could save yourself a trip tomorrow by going back down the hill and filling these two cans for tomorrow. Just remember which cans have set overnight." Ike then handed the bottle of chlorine tablets to Boston. He picked up the two cans and walked back down the hill. Going down wasn't that difficult but returning uphill with two cans caused him to stop and take breaks. Even after he had added the chlorine tablets to the two fresh cans he was still breathing hard. He walked back towards the chuck box. When he arrived, still breathing hard he asked, "where do I put these pills?"

Jo showed him a place on the top inside shelf, then said "You need to take it slow and easy. We're at a higher elevation."

He watched as everyone seemed to be doing something associated with the evening meal. Jiggs took the big grey coffee pot and headed towards the Lyster bag. Jiggs told Boston, "You might as well come along and see how we make coffee." Jiggs continued. "Fill the pot two thirds full of water." After doing this, both walked back to the chuck box. Jiggs then continued"Grab two fist fulls of coffee and drop it into the pot. Place the pot on that flat rock pushing it near the fire. Wait till it boils. Once it boils, pull it back away from the fire. You'll want to have some egg shells handy, so crack an egg, saving the egg for breakfast. After the pot has simmered away from the fire a few minutes, add the crushed egg shells. Push the pot back towards the fire and let it boil again. Then pour the coffee through a sock to catch the shells and grounds." Boston just looked at him a few seconds then said "you are kidding?"

"Or you could just pour the coffee grounds in a sock and drop it into the pot and forget about the egg shell." Jiggs commented.

"Really?" replied Boston.

"No, Boston he's not," said Ike. "You will get the hang of it after a couple of times." While Jiggs had been explaining coffee making. Ike took a short handled shovel and dug a small pit in the ashes. He then placed the kettle he was preparing in the small pit and covered it with ashes. Jo had placed biscuits in a similar looking pan but it wasn't as deep. She then busied herself spreading something on a tortilla, rolling them up, then cutting them in small pieces. Jiggs suggested to Boston, "you might want to hunt up some wood while we still have a little daylight."

Boston wandered into the nearby trees looking for something sizable for the fire. He didn't want to go too far on his first time out, so he stayed on the edge of the meadow. Soon he was dragging a good size dry limb back to camp. He realized this wood gathering was going to be more of a chore than he thought. The sun had dropped behind the mountain as he was returning to camp. With the setting of the sun, the air temperature seemed to fall as well. He was glad that he had remembered to bring a sweatshirt. Next time he would remember to bring that jacket he bought. The sound of Ike's voice calling, "Come and get it!" hastened him towards the camp.

They all enjoyed an elk roast with Rice-A-Roni, biscuits that melted in your mouth along with Jo's tortilla with cream cheese and jalapeño. Boston always thought food tasted better out doors and that thought was just reinforced.

After the meal, each one cleaned his own plate in what they called a wreck tub, and set them back into the chuck box. They would then retire back to the logs by the fire with their coffee and talk about the upcoming day or whatever topic was at hand. Tonight Boston commented about how good the meal was and that he never knew elk tasted so good. He commented that he had never seen it on a restaurant menu. "There's lots of things the people back East don't know about folks out West." Jiggs stated.

"Like what?" asked Boston.

Jiggs always spoke his mind and Boston knew he would get a straight answer. "Our work is hard. This is not a glamorous life like they show in movies. It's eating dirt, sweating, bleeding and sometimes dying. Yeah, we complain but so do most folks about their work. Wouldn't want to be fenced in by buildings and houses. We prefer the lonesomeness of the plains, prairies and mountains. We're individualist, to a fault maybe. Maybe even nonconformist. Not all cowboys are uneducated or shiftless. They read whatever they get a hold of, feed sacks, newspapers, journals and even books if they find them. But without those, they can read horses, cattle, the weather, the grass and even their fellow man. We'll do without luxuries in order to live the life style that affords us our freedom. We know we are never going to get rich or own a piece of land. So we attach ourselves as hired hands to those more fortunate. Not begrudgingly but earnestly and eagerly. A cowboy can always quit if he doesn't like the way things are going. But mostly having the freedom to be on the land, to work in such beauty surpasses any city. Enjoying a star lit sky in front of a fire we think surpasses the lights of any city. We take pride in our work, our gear, our life style. In the sight of others we may not appear to have much. But we have all we need."

Jo looked at Jiggs "I've know you a few years now, and that's the most I have heard you say at any one time. I think you spoke for all of us. We couldn't have said it any better. Bravo!"

Jiggs just sat there and took another drag off his cigarette and sipped his coffee. Boston wished he had a tape recorder. He wanted to recall every word Jiggs said.

As darkness crept in, the stars came out, more than Boston had ever seen before. They passed an hour talking about beautiful sights they had seen. Boston joined in telling about some sights he saw in Hawaii. They seemed very interested in his descriptions, even asked a couple of questions.

Before they retired for the night, Ike explained to Boston what they were going to accomplish in the next several days. In the morning they would ride up to the high pasture, more of a mountain side and push the cattle toward a large trap or pen at the bottom. This process would be repeated until they were sure that they had found all the cattle. Ike told Boston that cattle have a way of disappearing in timber and brush. There was water running through the trap so the cattle could stay there overnight. Before leaving them, a count would be made and a visual check for any sick cows. He drew out a picture in the dirt how and where he wanted each person to be as they entered the high pasture. They would follow each other along, or close to the perimeter of the pasture. Then slowly make a turn inward to form part of a circle. Each rider is to move slowly toward the cattle. Ike explained that if a rider or horse shows fear or lack of self-confidence, the cow or cows will pick up on it. A cow should move normally in the direction it is facing. Once the cow is moving, then begin to move or pressure her to go in the direction you want her to go.

Ike said, "Cows don't have lots of patience and they will get on the fight if you press them too much." He went on talking about being a little aggressive, but too much can result in a bad day. "Remember, if one gets by you, we can do another drive. Boston, all these horse have done this before, so don't be timid. The horse is waiting for direction. Keep your pace with us as we get to the bottom. Hold and wait until those of us further away come to you. Keep a distance and push them into the trap. Jiggs or I will work the gate to get you back out. If everything goes alright, we can sort and brand tomorrow."

Boston had been listening intently, but inside he was excited as a kid at Christmas. He began to understand the importance of having an experienced man doing the work he was going to attempt in the next few days. The evening seemed to disappear as fast as the wood in the fire. Jiggs got up to get his bed roll. Jo and Ike followed with Boston bringing up the rear. Ike was assisting in setting up the metal box which housed Jo's bed as Boston reached under and picked up his sleeping bag. "Good night" he said as Ike and Jo responded in kind.

Returning to the fire he noticed the size difference between his sleeping bag and the bed roll of Jiggs. It was much thicker more like a mattress wrapped in canvas. He wondered if his sleeping bag was adequate. Was there a reason his bag and Ike's were different? Boston was about to spread his bag out between the fire and big logs, when Jiggs spoke out "Your place is on the other side of the logs. Since it is your job to tend the fire, being the furthest away from it, you'll be the first one to get cold and you'll have to get up and put in another log. Oh, and remember the coffee." He then crawled into his bag. Ike then came over with his bag and unrolled it where Boston had intended on placing his. Boston was spreading out his sleeping bag and was the last one to crawl in. Boston observed the others had taken off their chaps laying them alongside their bedrolls and putting their boots inside the bedroll. His sleeping bag didn't give him enough room to put them inside so he left them out with the chaps.

Sleep didn't come as he thought about what Ike had said they would be doing the next day. The excitement of tomorrows work may be partly at fault for delaying his sleep. Laying there in the peace and quiet, except for an occasional pop from the campfire, he was captivated by the vast number of stars he was seeing. Dreaming that the next days work would be like what he had seen in the movies. This was what he envisioned the cowboy life to be like. His eyelids grew heavier the more the campfire burned down. The peace and quiet soon turned into dreams.

CHAPTER TEN

Boston tossed and turned as he tried to find a comfortable spot on his bed ground. He decided to get up and relieve himself. Slipping his boots on, he quietly walked toward the horse corral. Standing there he looked at his watch on his wrist. It said 5:15. When he had finished he walked slowly back to the camp. He looked up into the night sky, it seemed as if there were even more stars out at this time. He didn't see any moon and yet there was enough light to see where he was walking. Only embers were left from the night fire. He treaded quietly past the logs and chuck box to the wood pile. Picking up a couple of larger pieces and a number of smaller sticks he headed back to the fire pit. Using one of the smaller sticks to poke the undisturbed embers back to life, then gently laid into the hot coals the remaining small sticks. When they were ablaze, he laid on the two larger pieces of wood. The fire now gave off a nice light and illuminated the two sleeping figures in their bed rolls. Boston picked up the grey coffee pot by the bale handle and taking the lid off he poured the remaining coffee on the ground. Again he walked softly past the chuck box, wood pile and the bed where Jo was sleeping to where the Lyster bag was hanging. Filling it, as Jiggs had showed him, he returned to the chuck box quietly. Reaching for the coffee, Boston remember that if he put the coffee in a sock he didn't have to mess with egg shells. So he went back to where Jo slept and getting down on hands and knees he felt around until he found his laundry bag. He stuck his arm in up to his arm pit and then felt around until he felt a sock. Quietly he closed it up and gingerly walked back to the chuck box hoping he hadn't awakened Jo. Now, he grabbed the coffee, and taking one fist full out, he stuffed it into his sock and did that process again. As he held up the sock looking at the small lump in the bottom, he decided to add another fistful since he figured his hands were probably smaller than Jiggs'. He then dropped the sock into the pot. Continuing to follow instructions he push the pot out to the end of the flat rock so it was next to the fire.

Rather than sit around the fire he thought he could go out and try to gather firewood. As he walked away from the fire and the camp it became obvious that there just wasn't enough light to find wood. Besides he wanted to see what he was reaching to pick up. Heading back to camp he could see grey light in the east, and knew their day would soon begin. He really was hoping the coffee would be ready when everyone woke up.

Boston sat on the ground near the fire and was watching the eastern sky change from a faint grey to a brighter grey. Ike crawled out of his bed roll. "Good morning Ike. Coffee should be ready soon."

"Thanks. How did you sleep?" Ike responded groggily.

"Towards morning the ground got kind of hard." Boston stated the truth.

"Yup! If you're going to be doing a lot of sleeping outside, invest in one of these," Ike said kicking at his bed roll.

"I may have to do that. What store do you get one at?" Boston asked.

"Around here we just buy a big sheet of canvas and make them ourselves, or there are a few specialty shops that make them." Ike explained.

By now Jiggs was stirring in his bed roll and slowly crawled out. "Coffee ready?" he asked. Boston looked at the pot "Just started to boil." Grabbing the side handle of the pot with his sleeve he pulled it back from the fire. Boston went to the chuck box and took down three cups, which he set on the chuck table. He then returned to the fire for the pot, but wasn't sure how he could pour the coffee if he had to hold it with the ends of his shirt sleeves. Ike figured out his dilemma and handed him his wild rag.

"Use this like a pot holder."

Boston took it and began to fill the cups. Before he had finished the third cup, Jo showed up with her cup. He was filling it up but the coffee didn't seem to pour as evenly. It kind of dribbled out. By now the other two had come over to retrieve their coffee and overheard Jo ask, "Boston, did you make enough? It seems to be pouring like it's at the bottom of the pot."

"I followed Jiggs' recipe, two thirds full of water." Boston stated.

"Did you take out the egg shells?" Jo inquired.

"I used a sock instead of eggshells." Boston said proudly.

"Did you take out the sock?" asked Jo.

"No! Was I supposed to?" Boston responded.

They all chuckled a little. Jo got a spoon and dug out the sock. Holding the sock up with the spoon they all saw that it wasn't tied into a knot.

"Boston, you need to tie the sock into a knot to keep the grounds from coming out and then hang it off the edge like a tea bag. That way you can retrieve the sock after the water boils when you pull the pot from the fire." Jiggs continued "It won't be the first time any of us drank coffee with grounds in it. Besides we can strain it through a cloth if we really want to eliminate the grounds."

They all headed over to the fire to sip coffee watch the mountains come alive with light. Boston took a sip of his coffee. He could barely get it down without a grimace. He hoped the others didn't see. If yesterday's coffee was strong, this stuff was really stout. Almost gave one a bitter stomach. He didn't know if he should say anything. This thought was interrupted when Ike said "It sure is wake up coffee." He and Jiggs just kept sipping, Boston was embarrassed and kept his head down so his hat brim kept his face in the shadow.

Jo said "Mine is really hot, I think I'll add some water" and got up to walk towards the Lyster bag. Boston just kept his head down and continued to sip, although very small amounts, of his coffee. As they sat there Jo came back carrying a jar of water. She poured it into the pot and slid it next to the fire. Nobody said anything they just kept sipping on their coffee. Ike got up and brought a big skillet to the fire pit. He had first placed two logs across the fire pit and then set the skillet on the logs. He put some bacon in the pan and Jo was mixing up a pot full of biscuits. Jiggs had gotten up and disappeared behind the chuck box. Shortly he came back with a faded blue wild rag in his hand. With a stretched out arm to Boston, " You better have one of these. They are pretty handy for lots of things. Most of our equipment has a purpose. This piece of cloth has many purposes. I'll let you buy me a new one for Christmas." Smiling he sat down and sipped his coffee. By the time they ate their breakfast, the coffee was heated up again and they all enjoyed their second cup. Again, each one cleaned his plate, fork or spoon and cup. When everything was stowed, they headed toward the corral.

They each saddled their mounts with Ike assisting Jo with her saddle. Ike told them the order he wanted them to ride out in and to stay in that until they get all the cows to the trap. Quickly reviewing the instructions, they mounted up and headed out. Boston felt the instructions and review was for his benefit. Boston thought they rode about a mile when they came to a wire gate. Ike got down and opened it as the rest rode through and waited until Ike had the gate closed and he was remounted. The sun was over the tops of the mountains in the East, and Boston was looking and listening to all the sounds as the rode up a wide road, which they called a fire break. There were fewer aspen trees now as the trail sloped up gently. Off to his left was a fence line only visible through the gaps in the pine trees. The trail became narrower and the branches on the evergreens slapped against his legs and arms. Mentally Boston was reviewing what Ike has said that morning and the night before, when he noticed Jiggs turn to the right and disappear into the trees. Boston turned his horse where he was at and headed off the trail down the side of the mountain. He quickly glanced to his left and then right but the trees were so thick he couldn't see. He was not able to go in a straight line decent because of the trees but weaved back and forth trying to stay on his line. Continuing to pick his way through the trees he only heard the sound of the horses feet breaking branches, the branches slapping his legs, arms and face. Ahead of him he could see the trees were thinning and the pasture must be approaching. He tried looking left and right to locate Jiggs or Jo but didn't see anyone. Looking back to the front he saw a cow moving uphill towards his left. He was not able to move his horse to attempt to stop or turn the cow because of the trees. Remembering what Ike had said about doing another drive, he let it go past him. By the time he reached the edge of the valley, everyone else was there. Jo was off to his right waiting and Jiggs off to his left waiting. Past Jiggs he saw Ike move up to the farthest end of the valley. Jiggs turned to follow after him as did Boston and Jo, all moving at a walk. At the far end Ike crossed the narrow valley and went into the trees, Jiggs followed stopping at the edge of the trees. Boston continued to the end of the valley when Jiggs said he should take the drag position and stay at the bottom of the valley. He and Jo would work the flank, while Ike was pushing them out of the brush. Each one positioned himself and waited. Cattle were milling in the valley as the three of them rode forward slowly. The three of them moved the cows steadily down the valley. Once in a while a cow and calf would come out from the trees further up. Boston could see the trap and that Ike had opened the gate and then ridden out toward the tree line on the flank Jo was working. Jiggs positioned himself back from the trap but yet close enough that the cows didn't break back toward him. Boston steadily rode forward keeping a slow pace. The valley floor had become wider now. It was necessary that he ride a loop where he would walk toward one side of the valley and then loop back toward the herd going in the opposite direction, remembering not to get too close so the cows felt pressure. As Jo got closer to Ike's position, she dropped behind the herd to join Boston. The two steadily pressured the cows and calves into the large trap. They rode into the trap while Ike and Jiggs closed the gate behind them. Ike let out a whistle and Jo turned back, Boston turned to see what Ike wanted. He saw Jo turning back and followed her as Jiggs worked the gate, letting them out one at a time.

They sat on their horses as Ike asked if they may have missed any. Boston said one cow had gone past him and Jo said she also had one get by. Jiggs said that first part is pretty dense and he was sure there were more than a few hiding out there. Ike wanted to take a rough count so they all rode along side of the trap where the cows were now milling around. They rode in a line. Boston watched Ike as he stood in his saddle and began counting. When everyone got to the opposite end of the trap Ike asked what was the count. Boston said "I didn't know I was supposed to count." Jo gave her number and Jiggs gave his. Then Ike told them what he counted. All their individual numbers were close to each other but Ike said they were short of the eighty five head that are to be in this pasture. Ike paused for a moment looking back at the pasture, then at the timbered sides. Ike turned to talk to the three

"We are going to do another drive, only this time, Jiggs and I will push them out on this west side," he pointed to the side of the valley on his left. "Jo, you will start going into the trees on the far end. Sweetheart, on that side the trees aren't as deep. Take your time and be careful. You and Boston ride to the far end but give us some time to work our side before you start moving toward the trap. Does everyone understand? Any questions?"

Jo asked "What about the gate?"

Ike replied, "Jiggs will be coming back and will let himself inside the trap and hold those cattle at the far end of the trap. I will handle opening the gate and then assist in moving whatever we catch this time into our trap. If we miss them this drive, we can always make another round. OK?"

They rode off as Ike had instructed. Jo and Boston rode back up the valley to where it started. Boston remained in the valley as Jo rode up into the trees to Boston's left. Boston waited until he thought enough time had passed then decided to wait a little longer. A cow and calf came out on his right but forward of where he waited. He began walking his horse slowly staying close to the trees on his right hoping the cow and calf would come further into the valley. As he approached they did exactly as he had hoped. He glanced to his left into the trees and could see Jo was ahead of him. Still he kept his steady pace. Soon another pair came out of the trees on his right. They seemed to align themselves with the first pair. Jo had flushed a pair into the valley pasture. This forced Boston to begin his slow serpentine movement. By the time he got into view of the trap, Jo had joined him and together they pushed the eight pairs that were flushed towards the trap. As they approached Ike was again stationed to the right of the trap and the gate was open. Jiggs was holding the cattle as far as possible from the gate. When the eight pairs saw Ike they gradually changed direction and headed toward the gate. As this package of cows and calves began coming through the gate, Jiggs moved to one side of the trap to allow the new arrivals to go past him. Once the cows were inside the trap, Ike told Boston and Jo to ride into the trap and Jiggs would explain what they would be doing. The trap was a long rectangular area with the perimeter fenced with rails made of smaller aspen or pine trees. There was a fence line that divided the trap area into two parts, with alleyways at either end. One part was twice as big in width as the second portion. Jiggs stationed Boston in a spot near one end of the fence which separated the trap. Ike would position himself on the outside of the trap in line with Boston. Jo and Jiggs would cause the heard to move in a circular route around the outer edge of the trap. This would allow Ike to take a count of the cows as they passed between Ike and Boston. Once the cattle began milling in the direction Jo and Jiggs were pressuring them, everything went smooth. The count being finished, Ike opened the gate for the three riders to exit. This had taken the better part of the day and Ike wanted the herd to settle for the night and pair up again. Besides, any stragglers would come down to join the rest of the herd overnight. They exited the high pasture, securing the gate as they rode back to camp. Riding back to camp, Ike indicated his count was three cows short.

That evening at camp they discussed the work of the day and what would be ahead for Boston the next day. After chuck, they sat around the fire and sang old cowboy songs and gospel songs. Boston joined in if he knew them, but he was surprised that they sang songs. He only thought that was done in the movies.

CHAPTER ELEVEN

After breakfast they all rode back up to the high pasture. Boston was a little sore from yesterday's riding. It was more than he ever did at one time but did not want to mention his aches. Ike had previewed the days task and Boston had a general idea that today was branding. They secured the gate as they came into the high pasture. Seeing no other cows or calves outside the trap, they dismounted to prepare for the branding. Ike and Boston began setting up the Nordfork.

"Kind of a funny name." said Boston.

"It's named after the fella who invented it. His name was Nord from Oregon." Ike explained.

Boston pounded in a stake to which an inner tube was attached and then a piece of rope to a wish bone looking device which was affixed at the opposite end. Ike walked Boston through how this was to be used. Ike then asked Boston to explain and demonstrate to him, what he would be doing as a calf was being drug in. Meanwhile Jo and Jiggs were busy gathering wood and starting a fire and bringing the branding irons out to the fire. Then Jiggs and Jo pushed the herd into the larger side of the trap and secured the gates on each end of the barbed wire fence. Jiggs would be roping first and Jo would run the gate to allow Jiggs to drag the calf to the fire without letting any other calves or cows out. Once the calf was branded and vaccinated, it was released and allowed to wander in the narrower portion of the trap. When the branding was completed, the gates would be opened and the mothers could join up with their babies. Ike would be doing the branding, vaccinating and castrating. Jiggs mounted his horse and Jo opened the gate. Boston was looking down at the Nordfork and mentally going over what he was to do when he heard the gate open again and saw Jiggs dragging out a calve by its hind legs. As the calf passed Boston walked along side holding the Nordfork behind the calf's head. When the slack was out of the rope and the inner tube brought resistance, Jiggs turned his horse toward the calf. The calf was now stretched out as Ike brought the hot iron. The smell of burning hide was something Boston had never experienced and reacted accordingly. Ike looked at him, "You will get used to it." Ike then gave the calf a couple of shots. Just then Jiggs slowly release pressure on his rope and Boston lifted up the handle of the Nordfork. The calf stepped out of the loop and walked off, being hazed a little by Ike. Again the gate opened and Jiggs was dragging another calf to the fire. "Bull calf." Ike hollered as Boston guided the Nordfork behind the calf's head and then secured it in place. As Ike picked up his knife to castrate, Boston went for the iron. Turning back toward the calf with the hot iron he watched Ike lay two testicles in the ashes at the edge of the fire. Now taking the iron from Boston, Ike burned in a cinnamon colored IO on the calf's hide. Boston brought the needles and the calf was vaccinated.

This process repeated itself over and over and over. The only change was that Boston was now hollering out "Bull calf." There was a brief lull when Ike and Jiggs changed places to allow Jiggs' horse to rest. During that lull, both Ike and Jiggs stabbed their knives into one of the "Fries" at the edge of the fire and ate. Looking at Boston, Jiggs said "Ya want one? You don't know what you're missing!" Boston went over and using his new pocket knife stabbed him one, which after eating it, thought it was just like eating sausage. Ike and Jiggs laughed as Boston stabbed another. Jo stood by the gate shaking her head saying "Boys will be boys." Outside of this brief lull, they worked steady. The noise of the calves bawling and the cows bellowing reached a level which made it hard to hear someone talking. Focusing on the work at hand the noise faded into the background. Jo hollered "Last one," as Ike dragged it to the fire. Jo again closed the gate closest to the fire and walked to the other end where she opened that gate and allowed the babies to mother up amongst the bawling and bellowing. After taking long drinks from their canteens, they doused the fire. It was hot, sweaty and dusty work. Boston was relieved yet excited that he had participated in a tradition of the

West. With the fire out and the irons secure, they mounted up and again rode back towards camp. This time the sun had just gone down behind the mountains, and their breakfast had long since wore off. They were all anxious for supper.

By the time they got their horses stripped it was almost dark. Jiggs began working on the fire and Boston went to the Lyster bag. He poured in two of the cans and went down the hill to fill them up for tomorrow. He preferred doing this task in the evening rather than morning. He did not want to be the cause of slowing anyone up at starting of day. Upon his arrival back at camp the meal was in full preparation and coffee was boiling. He wondered off in a different direction in search of firewood. With the lack of light he was only able to find an armful which would be gone by morning and he would be back on the hunt again. He knew he needed to find a tree he could chop down or some tree that has fallen recently in order to have a supply on hand. When he came back this time supper was ready.

The food was wonderful as always and the coffee and discussion was always enjoyable, they even shared a few laughs. They even had compliments for how hard Boston worked and how fast he caught on to the Nordfork. Boston felt a real sense of worth and that he was contributing to this operation, but knew he had a long way to go to prove himself. Ike and Jo said, "Good night," as the bedrolls were retrieved and spread out. Boston had no more than taken off his chaps, boots and hat and laid his head on the ground when his eyes closed in sleep.

CHAPTER TWELVE

It was the beginning of another early day. Boston quietly and quickly went about his chores. He wondered what this day would bring, since he left the headquarters he was getting a taste of cowboy life. Living under the stars, sleeping out, sitting around a camp fire and riding a horse.

At breakfast Ike asked Boston to ride the fence and make sure it was secure. Today they would be pushing the herd into this pasture and it is important that the fence is standing and strong. Boston was thrilled that he was going to do something by himself on horseback.

Before he climbed into the saddle Ike came over, "Boston, I just want to say that everything we do is dangerous and this is not the place you want to have an accident. It may take hours before we would know and then hours before help can get to you. So if you're in doubt, always decide on the side of safety. You can see the fence from a distance and if you need to walk up to any point to inspect it, that OK. Just be careful. This is not flat ground." He handed him a small set of saddle bags. "Here's your fencing kit."

Boston took it and tied it behind the saddle, then got up into the saddle and looking down at Ike said, "Anything else?"

"Yeah, watch for slide rock!" Ike replied. Boston started at the fence behind the camp and began his first solo assignment.

He focused on the fence but also kept an eye out for firewood, at least while he was close to the camp. Riding along he thought about what Ike had told him about being safe. But what did he mean about slide rock? Why didn't he ask what he meant? He wasn't afraid of getting lost since he was inside a three square mile box and he just needed to find the pasture and there would be the camp. So far he had only found a couple of missing staples, as he entered into his third mile. Now the terrain was steadily going uphill. His horse was breathing hard, even though he was zig zagging to get up the steep incline. All the while Ike's words were echoing in his mind, "This is not a place you want to have an accident." A horse falling in this kind of terrain could cripple the animal and seriously injure the rider. Arriving at a place which allowed Boston to rest the horse, he reined up. He sat there motionless as he listened to the horse's deep breath, remembering how Jiggs had told him, " Take care of your horse so the horse can take care of you." The trees seemed to be so thick it was difficult to see where the fence went. The density of the trees blocked his vision. It was obvious he couldn't go any further up and the trees blocked him from going to his left. He would need to go back down until he could see another way to come up past this area of dense trees. Leaning back in the saddle and pushing his stirrups as far out front as possible, he turned his horse downhill. He had gone about thirty feet when he noticed a small game trail leading away from the fence. He turned his horse onto it. He was now moving away from the fence but when the ground permitted it he would double back towards the fence. In riding twenty or thirty feet further the trees now allowed him to go up hill again and turn past the thick clump of trees which had caused him to turn back. He picked up the fence again and continued on his way. He was able to see ahead as he rode along side of the fence, even though the ground where the fence stood was at his eye level. Ahead of him he saw a washout about three feet across and maybe two feet deep. He stopped at the brink to study a way around, when his horse leaped across the wash. The horses' feet cleared the wash but as they landed on the other side, the rock began to move, his horse struggled to regain it's balance. Boston himself was trying to regain his balance from the leap as his horse is desperately trying to regain its balance. Boston kept the horses' head pointed up hill as they began sliding downward. Finally regaining footing, his horse continued to attempt to go up. Boston realized that he needed to move across when possible, Even though this only took a few seconds to happen, Boston's heart was beating twice as fast. Once cleared of this rock area, he saw what he was dealing with, flat small rocks like chips. Laying there like stacks of chips fallen over, and then when pressure was applied they would slide. There was no doubt in Boston's mind what slide rock was and why you want to avoid it.

Boston arrived back at the campsite to see them enjoying coffee, their horses tied near the corral. "Sit a spell" Jiggs encouraged.

"How did it go?" asked Ike.

"It's good. Only a few loose wires. Nothing down." Boston reported.

As they drank coffee, Ike filled them in on the primary task for the day. Today they would move the cattle out of the high pasture down into the pasture where the camp was located. Boston was to ride into the trap and start to move the herd out so it could be pushed down into this lower valley.

Shortly after they finished their coffee, they mounted up and rode up the fire break opening the gate between the two pastured areas. As Boston entered into the trap area, Jiggs reminded him, "Move slow and easy. They will eventually drift the way you want them to go, don't try to push all of them." Boston would pressure them a little and then pause, they began moving in the direction to the far open gate. At first they trickled out and then the majority found the gate opening. He doubled back along the edge of the trap and began moving the remnant who would not turn or ran past him. When he got to the end Ike had come into the trap and the two of them pushed the remaining calves and cows out. Boston observed how Ike would press the cow or calf and then position his horse differently and the cow or calf would then move in the direction Ike wanted it to go. Boston commented to Ike how "You seem to know just what that cow is thinking." "Cattle know if you're inexperienced or a greenhorn. They are reading you and your horse. I was more aggressive and yet I knew when to back off and give them room. It will come with working and being around cattle." Ike continued, "But you did a good job for your first time moving cattle on your own." Ike then urged his horse forward ahead of Boston. Looking up, Boston saw the gate and realized his job was to secure it. He dismounted and shut and secured the gate. When he turned around Ike's horse was perpendicular to Boston's. "If you position your horse like this, you are preventing the horse the man is attempting to mount, from moving." Ike waited until Boston was mounted and then trotted off, turning back toward Boston Ike said, "It's a cowboy thing."

By the time the crew returned to camp, the majority of the herd was spread out in the valley along the stream. Boston rode up last as the rest set on their horses. When everyone had gathered Ike spoke, "Jo and I are heading back to headquarters. You've got enough meat in the cooler for a few days. We'll be returning with more provisions before you run out."

Ike had taken another horse from the corral which Jiggs had saddled with a pack saddle. As Jo and Ike rode off, Jiggs told Boston, "Loosen your cinch but don't remove your saddle. We'll have a cup of coffee and then check on the herd." The two stepped off their mounts and loosened their cinches. Then each poured a cup of coffee.

Boston was excited to spend time with Jiggs at the camp, he was hoping to ask lots of questions and maybe learn something about cowboying and Ike. "Jiggs, I'd like to learn more about you, would you mind if I asked you some questions?" Boston inquired.

Jiggs paused a little, "Not saying that I would answer, but go ahead and ask."

"I really admired how you rode that bronc at the rodeo. Could you teach me to ride like that?"

"Well, if you like that sort of riding, sure." Jiggs replied.

Boston was hoping for more of a detailed answer and he continued to ask, "Where did you learn to cowboy?"

"My dad at first, then other older men at some of the ranches I worked on taught me." Jiggs stated.

"How did you come to work here Jiggs?"

"Ike asked me if I wanted a job?" came the response.

Again Boston was hoping for a more detailed response. It wasn't easy carrying on a conversation with these short answers. Boston continued, "Where did you meet Ike?" Another pause as Jiggs got up and went to the chuck box, and returned with a couple of flat pieces of meat. Handing one to Boston Jiggs said,

"Lets eat dinner."

"What is it?" asked Boston.

"Dried elk meat or jerky, it will hold us until supper," Jiggs replied.

They sat there in silence chewing on the jerky. Boston wondered why Jiggs didn't answer his last question. Could it be they met in prison or maybe knew each other before, or did Jiggs stumble into town? Boston's imagination raced with all sorts of possibilities. Nearing the end of their dinner, Jiggs commanded, "Saddle up!" They set their coffee cups on the chuck box then walked over and tightened up their cinches. Boston rode along side of Jiggs as he explained how they would be spending every day for the next few weeks. Riding through the herd slowly watching for calves that were stressed, sick or lost, same with the cows. As Jiggs was giving pointers on signs that indicate a calf or cow might be sick. It would be necessary to rope the cow or calf in order to doctor the animal. He encouraged Boston to get a rope and practice roping a stump and then practice roping it from his horse, and to do this whenever he had a chance. Quietly and slowly they picked their way through the herd. Sometimes they would just be sitting their horses observing the calves and cow. This allowed Boston to observe how cows treated their calf and gave him some valuable lessons on their behavior. Jiggs informed Boston that the cattle may not be this bunched up tomorrow. "They will drift the entire fenced area, and it may take us a lot longer to check them. But now we'll just hang out here and make sure they stick to this bed ground." They spent the rest of the day staying on the perimeters of the pasture and later in the day did another slow walk through the herd. When they finally returned to the camp Jiggs suggested," Leave your horse saddled for now, just loosen the cinch. You never know if we'll need them before dark." Boston wanted to get some firewood and wondered if he could use Jiggs' rope to pull a tree back to camp. "Naw" he said, "don't want any dead spots in it, but you can use that clothes line affair under Jo's bed." Boston rode to where Jo's bed was located, got down and found the clothes line Jiggs was talking about. He remounted and started his search. On horseback with daylight he was sure to come across something. He was about to the far end when he spotted an old aspen that had fallen. He dismounted and tied one end to the bigger end of the tree trunk. He then walked back and looped it around the saddle horn. Not knowing how the horse would react, he walked the horse out slowly. The horse took the challenge and steadily pulled the log out to the edge of the pasture. Leaving the rope on the off side of his horse, he mounted slowly, being careful to place his leg under the rope. Then slowly he walked his horse back to camp. At the base of the knoll, he loosened his dally and dropped the rope. He then went and dismounted, loosening his cinch afterwards. Now he had a supply of firewood nearby and was pleased with his work. He untied the clothes line and placed it back under Jo's bed.

While Jiggs was pouring another cup of coffee, Boston picked up the water cans and went down the hill to fetch water. There was plenty of time and daylight for Boston to explore the stream. Leaving the water cans, he walked upstream. The creek became narrower with the water running faster. He then walked in the opposite direction past the water cans. Just around a bend where he was getting water, was a beaver pond. He walked up slowly and could see fish dart away to the far side. When he walked toward the dam itself, he saw more fish dart away. Returning to the water cans, he was hoping to catch some for supper. He would try and remember to buy some hooks and line next time he got to town. He filled the two cans and struggled back up the hill. After placing the chlorine tablets into the cans he returned to the chuck box. "Do you like trout Jiggs?" asked Boston.

"Can't say either way. It has been a long time since I had any," came the reply.

"I saw some down in the stream at a beaver pond, maybe I can catch us some," Boston said excitedly.

"When you gonna find time for that?" Jiggs inquired.

"I'll work on that!" said Boston.

For the next four days Jiggs and Boston rode through the herd and continued to check on it as it spread out into the trees. They did find a few stressed calves which they monitored. They also identified a few dry stock cows that didn't have calves. Jiggs made a note of their individual markings so he could find them again.

That night after supper as they sat around the fire, Jiggs informed Boston that he would be leaving around noon on Saturday and Jo & Ike would be relieving him Saturday night. This came as sad news to Boston, he was really enjoying being at the cow camp. He spoke up, "What if I don't want to leave?"

"That's the boss's decision, We are just the hired hands. You'll be back up here in a day or so, enjoy you time off. "

"What are you going to do?" Boston asked.

Taking a drag off his cigarette, Jiggs replied "I got a friend at another ranch I've wanted to see. I'll ride over to that outfit." He set his coffee down on the log and crawled into his bed roll.

The fire had burned down to coals, when Boston put a small log into it. He lay on top of his sleeping bag on this warm night. He just stared at the stars and listened to the noises. At dusk the coyotes would howl, once in a while he would hear a branch break in the trees. Cows would bellow for their calves, a horse would snort or nicker. He was amazed at how peaceful the night seemed. Clouds would silently glide past the stars. Sometimes the moon played a game of peek-a-boo with the fast moving clouds, as if darting in and out, trying to hide from him. Is this what the cowboys of a hundred years ago saw and heard? Then he remembered they took turns riding night guard. They had no wire to keep the cattle in place, or corral to hold the horses. All these sights and smells he wanted to remember. Somehow sleep seemed to steal his thoughts.

Boston awoke to the smell of coffee. Jiggs was sitting on the log a cigarette in one hand and cup of coffee in the other. "Tough night?" he asked.

"Yeah, I had trouble falling asleep," responded Boston.

"It's a wonder you can sleep at all in the bed you got. But then you young bucks can handle a lot. I think if I started out with one of those, I'd be so stoved up by now I couldn't straighten up."

Smiling Boston responded "I like the bed rolls you and Ike got but I never saw anything like those before. This is all I knew."

As he exhaled cigarette smoke Jiggs said, "If you're going to be serious about working on ranches and working with cattle, you need to get the proper equipment." Handing Boston a piece of jerky he continued, "Here's breakfast, grab a cup of coffee." Boston and Jiggs drank coffee and ate jerky in silence. Afterwards Boston did his chores of water and wood. Having a source of wood nearby made that task a lot easier.

When Boston had completed his chores, the two saddled horses and rode through the herd counting and checking on their health and location. When the two of them came back into the pasture, they could see that Jo and Ike had arrived with a pack horse of provisions. They visited awhile and Jiggs rode off in another direction from headquarters.

As they were watching Jiggs ride off, Boston was picking up his laundry bag and personal items. When he returned to his horse, Jo said, "Boston, you can use the truck to go to town so you can do your laundry and eat at the café. Before heading back up on Monday, please clean the corrals."

"I'll see you on Monday." Boston said waving a good by. He rode slowly past the herd and onto the fire break which lead down to the headquarters. The trail wasn't as hard to follow as Boston thought. There were plenty of fresh hoof prints and signs.

Arriving at the barn and corrals he led his horse into the coral and stripped off the saddle and bridle. He then threw out a flake of hay, followed by a check on the water tank. Walking towards the bunkhouse he realized he hadn't cleaned up in a week. He stripped off his clothes and walked to the shower. The water was warm and refreshing, as was his shave. He placed all his dirty clothes in the laundry bag. At the same time, he laid all his clothes out that he wanted to take back to camp. This time he was going to take a long underwear shirt to sleep in, it might help him get a good night sleep. Which is what he was looking forward to getting from the bed at the bunkhouse.

CHAPTER THIRTEEN

Rising early the next morning he hurried to do the chores and make sure the animals had feed and water. He then returned to the bunkhouse and picked up his laundry bag. Running back to the headquarters, he opened the truck door and threw in his laundry bag. The truck roared to life and he headed towards town. Pulling to a stop in front of the café, he went inside where he sat at the counter. There were only a few customers at this early hour. He ordered a big breakfast and just as he began sipping his coffee, Shylo walked through the door. "What are you doing here so early?" she inquired.

"I was just going to ask you the same question." Replied Boston.

"I sit in here to drink an orange juice to cool down from my run, before I head home" Smiled Shylo.

"Smiling back Boston inquired "Are you on the school track team?"

Shylo laughed, "No. I graduated about four years ago, I work at a hospital in Taos. I'm an anesthesiologist technician. I just like to run to stay in shape."

Boston was going to make a comment about her shape, but concluded it wasn't appropriate or gentlemanly. "Did you go to nursing school or something?" he asked. After taking a drink of juice, Shylo replied, "I am working towards an RN degree. I have a couple of semesters to complete yet, but working and going to school at night takes a lot of time." Boston's order came and he continued to listen.

"Go ahead and eat your breakfast before it gets cold." Shylo insisted.

Boston began eating, but it was hard to stop since he hadn't really had anything to eat since yesterday morning. He had almost finished his breakfast when Shylo spoke "I know Jo is a really good cook. Have you been missing her meals?"

Boston smiled, took a sip of coffee, "I haven't eaten since yesterday morning – I hurried to get down the hill to clean up and get a good night sleep. It wasn't until this morning I realized how hungry I was. I apologize for my manners. Can I buy you something?"

Shylo glanced at the wall clock. Smiling she said "No. I need to get home and get ready to go with grandma to church. Would you like to join us?"

"No. I need to do my laundry. But I have enjoyed our chat." Boston responded.

"You know your heart needs to be clean also, and at our church you will see how. I will do your laundry after church if you'll join us." Shylo pleaded.

"Maybe another time. I just want to get back to the ranch. Say hello to Adeline for me."

"I will, good bye." She got up and walked out the door. Boston thought to himself that he was not very considerate of her and hoped he would have another chance to talk with her. She sure was a striking young woman and he wanted to know if she knew anything about Ike's past. The waitress was filling his cup with more coffee when Boston asked, "Is the library open today?" She responded "No. Just us and the General Store, but only until two o'clock." Boston thought he would do his laundry and then maybe write a couple letters.

He left the café and drove to the wash house. After he had started the wash machines, he decided to walk to the general store. It would not only kill some time but would allow him to pick up that fishing equipment he thought about. At the General Store, he strolled up and down the isles, picking up some snack foods that he could take back to the ranch and maybe to camp. He purchased hooks, fishing line, and small sinkers. Walking back to the wash house people were heading to church or just leaving and going to the café. After two o'clock, the town seemed to shut down for the day. Everyone went home to relax.

Returning to the ranch he checked the horses and then went to the bunkhouse to unpack his clean clothes from the laundry bag and put in the clothes he was going to be taking to cow camp. Including the jacket he bought at Adeline's store.

CHAPTER FOURTEEN

Boston arose at early grey light, he dressed and throwing his laundry bag and jacket over his shoulder he walked to the barn and corrals. When he had finished his chores and feed and watered the horses, he saddled one for the ride up the mountain. He finished by tying his laundry bag around the saddle horn and led the horse out of the stall. He was hoping to get there in time for breakfast. But just in case he kept the apple he purchased yesterday in his jacket pocket.

Even in the early light the trail was easy to see, as he slowly made his way. He was excited to get back to the camp, and wondered what tasks they would be doing this week. This commute was very different from any other trip to work. There was no traffic to get ensnarled in, or traffic noise, the smells weren't there, and the flood of people when you arrived wasn't there. He decided this was the most fun and excitement he has had on any job. He realized that he was moving about rather freely, he didn't have concerns about parking, or tables at restaurants or smog filled air. Here it was clean, pleasant noises and surroundings, heck this didn't even feel like work.

When he broke into the pasture and could see the camp on the far end, it was difficult to contain his excitement. He began waving and hollered out "hello." He encouraged his horse to a trot until he saw the cows and calves in the pasture and then came back down to a walk. He felt the smile on his face was bigger than his hat brim. He went over to the corral. After loosening his cinch he went to the camp fire. As he walked toward the fire, he could see he missed breakfast. "Coffee?" Ike asked.

"Sure would like some" Boston responded.

"How was your day off?" Jo asked.

"Well, I went to town to do laundry and get some breakfast. While in the café, Shylo came in and we had a little chat."

Ike grinned as he said, "She sure is a shiner isn't she?"

"What does that mean?" Boston asked.

"It means she is pretty." Replied Jo.

"Okay, yeah, I agree she is good looking but we just talked over coffee." Boston said defensively.

"We're going to have to watch him closer." Ike teased.

"OK, that's enough," Jo went on to say," You were his age once. I remember, and the way I remember you weren't any different." As they continued to joke with each other, Jiggs came riding back into camp. "Good morning Jiggs! Have a cup before we start the days work." Ike commanded.

"Don't mind if I do," he said, stepping off his horse and letting the reins fall to the ground. There was more general conversation until Ike spoke up, "I'll be going over to the Goolsby Ranch to pick up a trailer to transport our dry stock to the sales barn. I will need the two of you," pointing to Jiggs and Boston," to separate them out and move them down to the trap at Nesbitt Creek. Two days from today you need to have them in the trap. Jo and I will be going back to the headquarters. When you two accomplish those tasks get back to the herd, I will join you up here in three days." Again they split up with Jo and Ike riding off. Boston quickly checked the camp for water and wood. The water needed to be refilled and he needed to cut some wood. He was about to head down the hill for water when he heard Jiggs holler.

Going back to the camp, he saw Jiggs was already mounted, "Tighten up your cinch." Jiggs said. Boston knew that meant he was ready to ride. Boston had no more mounted when Jiggs dismounted and walked to the chuck box. He returned with the ax, which he tied behind his saddle. Boston without saying a word followed Jiggs as they rode out. They rode in the direction of the high pasture. Arriving at the gate, they dismounted. Jiggs walked around and then looking at Boston he said, "We need to build a trap so we can temporarily keep these dry cows until moving them down the mountain. The gate is going to be one side, we'll build the other three sides from trunks of trees we cut down. We will need to have one we can quickly move across the trail after we push them into this trap. Savvy?" They walked into the trees where Jiggs selected three trees about six inches in diameter. "Cut down these three trees and remove all the branches." Jiggs instructed. While Boston began chopping away at one of the trees, Jiggs rode back to camp. Before the tree was felled Jiggs had returned, carrying that old clothes line rope. After felling the first tree, Jiggs took the ax and began knocking off the branches while Boston took a breather. When this task was done the tree looked more like a pole. Jiggs secured the rope to the bottom end and he and his horse pulled the tree into the road. This process was repeated until all three trees were felled and stripped of their branches and set on the road. Next they attached each end of the poles to live trees that were parallel to the fire break road. They did the same on each side of the road. The last pole which would form the fourth side, ran perpendicular across the road. And it rested on top of the other two poles and next to a live tree. They tested it for length and then brought it back out and laid it on the road. Each of the three poles would be affixed so they were about thigh high. Hopefully it was enough to deter the cows from leaving, at least for a night.

By the time this task was completed, most of the day was gone. While Boston was chopping on the last two trees, Jiggs would ride off and check the herd. Boston would have the trees felled and branches stripped before Jiggs returned. Riding back to the camp meant more work but the sun had just touched the mountain peaks and there would be enough light to get the water. After they stripped their horses, Boston went to fetch water while Jiggs began preparing the evening meal. Heading for the stream, Boston realized he hadn't eaten all day and now he felt pretty hungry. Just thinking about supper didn't help. Even though he had never tasted any of Jiggs' meals before, well that's wasn't true, they always seemed to consist of jerky. Boston was hoping this evening meal would be more than jerky.

Returning to the camp and filling the Lyster Bag, Boston told Jiggs he hadn't eaten all day, and he had forgotten about the apple he brought to snack on. "Bring it here." Jiggs said excitedly. Boston dug out the red gem from his jacket pocket and held it in his stretched out hand. Before Boston could retract his arm, Jiggs had snatched the apple and had it sliced up with the knife he was holding. Boston, thinking Jiggs wanted some of the apple to snack on, stood silently. Jiggs then lifted the cover of the Dutch oven, that was hanging over the fire and dumped the sliced apple into the pot. "Hey, what are you doing?" Boston questioned. It was the first time he ever questioned him. Jiggs who was squatting next to the fire looked up at Boston, "Thanks for contributing to supper! Coffee?"

Boston, thinking he was going to get reprimanded, quickly replied "Boy, that sounds great!"

Jiggs, who was busy stirring a pan full of sliced potatoes said "pour me one too."

Boston just smiled and he filled the two cups and returned the pot to the fire's edge. He was enjoying this time he was spending with Jiggs and knew by Jiggs teasing that he enjoyed being with Boston.

Sitting there waiting for the meal to cook, Jiggs complimented Boston on how hard he worked today, and did what he was told without any discouraging words. He continued saying, "Some greenhorns are always running off at the mouth thinking they know better or have done things different at home. Maybe because you don't know anything you stay quiet. There is nothing wrong with listening and observing, you're probably learning more."

"Thanks Jiggs, that means an awful lot coming from you." Boston said softly.

"Tomorrow will be another full day, trying to locate the dry cows and then get them into the trap." Jiggs stated.

"How do you know which are dry cows?" Boston questioned.

Jiggs, lighting a cigarette, replied, "Look at the bag on the cow. It won't be big and tight, which indicates the cow has milk. A dry cow has a small bag. But still we need to be careful by checking to see if the tits are shinny and hair wet to make sure a calf hasn't been sucking. Some first calf heifers don't have a big bag. If you spot one with a small bag, watch a little while to see if a calf is nearby or comes up. Like I said, this is going to be tough in the short amount of time we got. You not being able to rope makes it double hard." Boston again realized the difficulty he placed on everyone by not being straight forward. There was silence for awhile before Jiggs spoke, "Aw we'll manage, ain't nothing we can't figure out."

Jiggs and Boston picked up their plates and flatware and walked over to the pot. By now it was dark and the camp was lit by firelight. Lifting the lid, Jiggs stabbed a large piece of meat and set it on Boston's plate, then replaced the lid. Jiggs then cut the piece in half. "See any pink?" he asked.

"Nope." replied Boston.

Jiggs then took one piece of meat and set it on the other plate. He put a large baked potato on each plate. Then he again removed the lid from the pot and ladled out some sort of juice with pieces of apple in it. This he poured over everything. Handing a slice of bread about two inches thick to Boston, Jiggs said, "Dig in." Boston sat on the ground and began devouring every scrape of meat and potatoes, soaking up the juice with the bread. "Anything left?" he asked Jiggs.

"Take whatever you want." replied Jiggs.

"This is really good. What kind of meat is this?" asked Boston.

"Pork" came the reply.

"Without giving away any secret recipe, what makes it taste so sweet?" Inquired Boston. "Lick," said Jiggs with a smile.

"OK, what is this lick?" Sensing this may be a joke, Boston smiled.

"Well, it is kind of my secret. I use maple syrup to sweeten it up." Jiggs confessed. Boston finishing his second plate said, "I'll have to remember that. It's very good, can I get more?"

"Finish the pot, you worked hard today." Jiggs said with a grin.

Jiggs was leaning back against a log with his legs out stretched smoking on a cigarette by the time Boston finished his third plate. Looking at Jiggs, Boston thought that seemed pretty relaxing, so he asked, "Could I have one?" Without so much as a blink or word, Jiggs tossed him the leather tobacco pouch and papers. You couldn't say the two of them enjoyed a smoke, since one spent more time coughing then relaxing.

"Where did you cowboy Jiggs, before you came here? Boston was hoping Jiggs would answer and not change the subject. "Started out at the Pigeon Ranch south of here, then down to Arizona on a ranch near Kingman. From there I went to the Thomas Ranch in Nevada. Came back to New Mexico and went to the Bell Ranch, then up here to Colorado." Boston was curious "Why did you move to so many ranches?" Jiggs thought a little then said, "Well, when I was young I wanted to see different places and learn different things. I did learn how different ranches work, and I certainly have seen lots of wonderful sights. Sometimes the work is only seasonal and a cowboy moves on, or goes to town to find work. I never left an outfit in a tight spot, I always rode for the brand. I enjoyed being around cows and horses and people of like mind. I'd pick up odd jobs but to me they was all related to cowboy work. Now it's my turn to ask a question or two." Focusing directly on Boston's eyes Jiggs asked, "What exactly are you doing out here? You showed up under false pretense, and yet you are still playing your hand."

Boston knew that Jiggs would see through anything false. "Well, I thought by coming out here I might be able to write an article or book about what I learned. But please don't mention this to Ike or Jo." Boston pleaded.

Jiggs response was accurate and to the point, "Might write a book? Have you written anything outside of some paper for school? Have you written anything for a newspaper or magazine or some other copy that people read?"

Boston replied with a sheepish "No."

"Well, I ain't saying you can't write. I guess what I am saying is that if that's what you want to do, go after it with everything you got. Don't get side tracked, work hard at it. Just like I see you working hard at learning what to do out here. Give it the best you got, not just enough to get by. I think writing about something you know is a good thing. You wanted to know something so you are experiencing it. I think it makes a more believable story. Everyone works hard from little on, unless you were born into wealth. Nothing wrong with wealth, but people out here aspire to living life at it's fullest with what they got. They know and care about their neighbors and the neighbors feel mutual. This cowboy work is a job that not everyone wants to do. But those of us who do it desire to do it, and do it darn good no matter how difficult it becomes. Phew! I need a coffee and smoke. All that jaw jacking got me thirsty."

Boston poured each of them another cup. "Would you be willing to teach me to ride broncs?" Boston asked.

Jiggs dragged on his cigarette and replied, "That takes a lot of practice, and unless you're planning to chase the rodeo it may be a waste of time. "

"I guess you are right. I just wanted to learn from the best." Boston stated.

"Heck, I ain't the best. You should have seen Ike ride when he was in his prime, before he got busted up in that bad wreck. He might have been a world champion."

Being curious Boston asked, "What happened?"

Jiggs began, "He used to like riding those that others say couldn't be rode. This one snaky bronc showed up with just that reputation, so of course Ike takes him on. He mounted this outlaw in a corral and the dust and hair was flying. This Cayuse used all the tricks and a few never seen before. He headed toward a square corner where there was a good size water tank. With one jump the critter straddled the tank, two legs inside and the hind legs out. It reared up trying to get out of that tank, when it's hind feet slipped in the mud causing it to loose balance. It fell backwards onto the side of the tank. Ike was in the water, but still holding on. The horse kicked and rolled itself into the tank with Ike on the bottom. Those of us watching knew this wasn't going to end well for Ike, so we ran for the tank some with ropes. Before we got there that horse had gotten up, but this time Ike wasn't on board. Still in the tank it just jumped around like it was going to stomp Ike through the bottom. One fella got a hold of the braided bronc rein,and was able to lead that horse out of the tank. Another man and I fished Ike out, we could see his leg bone sticking out in two places and he was out cold. We laid him out and checked him over. We figured he broke his leg, arm, probably some ribs and maybe had a concussion. Since that wreck he doesn't intentionally ride outlaws. He ain't chilled, but doesn't see any need to ride them kind any more. There are too many good horses."

"I guess I'd better pay closer attention to what he tells me about horses." Boston replied. "You would do well to pay attention to what we all say." Jiggs replied.

The evening ended with the two of them staring into the fire. Each lost in his own thoughts. "I'm turning in." Jiggs said as he got up to get his bed roll. Boston followed silently. Boston's mind barely replayed any of the day's events before the weight of sleep pressed on him.

CHAPTER FIFTEEN

Morning crept into the camp without a sound or light. Boston stretched as he stumbled off to the woods. He hoped to have the fire and coffee going before Jiggs awoke. Being as quiet as possible, he poked the coals back to life and added small sticks. Eventually he had built a small blaze. There was plenty of cold, left-over coffee to be heated. Placing the pot on the edge of the fire ring, he headed for the Lyster bag. Grabbing the two empty cans he headed down to the creek. It was slow going in the dark, but he knew by the time he would be coming back up, the grey light of dawn would help.

After dropping in the chlorine tablets, he left the two cans at the Lyster bag and returned to the fire. Jiggs was sitting on the log with coffee in one hand and a cigarette in the other. "Weather is coming!" Jiggs blurted.

"What makes you say that?" Boston inquired.

"My bones are sore this morning, that's how I know." Jiggs replied taking a drag on his cigarette.

Boston chopped a little wood for the day and stacked it behind the chuck box.

While they were having breakfast, Jiggs laid out the plan for the day. They would start on one end and slowly move through the herd, looking for the dry cows. From previous weeks of observations Jiggs knew there should be at least three dry cows, and he told Boston their markings. They would try to cut them from the herd and then move them to the trap. If they can't cull and move them, then Jiggs would rope them and pass the lariat to Boston to drag to the trap, while Jiggs tried to rope another one. They ate a leisurely breakfast to allow it to get as light as possible so they could check the cows easier. After cleaning up, they saddled and mounted. Today, most of the cows were in the pasture or near the stream for water. They stayed near the edge of the pasture and walked their horses to the far end, all the while Jiggs and Boston were surveying the herd. Jiggs pointed out two cows which resembled the one they were looking for. Jiggs told Boston to remain and he would go closer for a better look. He returned and said that only one of them is dry, the other had wet hair and shiny tits. Jiggs pointed out the one they needed to cull out saying, "The trick is to get the cow to think it was moving in the direction it had chosen, but in reality it's being moved where the cowboy wants it to go. This takes patience and placing your horse in a position that is not threating and turning the cow to move in the general direction towards the trap." Boston nodded, then both moved out slowly toward the cow. They had been at this slow pace and process for almost an hour, when Jiggs signaled Boston to break away. Boston turned gradually away from the cow, as Jiggs pressed the critter into the trap, with Boston putting up the pole forming the fourth side. Jiggs was pleased that this one went easy but stated, "Hope the others go this good!" They headed back to the pasture, this time going down the edge of the woods opposite the camp. Everything was slow going as Jiggs and Boston keep a look out for at least two more dry cows. They both knew that getting the second and third cow into the trap was going to be difficult.

They located their second dry cow and this one also seemed to go along willingly. The one inside the trap remained there as the second one was introduced. This time Jiggs rode into the herd and Boston rode along the edge of the trees, hoping to get different cows to move towards the creek. On this pass they again culled out a dry cow, and the two of them worked slowly to move it towards the trap. While some distance from the trap, Jiggs told Boston, "Ride up and open the trap and position yourself to hold the two other cows there, But go slow." Boston broke off and in a wide arch passed the cow Jiggs was maneuvering. He did as Jiggs had asked and kept the cows at a far corner. After putting up the end rail, they weren't sure if there was another, but they needed to make another pass in order to see more of the herd. Again they went back. This time Boston went further into the trees hoping to push more cows down into the pasture below, while Jiggs slowly serpentined through the cows. Boston had ridden back and forth through the trees at a good walk. He felt sure he had pushed cows out, but only saw a few pairs leave. He had been scanning the trees when he herd Jiggs holler his name. He turned his horse downhill towards the pasture. Breaking clear of the trees he could see Jiggs had his rope around the cows head. The tug-o-war seemed to be in favor of the cow since Jiggs' horse was getting tired. As Boston came over, he came up behind the cow and Jiggs' rope went slack, the cow seemed to be co-operating more. Together they pulled and pushed the momma towards the trap. As they approached the trap Jiggs had been replacing coils in his rope while instructing Boston," Pull the pole back just enough so I can get inside with this cow." Boston did as instructed and Jiggs passed him with the cow close behind. Boston closed the rail and waited until Jiggs got his rope off the cow and then he again opened the trap just enough to let the horse and rider out. "Overall that went well," said Jiggs. "The real work will begin tomorrow. Let's check the herd and then go to camp." The two trotted back down to the pasture and then made another serpentine course through the herd. One on either side of the creek. Each one then returned through the timber along his respective side of the creek. They met back at the corral.

At camp, Jiggs began preparing supper while Boston chopped wood and made a fresh pot of coffee. He only needed to refill one of the water cans and again went down the hill. Jiggs had cooked some corn beef in a can and potatoes, with Hostess cupcakes for dessert. They reflected on the day and decided that things went their way and all in all they both were satisfied. "It's going to rain tonight, and depending on how much, it will affect how we will be working tomorrow." Jiggs commented. Sure enough, the wind had come up and clouds covered the sky. They let the fire burn down and secured or tied everything down. They crawled in early, as the rain began. Boston wore his leggings that night and brought his boot inside his sleeping bag. It was very tight and uncomfortable, he again wished he had a bed like Jiggs and Ike's.

It might be the thin mountain air, or the hard work. Maybe both that caused sleep to come early and fast.

Boston was aroused from sleep by something poking him in the side. At first he thought it was his boots, but it wasn't a steady pressure. Something was poking at him. He laid there or a couple of seconds with his eyes open, confirming that something or someone was poking at him. He rolled over and poked his head out against the wetness of his sleeping bag, to see Jiggs holding a stick. "Get up Boston."

Starring at the dark form against the background of grey clouds looked frightening "What's the matter?" Boston said groggily.

"Get up if you want some breakfast!" was the response.

Boston stumbled to the trees and back again only to realized his socks were now wet. He crawled head first into his bag to locate a dry dirty pair of sock and his boots. Sitting on his wet sleeping bag he asked "What time is it? I don't see any grey light anywhere!"

Jiggs was handing Boston a cup "Have some coffee and I'll explain. Oh yeah, here's breakfast," as he held out two pieces of elk jerky.

Boston sat quietly sipping coffee and biting on the jerky, while Jiggs just stared up at the sky.

Jiggs had finished his coffee when he said, "In about thirty minutes the clouds will clear, and we should have sufficient moon light to move those cows down the mountain. We will need to be down before it gets light."

Boston wasn't sure he had heard what he heard. "In the dark? Isn't that dangerous?"

"In case you haven't realized this or figured it out already, everything we do is dangerous," Jiggs responded. Boston didn't have to think very long to come to that conclusion.

120

Jiggs began spelling out their task for the day. Get those four dry cows off the mountain before it was daylight, without losing them and without having a wreck. Boston knew that word was not thrown about lightly.

His interest was piqued, but he wanted to know, "Why are we moving them at night?"

Jiggs explained, "It's a pretty big moon tonight and it will light the trail, the surrounding woods will be dark. The cattle will want to stay on the trail where they can see. We'll be going down some steep ground and if you think your horse is going to fall kick your feet out of the stirrup, and lean back. If your horse falls on his knees and starts to roll get off the saddle fast. You'll be able to find your horse at the bottom."

Needless to say Boston's pulse had quickened, there was tightness in his gut and he sensed fear in himself. Before anything else was said, Jiggs commanded "Saddle up." As they walked to the horses Jiggs made another comment, "Make sure your cinch is extra tight. Track him out in the corral before you bring him out, then dismount and tighten it again." Boston just listened with every particle of his hearing. He did as Jiggs had instructed, and soon the two of them were mounted and walking toward the trap they erected, in silence. Before the pole was pulled back, Jiggs instructed, " Boston, stay out of the trap until I have the gate opened on the other end. Then bring your horse into the trap and close the pole behind you." As Jiggs was entering the trap Boston quickly glanced toward the sky, the moon was at three quarters full. Just as quickly he brought his attention to what is at hand. Before Jiggs opened the gate he called over to Boston, "I'll take the lead, you take up the drag. Keep pressure on and don't lag. See you at the bottom." With those final instructions, Jiggs opened the gate, positioning himself so as to turn the cows when they started out. Boston by now had pulled the pole across and was mounted and pushing the cows out of the trap toward the open gate. When Boston went through the gate he saw Jiggs disappear into the blackness of the trees. The cows followed the fence line which separated the high pasture from the camp pasture. Boston saw a dark shadow appear further up and momentarily lost track of it, then it rose up. He realized it was Jiggs who was mounting his horse, it paused and then seemed to sink into the ground. Boston brought his attention back to keeping track of the cows in front of him, because he knew how fast they could disappear into trees. He kept counting to make sure all four were still in front of him, the cows paused when they came to a gate opening but continued through as Boston pressured them onward. Again, he watched as the lead cow seemed to melt into the earth. Finally Boston came to the crest of the hill, he paused for a second, then encouraged his horse forward. As his horse went forward Boston leaned back onto the cantle of his saddle, at the same time his pulse quickened. He fought off fear by focusing on keeping pressure on the cows and trying not to overcrowd them. He pushed his stirrups forward to keep his balance. He kept his horse at a steady pace. It was difficult to move to any side. He was just hoping the cows wouldn't try to turn. He still had the four cows in front of him with the dark shadow of Jiggs beyond them. Now this same dark shadow which previously caused momentary fear was now somehow reassuring. The decent seemed like an eternity but after three or four minutes he arrived at a bench, a flat spot, maybe ten feet wide. The cows slowed and he was able to move to the left or right as needed to urge them downward. Now that he had been through this descent once it didn't bother him as much as the first time the ground dropped away. The moon light provided enough light that one could see if there were any obstructions or if a cow had stopped. The cows also seemed to know this and they continued downward, sometimes running into each other and thus they were encouraging themselves. They continued past another two benches before Boston thought he could see the floor of the valley. As he urged his horse down this last slope, he became aware, the gait of his horse changed from a rocking motion from side to side as the legs of the horse moved in slow jerky steps. They were now sliding and then lunging forward trying to regain its balance. He knew they were on slide rock. He slipped his feet out of the stirrups, continuing to keep

122

them stretched out in front to be sure he could quickly get out of the saddle. He grabbed the saddle horn and leaned back as far as he could and still be able to see ahead of the horse. To him it seemed he was looking down at his nose when he heard the splash of water. His horse took a quick leap into the air. Being stretched out over the back of his horse and not having his feet in the stirrups. Boston was unable to maintain his grip on the saddle horn and fell backwards onto the rear of the horse. Then with one bounce off his horses' butt, he flipped over and landed face first into the stream. It happened so fast he himself wasn't sure how it happened, but he stood there in the stream thoroughly soaked. There right in front of him sitting on his horse was Jiggs with a big smile. "If you're done showing off, can we put these cows in the trap? I've seen trick riders perform a similar stunt and I think you can give them a run for their money." He laughed even harder and went to catch Boston's horse. Boston waded out of the creek as his horse was brought up. He remounted and they pushed the cows into the trap. They were willing to go since the grass was plentiful inside. Jiggs dismounted and began building a fire so Boston could dry his clothes. While he was in this process, Boston asked, "How often do you come down that slope?"

Striking a match Jiggs responded, "Never have. It sure can pucker your butt." They both laughed as a small flame arose from the pile of twigs. It was still early in the morning as they sat there in front of the fire, Jiggs smoking a cigarette and Boston holding his shirt over the fire on a stick. Their solitude was broken by the sound of a truck engine approaching. "That's Ike bringing the truck. You keep drying your clothes, I'll help load these cows." Jiggs stated. Ike backed the truck up to the loading chute and in twenty minutes they had the cows loaded onto the truck. The two men then walked over to the fire with Ike carrying a thermos. "I hear you decided to go swimming this morning," Ike said smiling.

"Hi Ike. Ya, I guess" Boston replied. "It sure was cold."

"Here, this will warm you up." Ike said, handing him a cup. The three of them sat there and enjoyed coffee as Ike laid out the rest of the day for Boston. Ike and Jiggs were going to the sale barn and then back to the Goolsby ranch. Boston was to head back to headquarters, then back up to the camp to check on the herd. We'll join up at the camp in the morning after breakfast. They doused the fire and walked to the truck loaded with the cows and Jiggs' horse. Boston mounted up and waved, receiving an "adios" from Jiggs.

As he rode back to headquarters following the directions Ike had given him. Feeling pleased with himself and the work he had done. It was mid-morning and he was enjoying his ride, he kicked the horse to a trot. It was about an hour later when was on the drive way to the ranch.

He put his horse in the corral and went to the bunkhouse to change clothes, they were almost dry. Having slept in them he felt he would put on clean clothes. In less than ten minutes he was back at the corral re-tightening his cinch. As he was riding back up the mountain he knew both Ike and Jiggs were pleased with him, even making fun of his water activities. He had never felt so pleased with himself and what he had accomplished. He sat a little taller in the saddle as he rode up the mountain to the camp.

CHAPTER SIXTEEN

Coming into the cow camp pasture, he headed straight towards the corral. He did a quick scan of the herd as he rode. He unsaddled the horse he was riding and caught another, quickly saddling it. He left it in the corral, then headed to the chuck box. He had never looked for food before in the chuck box. He just wanted something to eat and was hoping to find something quick and easy to make, and not jerky. He inspected each can reading the labels on how to prepare. He spotted the Spam can with a picture of Spam and eggs on the front. He knew he could make that. He poked around long enough in the fire and found some hot ashes on which he dropped a small amount of pine needles. When smoke started to show he fanned it with his hat until flames appeared, then added some tiny branches. He kept increasing the branches size until he had a nice fire going. He could now focus on the food. The only eggs that were left were the powdered kind. He read those instructions and began preparing that mixture. He opened the can of Spam taking out the meat. He cut the meat into thick slices laying in the hot skillet with some grease. In no time it was popping and sizzling, he then added the egg mixture. Trying to stir the eggs with the meat slices wasn't working so he cut the meat into small pieces. Just as he was hoping the meal was cooked in a short time. He scraped a pile of meat and eggs onto his plate. Setting the rest next to the fire, he began to inhale the plate full of eggs and meat. He ate it so fast he didn't remember tasting anything. The second plate full he ate slower, tasting the faint flavor of ham, although different, and the bland eggs, but he didn't complain. After his meal he seemed awful thirsty, so he grabbed a canteen and filled it to bring along on his ride. He re-tightened his cinch and started his rounds to check the cattle. He went into the trees to see if there might be some on the cold places. Those areas where there wasn't much feed but lots of shelter from wind and found nothing. He made one last pass through the herd and headed for the camp. The sun had dropped behind the mountain peaks and it was now dusk.

He unsaddled his horse and set his blanket and pad out to dry on the rail. Walking towards the camp he realized he left it without cleaning up his mess from the previous meal. He checked the meat locker and found one piece of meat marked "beef." He decided he would have that at breakfast since he didn't feel like frying anything. Once again he wanted something simple for supper. He remembered seeing a can of spaghetti and meatballs and dug it out from the chuck box. Supper didn't take long to fix, but the cleanup from the two meals seemed to take forever. He remembered that Ike had told him to keep a clean camp in order to keep unwanted guests away. By the time darkness fell he had finished cleaning the pots and stowed and secured everything. Having no one to talk with he stared into the fire and thought about the day's work. Just thinking about the mornings work made his heart race again. His thoughts were interrupted when he heard a snort. Was it from the horses, the cows or something else? He stood up and walked to the edge of the knoll, then went one direction and back the other way. But he saw nothing. He walked to where he stowed his sleeping bag and brought it back to the fire. Tonight he was going to sleep next to the fire and maybe a better night's sleep. After unrolling it, he crawled in. The fire still casting off a lot of light, prevented him from seeing all the stars, but it's warmth felt good. As he listened to the sounds in the night, sleep came without notice.

The sound of the camp robber birds woke Boston up. It was almost sunup, he wiggled out of his sleeping bag, putting on his jeans and boots. There was still enough water that it wasn't necessary for him to get any. He wanted to cut enough wood this morning to last a couple of days. But first he was going to fry that piece of steak in the meat locker. He built up the fire and hung a shallow pot over the fire, dropped a dab of grease into it, and went to get the steak. Placing the steak in the pan, the grease sizzled and popped up, causing him to retract his hand quickly. There was still plenty of coffee left from yesterday, which he had heated up. Pouring himself a cup he sat back and surveyed the scene of cows in the pasture under a bright blue sky with birds chirping and singing. It really was a peaceful setting. Time seemed to move at a slower pace in the West, or maybe it was the people. They didn't hurry from one place to another, everything moved slow and deliberately. This pace kept the animals calm and easier to work with. Nothing like the hustle and bustle pace where he came from. Everyone there seemed to be wrung tight like a towel, bouncing around like water on a hot skillet. This was the kind of environment he needed to free his mind to write, he thought.

He took out a couple of pieces of bread and made a nice steak sandwich for his breakfast, which he washed down with another cup of coffee. When he finished breakfast, he quickly cleaned up the camp, throwing out the water in the wreck tub and coffee. He then began chopping wood. As he worked he went over the things he wanted to accomplish in his mind. He would ride the herd and check each animal and then return. If there was time he might check a section of fence. He knew Ike was coming up probably about dinner time, so he wanted to get the herd ridden first. He saddled up inspecting each calf and cow. He wasn't sure what he would do if he found an injured or sick cow, but he was going to check on them anyway. The days were still warm so the cows would shade up in the trees, this always took longer to check on them. Boston looked up at the sun, it appeared to be directly overhead, he headed back to camp. Coming out of the trees so he could see the camp, there was nobody there. Had he got the instructions wrong? Ike did say he would be here today. Arriving in camp he loosened his cinch and put his horse in the corral.

He made a fresh pot of coffee and filled the wreck tub with clean water. He walked over to his Laundry Bag and took out his fishing gear, then picked up the one water can and went down to the stream. Leaving the can in the stream, he walked on to the beaver pond. Using his pocket knife, he cut off a branch from an aspen and made himself a fish pole. He attached about thirty feet of fine line, secured two fish hooks onto the line six of eight feet apart. About a foot behind each hook he attached a couple pieces of lead shot. He then started to pick up rocks along the stream's edge to find some type of grub or bug. These he put on the hooks. Then standing in the stream to avoid the trees along the shoreline, he cast the line into the pond toward the beaver dam. He laid the pole down on the shore and weighted it with large rocks. Returning to the water can, he hoped to have at least one trout later in the day and maybe two. Boston had just completed dropping in the chlorine tablets when he heard someone call, "Hello in camp." Boston walked to the edge of the knoll to see down the valley. There were four horses coming with three riders. Ike leading a pack horse and Jo, but the paint horse and it's rider he didn't recognize. Boston waved and continued watching trying to identify that third rider. It was the blond hair that tipped Boston to the riders identity, it was Shylo. Boston opened the corral gate and then took the lead rope from Ike. Boston said

"Hello Jo, Shylo, I wasn't expecting anyone but Ike."

Ike quickly responded, "I didn't want you jumping in the stream again like you did yesterday, so I didn't tell you."

Boston just smiled. Ike and Boston removed the canvas panniers from the pack saddle and carried them to the chuck box. "You're probably short on provisions," Jo commented. "Yup! Ate the last piece of meat this morning." Boston replied.

Shylo shut the corral gate and then joined them at the chuck box. "It seems that every time I see you, you're either eating or talking about eating." she kidded Boston.

They all chuckled and busily restocked the pantry in the chuck box. "We brought fresh eggs, bacon, beef, elk meat along with other canned goods. Tell me how are things here." Ike remarked.

"I checked the herd this morning and they all looked fine. My count was eighty seven including the bulls. I didn't get any part of the fenced check." Boston reported.

"That's a good report, Boston. Lets you and I ride through once and then come back for coffee." Ike suggested.

They went to the corral and tightened their cinches and rode slowly into the herd as Ike checked the cows over. Returning to the camp, the women had coffee and pieces of a cake set out. They all enjoyed the cake and coffee. While Jo and Shylo were tiding things up, Ike asked Boston to join him at the corral.

Boston came to realize that Ike and Jiggs didn't talk much but when they did talk something was on their mind and they spoke it straight out. They stood there looking at the horses when Ike began "How are things with you? You still like this ranch life?"

"Sure." Boston quickly replied.

"You have come a long way since you first showed up at the ranch, but there is a lot more to know. All of us are pleased with your attitude of trying, even if you are not sure if it's right. Sometimes knowing the right takes a lot of trying. Yesterday, when the two of you moved those dry cows down the fire break, that really surprised me. First, that is not normally how we get to Nesbitt Creek trap. Jiggs gave his explanation, not that I asked him, but he knows how I think. I might have done the same thing. It was his call and he was in charge of the task. The job got done without anyone getting hurt."

"Did I mess up?" Boston quickly interjected.

"Heck no." Ike said emphatically. "I'm very pleased how well you did. But the next few days we have another job. The three of us are helping over at the Goolsby Ranch. My dad started helping them with branding when he first came here, and now it's just something we do each year. When we work over there Mr. Goolsby is Owner and Mahlon, his son, is the boss. Whatever they say goes. You, me and Jiggs will take our orders from him. They have their own hands and we are not given any special privileges because we're neighbors. Right now, Jiggs is at the ranch helping with the gather as our rep. If any of our cows or calves are in their herd, Jiggs will mark them and they will be sorted out later. You and I will be leaving later today bringing all the gear, so bring what you need for two or three days. A couple of other things you will need to know. I told Mahlon that you do not rope, so he assigned you to the ground crew. You worked it for us, you may be at it possibly for two days. The other ground crew members will get breaks but you won't. It's going to be tough. Just stay at it without a word and you'll be alright. Also Mahlon told me he's got a young man who is trying to prove himself and wants everyone to know how good he is. If he wasn't as good as he thinks he is, Mahlon would have sent him packing. My advice to you is stay clear of him. Now let's start loading up our bed rolls and war bags."

"Whose going to take care of our herd?" Boston inquired.

"We got two pretty good hands in those women over there," as Ike pointed his thumb over his shoulder.

They packed the two relief horses with their gear. "Let's mount up." Ike commanded, then handed a lead rope to one of the extra horses. "It's all yours ladies. See you in a few days sweetheart." The two headed up towards the gate at the upper pasture. Boston wanted to turn back to see if Shylo was looking, but thought he'd better not. As they rode off they heard the ladies say "good bye." They both waved and kept riding.

CHAPTER SEVENTEEN

As they rode towards the gate Boston asked, "Are we going down the fire break again?"

"Only if you want to" Ike replied with a laugh.

"Yeah, once a week is enough for me." Boston said chuckling.

Boston got dismounted and looped the lead rope around the horn. He then moved the pole from the trap they built allowing them to enter into the high pasture. They rode to the other side and then followed the fence line up to the corner where there was a small gate, just big enough to allow a horse and rider through. Again Boston dismounted and opened the gate. He walked his horse and the pack horse through the opening. He handed his horses' reins to Ike and went back to secure the gate. Upon securing the gate he walked back to retrieving his reins from Ike and they continued on. They now were on a small trail that gradually meandered down the mountain. Sometimes it was steep with switchbacks, other times it seemed almost level. The last five or six feet was a little steep before ending in the creek, but it didn't bother Boston.

He threw his legs forward and leaned back as his horse stepped into the water. "Two miles downstream is Nesbitt trap." Ike commented. "Have the urge to swim yet?"

"Real funny," replied Boston.

They rode alongside a two track road for some time until they came to a cattle guard in the road. Next to the cattle guard was a gate in the fence line which Boston opened allowing them to go through and then closed. We're now on the Double OO Range." Ike informed Boston. They rode for another hour before seeing a wagon and large tent in the distance. Beyond that a small dust cloud was in the air caused by a remuda of horses.

As they came closer Ike said, "I will introduce you to the Goolsbys." They slowly approached two men seated on horses, one a white horse the other a black. As they came closer, the two men swung their horses around. "Ike, we were wondering when you would arrive." Said the older man.

"Sorry if I'm late. I had to pick up my man here before coming down the mountain. Mr. Goolsby and Mahlon, I would like you to meet Boston. Boston this is Mr. Goolsby and Mahlon."

"Boston it's nice to meet you." Mahlon said. The older man just looked.

"It's a pleasure to meet you, Mr. Goolsby and Mahlon." Boston replied.

Ike again informed Boston, "Mahlon is the cow boss. You do as he says, when he says."

"Yes sir!" responded Boston.

"Stack your beds by the wagon and we'll ride out to help bring in the herd." Mahlon instructed.

The two rode toward the wagon and tent as Ike said, "You ride behind me or Jiggs or else be the last rider at anything. There is an order here and doing that you'll fit in." Boston rode on in silence toward the wagon. They quickly tied the extra horses to a picket line, stacked their gear and re-mounted to meet up with the Goolsbys. To Boston it seemed like they were riding through a pasture, but Ike informed him it was the trap where the work would be done. They rode about a mile to a corner gate, Boston dismounted and opened the gate. "Leave it open." Mahlon instructed, as Ike waited for Boston to mount. Maylon and his father rode at an angle away from the gate and Ike and Boston followed. About fifty yards away from the gate, Mahlon and his father made a ninety degree turn and kept riding. Ike and Boston reined up and waited watching Mahlon. While they waited Ike explained, "As the point man or men arrived in front of the herd, they would pass between us and the Goolsbys. The outriders would come up and get in line with us until the drag showed up. As the drag riders came abreast of the first set of outriders, the outriders would get in line with the drag riders and keep moving the herd slowly. Each outrider pair would do the same until the entire herd was in the trap. Boston you will be last and you will need to secure the gate."

"Got it" Boston replied.

Ike moved away from Boston about fifty yards, the four men sat and waited. The point men came into view with the cattle following. The front of the herd was visible but a cloud of dust started rolling up in the middle of the herd which obscured the remainder of the herd. Boston was amazed at the size of this herd, he had never seen so many cattle. He had a ringside seat and was enjoying what was playing out in front of him, especially since Ike explained how it was working. Boston initially watched the cows as they went by, the dust boiling around the animals. As the dust became thicker, he kept his eyes on Ike, waiting for him to move. For Boston, Ike was the only person he needed to be watching. There was a glimpse of two men at the center of the drag, almost totally covered in dust. These men were the ones who were there the entire time. Boston watched Ike pull his wild rag over his nose and mouth. Boston's was in his jeans under his chaps, not a chance in retrieving it at this time. He saw Ike turn and move toward him, he would be next. As the riders came forward he could see they all had wild rags over their mouths and noses. Boston turned now and rode between Ike and the fence line, the wind being in his favor causing most of the dust to drift away from him. The entire herd and all the riders had gone through the gate. Boston dismounted and closed and secured the gate. He was just mounting his horse when Ike rode up. "Mahlon wants us along with a couple of others to hold the herd. I'll show you where to position your horse, and keep a distance from the herd so they don't feel pressured."

Boston replied "Yes sir."

Ike then rode off to another position to the left of Boston. Boston sat there on his horse, keeping one eye on the herd and the other on Ike. By now the dust had settled, and Boston could see they were holding the herd next to a pond. There was still a lot of bawling as the babies hadn't all mothered up. On the other side of Boston was the fence line. Ahead of him past the pond was the tent and wagon where considerable activity was taking place. From his vantage point he noticed some cowboys changing horses and wondered if Jiggs was doing the same. He saw that Mr. Goolsby was riding up to each posted rider, pausing then going on to the next. Finally Mr. Goolsby rode up to Boston, "Head on in and get some chuck. You did a nice job today."

Boston didn't think he did anything but said, "Thank you Mr. Goolsby! Do you want me to ride in with you?"

Mr. Goosby replied, "No. I want to check the herd over myself."

Boston turned his horse and slowly rode toward the tent and wagon. Up ahead he saw Ike had already arrived at the wagon and tent. He wanted to observe what he did so he could imitate those actions. He saw that Ike was stripping his horse and leading him into the rope corral. He then retrieved his saddle, blanket and pad and was walking past the wagon when Boston arrived. Following Ike's lead, Boston lead his horse into the rope corral and then picked up his saddle, pad and blanket walking past the chuck wagon. He saw Ike standing where he had laid out his saddle. As Boston laid his saddle down he inquired, "Do I do the wood and water here since I'm the low man?"

Laughingly Ike said, "Nah, they have their own hoodlum, to help the coosie, the cook." About this time Jiggs walked up covered in dust, "I'm headed to the wash tub to clean off some of this dust." dropping his tack.

As he walked away, he took his hat and slapped it against his leggings knocking the dust off it, before placing it back on his head. The camp was full of talk and laughter when the cook called everyone to chuck. The line quickly formed as Ike and Boston found a place. There were lots of good comments on the food and its flavor, the cook just smiled. Boston knew that he ate whatever the cook put on his plate and if there were extra, he might get seconds. The camp quieted down briefly as they sat and ate their chuck.

This was a great time of camaraderie among the cowboys. Ike and Jiggs wandered amongst them renewing friendships. Boston was enjoying listening to their tales and stories as they ate and drank coffee. A few feet away from Boston was a young fella who looked of high school age, who spoke to Boston,

"What's your name? Mine is George Roebuck, they call me Sears."

"H. B. Sullivan, but they call me Boston," hoping that would end the conversation about names. His hope was dashed as it continued,

"You from Boston then?" inquired Sears.

"No, it's just what I'm called," responded Boston.

"How did you join up with those two jail birds?" Sears asked.

The statement puzzled Boston and yet confirmed something he thought might be possible. Before he could respond, a deep voice from somewhere behind Sears yelled out, "Watch your mouth Sears!" Boston quickly turned his head to identify whose voice it was. Turning his head back towards Sears, he began to say "Well…"

Then the next fifteen seconds seemed to flash by like lightening. Out on the edge of the firelight appeared Jiggs who must have just stumbled or tripped on something as his coffee cup seemed to launch itself straight at Sears' lap, as Jiggs was falling down. "Aaah" yelled Sears as he leaped up. "Can't you hold your cup old man?"

Picking up his cup, he turned around and went for more coffee. The whole group burst out in laughter, except for Sears and Boston. The group then started spinning tales of things that happened at various ranches or rodeos where they worked at the time. Slowly, one by one they began seeking their bed rolls. Boston did the same, followed later by Ike and Jiggs. Everyone knew tomorrow would be a busy day.

The call to breakfast came before day break. This time the chuck line took longer to form as the men slowly came out of their beds. They lingered longer over their serving of eggs, biscuits, gravy and potatoes. The coffee, coming from a bottomless pot was especially good on a cool morning. Just when the quantity of conversations picked up, Mahlon stepped out and began giving instructions and work assignments to the men. Jiggs and Ike were mentioned with the group going out to sort cattle. The only ones not moving were the cook, the hoodlum and Boston. Mahlon looked at Boston and the hoodlum, whose name was Pogue, "You two go out there" pointing out in front of the wagon, "about fifty yards and build two fires." Boston and Pogue picked up some firewood and went out in the general direction Mahlon had pointed. They began building two fires with about fifty feet between them. Even though Pogue was the lowest man on the crew, Boston knew that he had experienced all this before. Boston was determined to watch what he did and learn. A pickup truck full of boys came rumbling out into the pasture, "There's the ground crew from the city school." Pogue stated. Boston took a liking to Pogue, he was maybe sixteen years old, big for his age, who talked slow and moved deliberately at his work. "Mr. Goolsby always hires some school boys to help. I got started that way out here. I hope these are good workers." Pogue explained. As soon as a good fire was going another man, a little older than Ike but not as old as Jiggs, came by and laid some branding irons in the fires. He then had the school boys carry some boxes marked with red crosses on them back to the fire.

Boston asked "What are the boxes for?"

The man replied in a deep voice, "They hold our vaccines, needles and syringes and such. Hi, my names Naught."

Boston heard of strange nicknames before and replied, "Not? Or Like K-N-O-T?"

The man smiled, "My name is Naughton Dewey. They shortened it to Naught, N-A-U-G-H-T."

Boston responded "Pleasure to meet you Naught, my name is Boston."

The introductions were interrupted as Mahlon called out instructions to the ground crew.

Because the town kids weren't as big, Pogue and Boston were the flankers and two of the town kids ran the irons, but Pogue and Boston were told to give the kids a chance at flanking as well, thus they would get a break. Mahlon and Naught were doing the vaccinating and castrating.

Boston asked Naught, "Do you use a Nordfork or dead stick?"

"Nope, just the flat ass method" Naught responded with a smile.

Boston knew what he was talking about since Ike had demonstrated it and then Boston demonstrated how it was done with a calf to show Ike he listened and knew what to do. The flanker's job was to throw the calf to the ground, making sure the proper side was up for branding. Another man, a school boy, would hold the calf's neck down with his knee and then hold onto one of the front feet. The calf would be vaccinated and castrated if necessary, and then released. As the ground crew got up, a roper was ready to drag another calf to the fire, and the process repeated itself.

Once everyone had their assignment and knew what to do, they got into position forming a line of men between the two fires. You could almost feel the excitement a minute before the first cowboy was dragging a calf in by its hind feet. The first cowboy went to the other crew, but directly behind him was a second cowboy dragging a calf towards Boston's crew. Momentarily Boston glanced at the other crew watching Pogue, then he brought his attention to the calf that was being drug to him. The roper slowed his horse down just as the calf was at Boston's feet. He and the high school kid grabbed the calf's legs with Boston sitting on the ground stretching out the calf's hind legs and the school kid placing a knee in the calf's neck and holding onto one of the front legs. Their first calf was a heifer. She was vaccinated and branded then released. The excitement settled down after that first calf. Boston was mindful that the calf needed to be laying so the proper side was up. The next calf was laying on the side to be branded. The calves were small enough that Boston could grab the roped legs and flip the calf over, thus exposing the side that needed to be branded. After they worked a half dozen calves, a rhythm was established and things seemed to be going along fine. Boston was in his position flat on the ground with his back toward the other crew. A rider was dragging a calf to that crew when he hollered out "Colt." Boston didn't understand what that meant, he just kept focused on his task at hand and doing the best he could. Boston was in the process of releasing the calf they had worked, and began to get up off the ground. It was at that time the horse dragging the calf to the other crew's fire shied. He could hear various voices from the other crew calling out phrases like; easy now, careful, keep him moving. By now the riders' rope began to slack, soon the calf would be up and running or break lose altogether if the crew didn't act. The flankers moved out to secure the calf, but all this commotion seemed to startle the horse even more, and it just wanted to leave the area. The rider was doing a good job of keeping the horse under control. Once the ground crew had secured the calf and freed the rope the rider left the branding area. Maylon spoke to both of the crews, "We're going to give Sears a couple of more tries with his colt at dragging to the fire, but everyone move slow and careful when he come in again." There was only one way the colt would get experience, and that was to go through the process. Boston especially knew how it felt to go through a process. At least another dozen calves went through the branding area before "Colt" was hollered out. This time everyone paused and watched as Sears brought his colt toward the fire Boston was working. Again the horse shied from the crew but not to the extent it had previously. The crew waited until the colt had dragged the calf past them before springing into action. By the end of the day the colt was taking to the job like a veteran.

As the day wore into the noon hour, the crews, ropers and horses were beginning to tire. The days of August were hot and this one was exceptional. Boston had taken his turn with the branding iron and even tried his hand at vaccinating a time or two, but left the castrating to Naught, although he observed and listened to Naught carefully. One of the cowboys in an attempt to give his horse a break roped a calf by the neck. A flanker, on the other hand, has to work harder to catch and then throw the calf. Boston's muscles were already sore as he ran his hand down the rope to the calf. Grabbing it by the front leg and reaching under its flank he flipped it, or threw it to the ground, the other flanker jumped in to neck it down and release the rope. "Doing it this way takes too much out of you." said Boston between deep breaths of air.

Ropers came and spelled the members of the ground crew for a while, so they could get refreshed with drinks from the coolers. These metal coolers were set up near the branding crews, and stocked with water and pop under lots of ice. Boston took a piece of ice and ran it over the back of his neck and over his face. There was so much dust on him the ice resembled a piece of clay when he was finished.

Everyone now seemed to be moving at a slower pace, methodically going through the motions. Those working the ground crew began talking to the calves. "Be sure to tell your friends where you got that," "Wear it with pride!" "You're one of the gang now," or "You'd better behave or I'll tell your momma on you." All these comments seemed to help lighten the work. The ropers were getting tired too and weren't paying close attention as they brought the calves to the fire. Another calf was being brought in by its neck to the other crew, but the roper was bringing it in too slow. Boston was not aware of the situation since he was focusing on the castration being performed on the calf he had stretched. The neck roped calf, by being brought in too slow was allowed to run and bounce along behind the roper's horse. The calf darted away from the crew waiting for it, and into the area where Boston was working. He was just getting up from the ground, and had positioned himself inadvertently between the calf and the roper. Those two, of course, were connected by the rope, which caught Boston in the middle of his chest, knocking him to the ground. As he fell he grabbed the rope, which put tension on the rope between him and the horse. The horse sensing this tension, pulled harder. While on the other end of the rope, the calf sensing the additional slack in the rope took off running. When the calf took off, it was only six feet away from Boston who was now stretched out on the ground. Resulting in Boston getting tangled in the rope and being stepped on vigorously from boot to hat by the calf as it was attempting to get away. The two ground crews assessed the situation and jumped in to secure the calf and allow Boston to get out from the rope and calf. Boston wasn't hurt but his shirt had a few new holes. There was no blame or fingers pointed, they just wanted to know if Boston was alright. It all happened so quickly and it could happen to anyone of the men on the ground crew.

As the sun dipped behind the peaks, the last few calves were dragged to the fire. The calves and mothers began joining up. The constant bawling and bellowing hadn't phased Boston. Each crew began cleaning up around their branding area smothering the fires with dirt. Some of the riders carried the boxes and branding irons back to camp. When everyone arrived at camp, the cooler was brought out stocked with beer. Everyone had a beer except Ike and Mr. Goolsby, they had coffee. Even the high school kids were allowed a beer, but that was all. They weren't allowed to have seconds and were told that when the cooler was brought out. There was plenty of conversation and laughter among them all. When chuck sounded, everyone was served steak, fried potatoes and peach cobbler. Once again as they ate the conversation subsided as they enjoyed the food.

Boston found Pogue sitting in back of the chuck wagon and sat down beside him. Soon the men would come back for seconds on the coffee and the conversations would increase. "Are you going to join the rest at the fire?" Boston asked Pogue.

"Naw, my day will start early helping the coosie." Pogue replied.

"I sure enjoyed working with you and hope to see you again." Boston said sincerely.

"I hope next time I can get off the ground crew." They laughed as Pogue continued, "Mr. Goolsby said I can jingle horses by this fall and maybe join the wagon for Spring work." Getting ready to leave, Boston said, "I hope you can make a hand. Good luck." Shaking his hand. Boston walked to the coffee pot and helped himself to a refill and then sat down near Jiggs and Ike. As he sat on the ground they were listening to someone's tale of bygone days. When that tale had ended, Naught asked Jiggs to recite his poem. He was joined by others with encouragement. Boston was shocked. A cowboy that likes poetry, they don't say that in the movies. Jiggs reached inside his vest, and pulled out a waxed paper neatly folded. As he was carefully unwrapping it he was saying," Let me give you the lay of the land so to speak. I was working on a ranch in Arizona and a lady was visiting there from up north. She wrote this poem and gave it to me. I don't know why, except that I might have been the best looking of the bunch." There was lots of laughter and then quiet as he finished unpacking the tattered paper from its waxed paper shroud. "Her name was Jamie and it goes like this:

"Oh! For the days when the West was young. For freedom of life, and the poet's tongue. To sing of its praises grand. Where the cattle roamed on the grassy plains and the crossed mustang with the braided mane sped o're the dim trails fair. Give back the days of the round up scent, the cowboy's song on the night herd beset and the brands and sizzling hair. Take back your fields of waving grain waft us the odor of sage brush again. Leave the coyote in his lair.

The roar of the auto, that passes the street has silenced the song of the horses feet and brought to our homes more care. The old saloon, with its polished bar, was a health resort, beside the car that is filled to the seat with the devil's brew, and all of the youth are in the devil's stew. Give back the days when man loved right and practiced it, with all his might. Wore his gun as the dude, a cane, carried a slicker for the rain. Rode home to the houses not in a row. His family was there, no picture show, no joy rides after. They called us tough but we all know, when we had enough. Give back the days when the West was young and we'll sing and praise with lusty lung. How heedless to wish for those by gone days when progress and crowding has changed her ways. Let us think of the days with memory thrilled and give thanks to Him for the gifts fulfilled. For having lived and known how fair were those pioneer days which have passed as air."

It was quiet as Jiggs refolded the paper and replaced it in the pocket he drew it from. The men were still absorbing the words when one finally spoke up, "We're sure a lucky bunch to have work in open spaces, to have good chuck and entertainment to boot." Everyone agreed with laughter and cheers.

Boston glanced around at the men, and he understood these men truly loved what they do for a living. They are not looking for a big check and no one has any benefits. They bring their own gear. They do it out of the love for it. All these men yearn for those days gone by, yet are content to still work cattle and horses in the wide open. One has to live this life to really understand how they feel and think. It was a good thing to come out West in order to get a feel of what it is like. Boston was sure all this experience would help him to write a book or article.

As the night before one by one they slowly began to drift towards their bed rolls. Boston went first, then Ike, and finally Jiggs. Boston sat down and removed his boots and laid back on top of his sleeping bag. Ike started talking to him, but Boston was asleep before Ike had finished his sentence.

CHAPTER EIGHTEEN

Ike aroused Boston early the next morning. After they had rolled up their bed rolls, the three of them headed towards the wagon, just as the coosie was calling out, "Come and get it." Pogue was already sitting next to the wagon eating his breakfast. Boston said "Good morning." He looked up, with a mouthful of food, raised fork to acknowledge his good morning. The response from the coosie was a little different when he said "good morning" to him. "Morning it is!" the coosie went on, "Good is just your opinion, and I ain't interested in your opinion." After the three had been served and were finding a place to sit, Jiggs said, "Coosie's a little grouchy, glad we are striking out today." They ate their biscuits and gravy in silence, acknowledging good morning greetings while sipping their coffee. "Let's drop our dishes in the tub and saddle up," Ike commanded. They saddled their horses and tied Jiggs' and Ike's bedrolls to the extra horses. Boston tied his sleeping bag behind his saddle. The three walked with their horses over near the tent. They said good bye to the Goolsbys, wishing them well and letting them know they will help if needed. Mahlon came over and shook the hand of each of them, thanking them for all their work. Even telling Boston he is welcomed anytime at the OO Ranch. The three mounted up and Jiggs turned around waving his hat and hollering, "So long boys!" Various responses came back from the camp as they rode off.

By now it was almost dawn and plenty of light all around. They coaxed their mounts into a trot with Boston bringing up the rear. Again Boston was standing tall in the saddle, pleased with himself that he represented the IO Ranch especially Ike and Jiggs. It was hard work and he was still a little sore but awful proud. Little was said until they rode off the OO Ranch land. Their conversation started with all they had done and that it went well and nobody was hurt. How they enjoyed working with some of the men, especially those who were good with a rope or sort off a calf. Boston mentioned about Jiggs spilling his coffee on Sears. Jiggs began saying "Huh, I had ridden with that Texas wind bag most of the day at drag. All he talked about was Texas and how things were done down there. I had it to the brim. He'll learn that not every range is the same as Texas and that what works there may not work in other places. He's not ready to listen to anybody, he's too full of himself. I wasn't going to waste my words on that knot head. So I thought I could embarrass him some with a little coffee in the lap. I was hoping he'd go and change shirts." Changing the subject Ike said,"Boston you did our outfit proud, you did a great job. Everybody said you had a lot of try."

"Thanks Ike," Boston continued with his reply, "I learned a lot about branding, vaccinating and castrating. But I really think I should learn to rope so I can have some fun like the rest of you did."

"Yup," Jiggs interjected, "Nothing more fun than roping and dragging calves to the fire. Unless you like being stomped into the dirt by a calf." They all laughed.

They arrived at the empty cow camp just before noon. "Where are the girls?" Boston asked.

"Hey Ike, he misses his sweetheart Shylo." Jiggs said teasingly.

"Sure sounds that way. They must have just left, there is still smoke at the fire pit. We'll let you write her a note and I'll have Jo take it to town for ya." Ike cajoled.

Jiggs picked up the banter, "Sure we will, the next time we find extra paper."

Again they all laughed. As soon as they put the horses in the corral, Boston checked the water supply. It was two cans low and the wood pile was low as well. Boston grabbed the two cans and headed down the hill. By the time he arrived back at the camp, Ike was just leaving the pasture. "Just the two of us again." Boston stated. "Yup! Lets check the herd and have an early supper." Jiggs suggested.

"Fine with me" was Boston's response.

The two re-mounted and headed out across the meadow. In a few hours they had reappeared and were headed back to camp. They loosened their saddles and secured their tie downs. Arriving back at camp this time, Boston remembered that he was going to check the fish line.

"Don't start supper until I get back up the hill. We may be having fish."

Jiggs replied, "Fine with me. I'll fix coffee."

In a matter of a minute, Boston had made it to the creek. Arriving at the beaver pond, he found his makeshift fishing pole. Nothing had changed. He picked it up and slowly retrieved the line. He could see that he had caught one, but continued to bring the line in slowly until he saw the second fish. Jerking the line quickly to set the hook, he steadily pulled the line in until both fish were on land. Taking out his pocket knife he cleaned them and with a fish in each hand, he started back up the hill.

"Fish for supper!" Boston announced.

With a big smile Jiggs said, "Great. I'll slice up some potatoes to fry."

Having filled the hole in their stomachs with fish, potatoes and fruit cocktail, they settled back with their coffee and Jiggs enjoyed a cigarette.

"What's next Jiggs?" Boston asked.

"What do you mean?" Jiggs queried.

"I meant what other task do we do now?" Boston said, rephrasing the question.

"Oh let's see. It's almost September, so in a few weeks the herd needs to be moved to winter pastures. Then we sort cows and calves, sort the calves by their gender and ship along with a few other things."

Boston thought a moment, "So we can relax for a few weeks?"

"Relax?" Jiggs began, "I don't think making wood, baling hay and stacking hay falls under relaxation. But I'll be sure to mention to Ike how you think that would be relaxing." They both laughed.

It was a day later when Ike came into camp. He took Boston and again they rode to the high pasture, through the gate all the way to the other end, just like they did, heading to the Goolsby ranch. Only this time they went to the opposite corner. In this corner was a larger gate with another fire break on the opposite side. Ike was explaining as they rode what task was assigned today and maybe the next few days. "The herd will be brought down this fire break to the Meadow pasture below where there is live water and a good set of pens to work them. Afterwards the herd will be moved to winter pastures."

"Funny name," Boston commented, "It's the same as saying woody log."

Ike looked over at Boston with a smile and replied, "That's the name of the owner, Shylo Meadow."

Boston looked back at Ike and replied, "I didn't make the connection. How does somebody so young own property, if I can ask?"

"She inherited it from her grandfather. Folks out here like to keep their land in the family." Ike informed Boston.

As they rode the gradual descending fire break, which wound around one mountain and then dropped down into the pasture, Ike was pointing out some dead standing trees which needed to be cut down. By eliminating these trees, they would not have to worry about anything falling onto the fire break and obstructing the herd when it was time to move. Upon reaching the pasture, the two rode to the far end where the pens were and exited through a gate onto the county road. An easy three mile trot and they arrived back at the headquarters.

Ike and Boston ate their dinner at the fire pit near the house. Jo was gone so the two of them ate baloney sandwiches and apples. Ike gave Boston instructions on how to use the chain saw, including how to sharpen and tighten the chain. After their brief dinner, they put the chain saw and a can of gas in the pickup and drove back to the Meadow pasture. Ike demonstrated to Boston how to fell a tree and get it to fall in the general direction you wanted it to go. Once the tree was felled, all the branches needed to be cut off so the trunk of the tree could be dragged out. The branches, or slash as it was called, needed to be removed from the fire break. Ike showed Boston a ravine in which the slash could be thrown into. For the remainder of the day Ike showed Boston what he needed to know about tree cutting and care of the saw and safety procedures.

For the next week, Boston drove to the pasture with a sack lunch Jo had prepared, while Jiggs stayed with the cattle and Ike was taking care of other ranch business. At night Boston was again sleeping in the bunkhouse but missed laying out on the ground. He would drive the truck up the fire break as far as he could and then cut the dead trees. Each tree trunk was cut into a ten or twelve foot length to make it easier on the horse when it was time to drag the tree out into the fire break. Sometime the horse would drag it further down the hill, while at other times the truck worked well. Using the truck allowed him to tie two or three trees onto the back and pull them to the headquarters. After a week of cutting, trimming, and dragging logs, it now was time to cut the wood into fifteen inch rounds and split these so they could be used in the stove or fire place. Ike again demonstrated to Boston how to use the wood splitter and where to stack the firewood.

After the first day of splitting and stacking the wood, Jo came out and asked Boston to split enough wood to take to Miss Adeline in town. She showed him some side boards that Ike had made for the pickup which allowed the truck to carry more wood without any falling off. Boston installed the side board and then spent the rest of the day splitting wood and filling the pickup.

At supper he told Jo and Ike he was taking the wood to Adeline in the morning. He asked "Is there was anything you need me to pick up for you in town?" They concluded there wasn't anything they needed. He was hoping that would be the case so if he ran into Shylo he would be alone, and wouldn't have to get back immediately.

After chores the next day, he got into the truck and headed to town with the load of wood. Jo had given him the address and said it would be easy to find. With so few houses and streets, it wasn't any problem locating Adeline's house. Boston knocked on the door and waited. He knocked again, but still no one came to open it. He then walked around to the back. The back yard was very neat with wild flowers growing around the edges. There she was on her hands and knees pulling weeds from the wild flowers.

"Excuse me Adeline, Good morning," Boston said hoping he didn't startle her.

She turned, "Good morning Boston," she began slowly standing up, "Shylo isn't here." "Oh, I'm not here to see her. I brought you a load of firewood." Boston responded quickly.

"Why that's very nice of you." Adeline said as she walked back toward the house, "I will show you where to put it. You can put it in there," Adeline said pointing to a small basement window. "That goes to the wood room," she continued. She then took him inside to the basement and showed him the window from the inside saying, "You will need to unlock it and push it open from down here."

He did as she said and went back upstairs to move the pickup as close to the window as possible. He began dropping pieces of wood through the window until he had off loaded half of the load. He then went back inside to the basement and began stacking the firewood. There were only a few pieces remaining from last season. When he had all the wood stacked, he went upstairs to begin dropping the rest of the wood through the open window. When the truck was empty, he walked back to the basement and again stacked the remaining wood. With the task of stacking the wood complete, he stood back and realized what he thought was a lot of firewood didn't even fill the room half way. He replaced the window and was heading back outside when Adeline asked, "Would you like some cookies and coffee?"

Boston replied, "That's not necessary. I'm fine."

Adeline went on, "I know you are, it's just a small way I can say thanks."

Not wanting to hurt her feeling Boston said, "Sure, why not!" as he followed her to the small kitchen. There were two chairs at a small table, white painted cupboards, a sink, a small stove, and refrigerator. Boston pulled out a chair for her to sit down as she retrieved the cookies from the bread box on the counter. She set out two china cups on saucers and invited Boston to sit down. She took from the stove a small stainless steel pot and brought it back with her to the table. She inquired, "Do you need sugar or cream?"

"No thank you Ma'am." he replied.

She poured the coffee and then sat down. Boston had just lifted the cup off the saucer when he heard, "Thank you Lord, for the wood and this food. Bless Boston in what he does today. Amen."

Boston had quickly set his cup down and bowed his head, hoping she hadn't noticed. When he looked up Adeline was smiling and said, "What are your plans?"

The question caught Boston off guard, "I guess I will head back to the ranch and get another load of wood, so I can fill you wood room."

Adeline laughed, "No, no. Your plans for your life is what I meant."

"I've finished college but, I'm just not sure what I want to do in life." Boston responded. Adeline setting her coffee down said, "You haven't found anything that brings you joy?" Looking somewhat puzzled Boston replied, "I didn't know you were supposed to have joy in your occupation. I just thought you were to like what you do for a living."

"Oh, that's part of it, but it's who you do it for is where the joy comes in." Adeline continued "Take Ike and Jo for instance. They work hard to make their living at ranching. They know that their skills and talents were given to them by the Good Lord. So in turn they want to please Him by doing the very best job possible. They don't work that hard to please themselves or someone else. They do it to please God. They let God have an active part in what they do. The Bible tells us to do things to please our Master. We will find our joy when we do what pleases Him."

Boston really wasn't ready for that, "Well I don't know much about the Bible, but I know I want to work."

"And that is how God designed us. The Bible says it will light up our path so we can see the way, and then we will know the truth and the life." She continued, "God brought you here for some reason. He may have put something into you that made you come here. I do know that Jo prayed about where to place an ad for your position, and then she prayed over those who responded. So whether you know it or not, God is already playing a role in your life."

Boston listened and sipped his coffee. "I'd better be going back if I plan to bring another load tomorrow," he said taking his last swallow. "Thanks for the cookies and coffee," He exited the house to the truck. His mind soon forgot what Adeline had said as he traveled down the windy dirt roads back to the ranch. Upon his arrival, he parked the truck near the wood pile and began splitting more wood. By supper time Boston had split enough wood but hadn't gotten the truck completely loaded. At supper he explained that he was taking another load into Adeline. Boston explained that his first load he brought in was small and didn't fill her wood room. They were pleased that he was willing to cut additional wood so she would have a full wood room. After the meal he excused himself to continue loading the truck. It was dark when the last few pieces of wood were thrown on the back. Just as he was heading towards the bunk house Ike intercepted him. "Boston, after you deliver the wood, I would like you to get the elevator down from the hay loft and sweep the loft out." Ike shouted.

"Yes sir, good night Ike," Boston responded. Continuing his walk to the bunkhouse, he wasn't sure what an elevator was but figured it would be a large object which he would recognize. A warm shower and a comfortable bed relaxed him into sleep.

After breakfast was over, Boston asked Ike, "Do you want me to get the hay loft and elevator ready this morning before I go into town with the wood?"

Ike looked at Jo and turned to Boston smiling, he said, "Well, if you deliver the wood in the afternoon you might have a better chance to see Shylo."

By now Boston was onto Ike's humor, so he smiled and responded, "Heck, maybe I should deliver it this evening and then my chances would greatly improve."

Jo, not wanting to be left out, chimed in, "Maybe I should deliver the wood and then I could visit with Adeline and Shylo over supper. That would leave the two of you to cook supper."

Boston quickly responded, "Since I'm not a very good cook, I'll get the hay loft and elevator ready and then go to Adeline's with the wood."

"Good," Ike stated and then he continued, "Now that we know who is doing what, Boston, make sure you put the end of the elevator, where the motor is attached, on the ground and not in the hay loft."

Boston excused himself and headed towards the barn. Climbing into the dark hay loft he made his way to the large door at the end. The door was outlined by the light filtering in around the edges. By the time he got to the door, his eyes had become more accustom to the dim light in the loft. There at the base of the door was a rope tied to a metal eyelet in the loft floor. He undid the rope and let the large loft door fall away and back against the outside barn wall. The loft was flooded with light from outside, dust particles seemed to dance on the sunbeams. Lying stretched out across the loft floor was a long rectangular channel device with links running the entire length on top. The two sides were eight inches high. Since this was the only thing up there, it had to be the elevator. There was an electric motor sitting on the floor at one end of the elevator. He walked to that end and examined the elevator and the motor, then walked to the other end and studied that end for a moment. Concluding that the motor was taken off after the elevator was hoisted to the loft. He then realized the elevator was sitting upside down on the loft floor, making it easier to slide the elevator out the door or along the loft floor. He positioned the elevator in front of the opening of the big door and taking a hold of the opposite end pushed the elevator out the door. The closer he got to the opening the lighter his end was becoming. He now was hoping he could hold onto the elevator and not let it drop to the ground as his end came up off the loft floor. He wasn't pushing as much now, more just holding on trying to control how fast his end was rising. About the time he thought it was going to get out of control, it stopped. He walked to the door opening and looked down to see the opposite end resting on the ground. He picked up the motor walking to the opening in the floor. While carrying the motor he realized it was too heavy to hold in one hand, let alone try to hold it and climb down. Leaving the motor on the floor, he went into the shop and located a bucket and rope. Returning he placed the motor into the bucket and lowered it with the rope. He then took it to the elevator so it could be reattached to the motor mount. When he had finished that job, he returned to the loft with a broom and swept the loose hay towards the opening where the ladder from down below came up. This chore had taken him less than two hours.

He checked the load of firewood to make sure that none would fall out on the trip to town. Driving back and forth to the ranch was nothing like driving back in Connecticut. He could enjoy the scenery and even look for wildlife as he drove. Driving in the daylight made it easy to spot wildlife, it was at dusk or early morning when he would see the deer or elk move about, and was glad he didn't drive at those times. He was driving rather slowly and had no reason to hurry, in fact the later he arrived the better he would like it. He knew Shylo was to be arriving back from where she was working sometime today. Boston backed the truck up so he could begin to unload, but wanted permission to enter the house to open the window. He knocked at the front and back doors with no answer, walked to the back yard but she wasn't anywhere around. Knowing that he told her he was bringing another load of wood, he entered the house heading to the wood room. On his way the telephone rang, and remained ringing even after he opened the window and came back up the stairs. His folks always required at least one of them are at home when someone came to install, fix or repair anything. All the neighbors did the same thing, they weren't as trusting it seems as the people in Wages. He worked steady unloading the wood, until half of it was dropped into the basement. He then went back inside and began stacking it neatly in the wood room. While he was doing this he heard small footsteps upstairs. Exiting the wood room he stood at the bottom of the stairs and hollered, "Adeline, I'm in the basement stacking the wood." He could tell she was in the kitchen when her response came, "Thank you. When you're done, come join me for some cake." Returning to his task of stacking the wood, the telephone rang. The house was small and it was difficult not to eavesdrop on the one-way conversation. At first he wasn't sure who she was talking to, until he heard her say, "That young man Boston is here, do you want to talk with him?" Now he was sure who it was. He just wished he knew what Shylo was saying. The conversation ended rather abruptly and the upstairs was quiet except for some footsteps from time to time. On his way back upstairs he said he was almost finished and when he had completely off loaded the truck and stacked the remaining wood, he would come to the kitchen. Hoping that when the work was done he could ask Adeline what Shylo had called about. This gave him incentive to hurry with completing the stacking of the wood. Boston closed the window when he finished stacking the wood and closed the door. Going upstairs he let his boots land heavy on each step, hoping that Adeline would hear him coming up the stairs. There on the table were two slices of chocolate cake. Adeline was bringing the coffee pot to the table to fill the cups, when she said, "Come sit," pointing to a chair. Boston sat down as Adeline poured the coffee into the china cups. When she sat down and took a sip of coffee she said, "Shylo called on the telephone this afternoon to tell me she has to work for one of the other girls who had to see a sick family member." Adeline paused and sighed before continuing with her thought, "I was so hoping to see her. She brings excitement to this house, I get kind of lonely when she's gone too long."

The news didn't exactly hit the high notes for Boston either, but expressed his condolences and hidden feeling when he said, "That's too bad."

Adeline continued as she picked up her fork, "That girl works too hard. It seems that is all she does."

They sat quietly eating the cake and sipping the coffee. Adeline had taken a sip of coffee and was about ready to take another bit of cake when she asked, "Boston are you going to heaven?"

Boston coughed and choked on his cake, as he reached for his coffee to clear his throat. "Well, uh I guess. I'm a pretty good person." He quietly replied.

Adeline responded gently, "Being good has nothing to do with getting to heaven. We are saved by grace, not by works, otherwise we could brag about how good we are. The only way to get there is through Jesus. He even said no one gets to the Father, except through Him. That means you have got to believe in Him.

Do you know Him?"

I know at Christmas we celebrate His birth, but I'm not a regular church attender." As Boston continued to answer, "I never had much interest in religion and I don't fault people who do."

Again Adeline responded eagerly, "Oh I don't think much of religion either. Jesus is not about religion, it's about a relationship. It sounds like you have never met Him. I know He wants to meet you."

By now it was easy to see that Boston was a little uneasy, with all the shifting in his chair and moving his legs about. He wanted to get away so he said, "I need to be going back to the ranch. Ike has some other chores for me to do."

"Oh, sure, sure!" Adeline said apologetically then concluded, "I want to tell you about Him the next time we meet."

Boston got up to leave when Adeline said, "Oh! I almost forgot to tell you. Shylo wants you to call her tonight."

Boston's face lit up, "Did she say why I should call her?" Then saddened a little as he said, "Doesn't she know there is no phone at the ranch?"

Adeline paused then spoke, "That's right. Ike didn't want anyone calling after…" her voice stopped in mid-sentence.

"After what?" Boston voice sounded demanding.

"Oh it's best he explains. I'm not one to talk out of place." She replied.

Boston turned, placing his hand on the door to push it open. He paused and then said, "Thank you Adeline, Good bye."

She waved and said "Good bye."

On the drive back to the ranch he thought about the comment Adeline made about the telephone. Why would he not tell me he had a telephone or give me the number so I could have left it with my parents? The more he heard, the more questions he seemed to have concerning Ike. He would have to wait for the right time to ask for answers. When he returned to the ranch he parked the truck and cleaned up for supper. He had screwed up enough nerve that he would ask about the telephone.

During supper he was telling them about the elevator and then hauling the wood to Adeline's house. He mentioned that Adeline said Shylo had called and she wanted me to call her tonight. "Do you have a phone?" Boston asked bluntly.

"Yup!" was Ike's reply, "We keep it unplugged, so we can get things done around here. Neither one of us are jabber boxes. Do you want to use it?"

Boston paused for a while before he replied, "No, not tonight."

Ike just hooted, "Jo, here is a guy who wants to spark a gal and when she asks him to call he gets cold feet."

Looking at Ike Jo said, "Yeah, it sounds like a fella I knew in high school."

Boston interrupted their banter, "Aw, she is not at home anyway. She took a shift for somebody else." Changing the subject he asked Ike, "What are the plans for tomorrow? More chopping wood?"

"Tomorrow we're all going to hay, so rest well tonight, because It's hot and dusty work."

CHAPTER NINETEEN

The next morning after breakfast and chores, Boston would ride with Jo and Ike to the hayfield. Ike helped his neighbors for years put up hay. In turn they would trade him hay for his labor. The hay was fed to the cattle during the winter months. When they arrived at the hayfield, five or six miles away, Ike and Boston got out while Jo returned to the ranch. Her job was to make the lunch for the entire hay crew and their families. They walked toward some equipment parked on the edge of the mowed hayfield. Two men were greasing the machinery while a third man was out in the field walking. Suddenly he would reach down, picking up a handful of hay and twist it. He would then move to another area in the field and do the same thing. Ike walked over and began conversing with the two men doing maintenance on the equipment. He returned shortly and informed Boston, "Your job will be stacking the hay on the wagon and then taking it through the gate," pointing in the distance, "then follow the range road to the farmstead. At the farmstead there will be some folks to help you unload the hay. Once we get their barn full, then the loads will go to the winter pastures and finally to our hay loft. The first wagon load may take you a while. You'll be doing it all by yourself. I'll show you how to start and stack, after that, it's all yours. I'll be on a baler, so at first you will be following me. Later you can start wherever you want. Follow me and I'll show you the truck you'll be driving."

Immediately Boston's thoughts turned to his struggle in learning how to drive Ike's truck. Now he will be towing a trailer. This could be a disaster. He had never pulled anything with a truck. Walking up to a truck much newer, Boston now became nervous that he might wreck the engine or transmission.

"Boston this is your dream truck." Ike stated.

"Why do you say that?" Boston responded.

"It's an automatic!" Ike exclaimed. "You will still need to start in low, especially with pulling a load."

"I can breathe a little easier now" Boston stated, causing the two to laugh.

On their way back to the hay equipment two men were driving off with rakes. The third man gave more instruction to Boston on driving to his farmstead.

It was almost mid-morning by the time Ike and the other man started moving the balers out. The two men raking had each made a pass, forming a nice windrow behind them. Boston drove the truck to the wagon and hooked it onto the truck securing the lynch pin with a large clip. He then slowly headed toward the baler Ike was driving. Ike had started down one windrow and after kicking out a couple of bales would stop and go back to check each bale. Boston would then drive up and pick up those two bales. After Ike had done this four or five time, he came back to Boston and showed him how to stack the hay bales on the wagon. He said not to stack them any higher than five layers, start in the front and work your way to the back. For the rest of the morning Boston would place a few bales on the trailer, then climb on and stack them. It was a slow process and a lot of climbing up and down. Ike had told him to bring his gloves to protect them from the wire holding the bales together, he was certainly glad he did. It took sometime before Boston had loaded the wagon and slowly made his way to the farmstead, being careful not to lose any bales. Coming down the drive way of the farmstead, two boys he guessed were junior high age came out to meet the truck. They told Boston to drive into the barn and they would help him unload the wagon. The barn was much bigger than the one at Ike's place, but the drive-through part came in very handy. It took a whole lot less time to unload the wagon then it did to stack it. He got back into the truck and pulled out of the barn heading back to the hayfield. Remembering that he could begin stacking the second wagon load anywhere, he stayed near the gate that leads to the farmstead. He would drive between the rows of bales and at first was able to pick up six or eight bales before moving the trailer. Then climbing onto the trailer, he would begin stacking the bales. Once he got the hang of it, it became routine, except the more bales he stacked on the trailer the fewer he could pick up before he had to stack them. It was close to noon by the time he had the second wagon load ready for the farmstead. Slowly leaving the field he headed toward the drive-through barn. The two boys had stacked the other load neatly and were waiting for his arrival. The three began the unloading process and in a short while Boston was ready to head back to the field. This time the two boys rode with him on his return trip. Upon their arrival the two rakes had come out of the field leaving the two balers to continue slowly down the windrows. Boston drove out into the field where he had left off thinking the two boys were going to help him in stacking the hay onto the wagon. As soon as he stopped they ran over to where the tractors with the rakes had parked. The process of picking up the bales, then driving forward, picking up more bales, then stacking all the bales he had placed on the wagon, continued. He had just finished stacking the bales on the front of the wagon when he noticed the balers headed in towards the location where the rakes had park. He continued his work until he saw Ike walking towards him. He stopped so he could hear what Ike was yelling about, "It's dinner time!" waving his arm he continued, "Come and get it!"

Boston got down from the wagon and trotted to catch up with Ike. "There's a lot of bales out here yet." Boston stated when he caught up with Ike.

"Yup, after dinner we'll all be picking up bales until the field is clean. Then tomorrow we will start again." Ike replied.

"Why don't you keep baling and then pick up everything after it's all baled?" inquired Boston.

"You don't want to have hay get wet after you bale it. If it's wet before you bale, you'll just have to wait till it dries. But if the hay is wet when it goes to the barn, it could start a fire. Besides, this time of year is our raining season."

Boston realized there was a lot about all this ranching stuff that he didn't know.

By the time Ike and Boston arrived at the small grove of trees, Jo was there along with another lady who Boston thought was from the farmstead. Everyone sat on the ground or leaned against a piece of equipment or truck. The food was set out on the back of Ike's flatbed truck. There were cold cut sandwiches, chips, potato salad, ice tea, carrots & celery, soda pop and pie along with thermoses of hot coffee. Everyone had plenty to eat with very little left over. The ladies packed up anything that was left, except the drinks were left in a cooler and stashed under a tree. Jo left for the ranch while the two boys rode with their mother back to the farmstead.

After dinner all the men went out toward the hay wagon to load bales. They told Boston to put the truck in four wheel high and shift to the low gear. Then just steer unless somebody hollers "Stop." Boston did as he was told, as the four men picked up bales from the field, while two others stacked what was placed on the wagon. In no time Boston heard the word "Stop." Boston didn't feel like he had done much of anything, but the owner of the truck said he did his share on the first two loads. The owner and another man drove the load to the farmstead to be unloaded. The rest of the men sat down on bales and rested while waiting for the truck and trailer to return. Boston looked at these men, they wore bib overalls and not jeans, work boots instead of high heel boots, and straw hats instead of felt.

The truck returned and again Boston drove, with the other four men loading and stacking. This process was completed three more times before all the bales in the field were picked up. After the field was cleaned the owner and his three men all rode back to the farmstead, while Ike and Boston waited by the cooler under the trees. They each helped themselves to some ice tea while they cooled off. When the truck returned it was not pulling the trailer, when it drove up to where they sat. Boston climbed into the bed of the truck and Ike sat in the cab. The truck slowly headed out to the county road and back to the IO Ranch.

When they got out of the truck at the ranch, and waved as the farmer drove away, Ike said, "Tomorrow we stack for ourselves, if the weather holds. The first load will go to the farmstead, but the next four will go to the winter range, then two loads up here to the barn." Ike explained.

"Then will the haying work be done?" asked Boston.

"For you probably, but I will need to continue baling for them another two days to make the trade fair. See ya at supper."

Ike turned towards the house. Boston went to the bunkhouse to clean up before supper.

The next day was a repeat of the first except for the dinner. Each man had brought a sack lunch which they snacked on as they continued to work. Boston stacked the first wagon by himself, then drove it to the farmstead. He was not able to drive through the barn this time since hay had already been stacked in that alley way. He drove the trailer up close to the barn, so the three of them could unload the wagon. When the wagon was empty, the remaining alley way had been filled. Boston waved good bye to the two young helpers and returned to the field. He began loading and stacking the wagon again not knowing where the next load would be going. Before he had gotten very far, one of the men driving a rake had come out to help him. He was placing the bales on the wagon and Boston was stacking them, even with just two people this process went faster. When this second wagon was loaded, Boston got into the truck which the other man was driving and asked him, "Do you know where this load is supposed to go?" "Sure. We'll just stack it on the edge of the field," the man responded. He drove the truck over to the side of the field and then stopped. Boston climbed up onto the wagon and began dropping bales for the man to stack. This process went on until the last two tiers of hay, Boston then would grab bales from the wagon and help stack. Driving out into the field after offloading the wagon, the man said "We'll stack the wagon seven high, since we aren't traveling as far to unload the hay." This time

Boston placed the bales on the wagon and the other man stacked them on the wagon. Half way through loading the trailer, the second rake man came over and was helping place bales on the wagon. Soon they were hauling this load to the edge of the field. The last load that was taken over to the edge of the field. All four men were loading or stacking which made the work much easier and three times as fast.

When it was time to load the first wagon which was to go to the ranch, only Ike and Boston were loading and stacking. The other men were moving equipment to the next field. Ike drove the hay wagon back to the ranch to be unloaded. He instructed Boston to throw off bales while he unhitched the farmers truck and hitched his truck to the hay wagon. After Ike had exchanged trucks, he brought an extension cord to be plugged into the electric motor mounted to the elevator. All the while Boston was continuing to drop bales from the wagon. Ike then said, "Boston, that's enough for now. Go up into the loft and I will start sending some bales up the elevator." Boston climbed down from the wagon and went into the barn. In half a minute he was looking down from the big loft door, "OK, I'm ready." Ike plugged the extension cord into the electric motor and the elevator came to life. Placing a bale onto the elevator he watched how it went up and at what height it arrived to Boston. He then adjusted the elevator by moving it back a little so the bale would arrive at waist high when getting to Boston. Carrying the bale to the back side of the barn and then returning to the elevator, allowed for the next bale coming up the elevator to fall onto the floor. This process was repeated over and over until the wagon was empty. Then Ike drove his truck towing the wagon while Boston followed with the farmer's truck. When they arrived back at the hayfield the other men had returned and all four helped in loading the wagon. When the field was cleaned of bales, Ike and Boston returned to the ranch with their second load. By now the sun was just touching the peaks of the mountains. The two worked steady until all the bales were stacked into the hay loft. Ike and Boston pulled the elevator up into the hay loft and secured the loft door. By the time they had finished and cleaned up for supper it was after eight thirty. At supper Ike told Boston he would be bring provisions to Jiggs in the morning after breakfast and chores. "Can you load the pack saddle and panniers yourself?" Ike inquired.

"I think I can," he paused then continued," I would feel better if you check my work. I"ll do it first thing in the morning before breakfast so you can check it" Boston said energetically.

"That's sounds fine." Ike acknowledged.

Saying "Good night" he returned to the bunkhouse to clean up and sleep.

After breakfast, Boston went about his chores as Ike checked the pack saddle. "Good job Boston. I'll get the pannier. Jo should have the supplies loaded by now." Ike returned to the house as Boston continued to clean the barn and corrals. He heard Ike coming and went to assist with loading the panniers. When Ike had lashed down everything, he said, "I'll be looking for you to be back here in a couple of days. I want you to straighten up the camp, with a good supply of wood. The nights will be getting cooler soon and we need to be ready."

"Yes sir," Boston's response didn't hide the excitement that he felt. Boston mounted his horse and taking the lead rope from Ike said, "See you in a couple of days. Be careful in the hayfield!"

He then turned his horse around as he and the two horses started up the trail behind the cabin.

Heading up the trail, the air became a little cooler, he looked up through the evergreens and aspens to the bright blue sky. He realized this is what he dreamed about doing in some fashion, being alone riding off to handle some task. Now he really felt like he was starting to do cowboy work, or at least another phase of it. This was a lot more fun than haying, but haying was a little above fencing or at least the digging holes portion of fencing. He remembered Jiggs telling him, "All jobs are important, you have to do all of them to make it work." Hopefully he was gaining an understanding of ranch life and western living. He felt at ease, almost peaceful, the sounds of the magpie or camp jay echoed out his approach. The rhythmic sound of hoofs echoing off the trees and the sound of a creaking saddle all added to the serenity he felt. These inner feelings were interrupted when he heard someone call his name. He quickly looked all around but didn't see anyone. Again his name was called out, he responded with "Yeah?" a little hesitantly. "Rein up," came the response and with that he knew it was Jiggs, and complied to the request. Sitting in the saddle he looked around but still had not seen anyone. Now he could hear the breaking of branches somewhere in front of him. Through the trees he could see Jiggs and his horse picking their way among the trees. "Did you lose the trail?" Boston asked sarcastically.

"I might ask that of you since you're on the old trail." Came the quick response from Jiggs. "I am?" Boston said, as he tried to remember if he missed something, after all he thought to himself, I was day dreaming. Boston then asked, "Where's the new trail?"

"Just relax, I'll show you when I get there," As he made his way towards Boston. "I've been looking for strays, a tree took out fifty feet of fence the other day, and I spent most of the day cutting it from the fence. I counted heads and came up a couple short. I found one on the other side of the fence, and persuaded him to come back home. I'm still looking for the other calf. I saw you from that rock ridge bring the provisions and thought I would ride up with you." Jiggs explained.

"So where is the new trail?" Boston asked expectantly.

Jiggs smiled when he said, "Well the old and new is the same but I had you thinking didn't I?"

They headed to camp with Boston leading the way. At camp, they unsaddled the pack horses and unloaded the provisions into the chuck box. Once the provisions were stowed, Boston quickly checked the wood pile and then headed towards the Lyster bag. Hollering over his shoulder to Jiggs "I'm going to fetch water!" then picked up the two cans and started down the hill to the creek. Boston knew Jiggs would rather cook than fetch water. Carrying the two cans up the hill was always a chore, but with a short rest he would regain his air. Dropping the chlorine tablets into the cans, he turned his attention to cutting firewood. The dead tree he had dragged in a few days back still offered up some firewood. He chopped away at the dead tree trunk, as Jiggs prepared the meal. It was sometime before Jiggs hollered "Come and get it," but the wait was worth it. He made a small roast with cooked carrots and potatoes with can peaches for dessert and coffee. Sitting back with their coffee while Jiggs was building a cigarette Boston said, "It sure was a beautiful day today!"

Without looking up from rolling his cigarette, Jiggs replied, "Yup! But the best time of the year is just ahead. Soon the leaves on the aspens will turn golden, the elk will be bugling and the morning air will seem cold. Yet in a couple of hours it will have a crispness, there will be ice particles on the edges of streams. I tell ya Boston it doesn't get better than that."

Pausing a little before replying Boston said, "After this warm weather, that sounds like a welcome relief."

"Yeah, it's when all the men in town wish they could be camping out. Ha! See we do have a good life." Jiggs said philosophically.

Boston sat and listened to tales Jiggs told of his cowboy days when he was Boston's age. In those days the old boys he worked with started their cowboying while New Mexico was still a territory. "Boy did they have some tales" Jiggs said smiling while shaking his head. Boston let Jiggs talk on into the night, savoring every minute the old cowboy talked. Boston remembered at the Goolsby gather the cowboys called campsite fires "Liars Fires" but still Boston listened intently. The fire had burned to coals before they got into their bed rolls.

Boston came awake to the smell of coffee and bacon frying. It was still grey light but he normally didn't sleep this sound. His movement brought a comment from Jiggs, "You going to sleep the day away? We need to be in the saddle at day break." Boston was still drowsy as he stumbled around. A few sips of Jiggs' coffee chased the sleepiness and grogginess away. After a quick bacon sandwich breakfast, Boston busily straightened the camp, securing the food box and pantry. Boston saddled his horse and put the pack saddle on another horse, then secured the empty panniers onto the pack saddle. Jiggs rode off in one direction while Boston headed toward the trail leading to the headquarters. By the time Boston had cleared the pasture, the sun was above the eastern peaks. It was another beautiful windless day similar to the previous day. As he slowly rode down the trail listening to the surrounding sounds, he noticed his horses ears stood straight up and the paced slowed even more. He paused and slowly scanned into the trees. Normally the horse's ears would be moving forward and back listen for any verbal commands from the rider. Jiggs always mentioned about being sensitive to your horse "they see or hear things we don't." Then further down the trail he saw a bear, taking its time checking out different trees or logs and just lumbering along. Boston and the horses stood motionless as they observed their neighbor in the mountains. Boston kept scanning the woods trying to determine if there were any cubs. The bear eventually moved off, but still Boston waited to make sure the area didn't have any straggling cub. Slowly he moved down the trail being more watchful than he previously had been. This area did have other predators and some are pretty good size. He could see why Jo carried a pistol as she traversed this trail.

When he arrived at headquarters, nobody was insight or came out of the house. He put the horses into the corral and hung the panniers in the barn along with the pack saddle. After throwing a couple of flakes to the horses, he went to the bunkhouse to clean up and fill the water tank, so he could shower later in the day after the sun heated the water a little. He washed and shaved, put on a clean shirt, and headed back towards the barn which needed cleaning. Starting with the corral he picked up manure and in general cleaned it up, then went to the barn where he swept out the alleyway and made sure everything was in its place. Finishing these chores, he walked over to begin splitting firewood for the house. The bacon sandwich he had for breakfast had worn off and the growling of his stomach was getting louder. As he was wondering what he could get to eat, a truck came onto the drive towards the house. He didn't recognize it so he stood watching it approach the house. As it approached, he recognized Jo and Shylo driving what must be Shylo's truck. They were laughing, like his sister does when she arrives with her girlfriends, must be a girl thing he thought. He waved and walked over to the truck as it came to a stop. Boston greeted the two with a big "Hello."

"Shylo offered to give me a ride so Ike can have the truck to drive home when he's done haying," Jo began explaining, "We're going to have a bar-b-que to celebrate the end of haying. Boston, you might as well start by building a nice bed of coals."

Smiling, Boston responded, "Sounds like fun, I'll get right on it." Turning his attention to Shylo he continued, "It's nice to see you too Shylo."

"Thanks Boston, and thanks for stocking the wood room." Shylo smiled and then looked toward Jo saying, "Do you need any help right now?"

Jo stopped on the stairs and said, "No! but I'm sure Boston would like some company." Shylo turned back towards Boston who was picking up some smaller pieces of wood for fire starters.

"I'll get some matches out of my truck," Shylo said as she turned and walked back to her truck. The two met at the fire pit where Boston was placing the smaller pieces of wood along with some dry pine needles. Boston completed arranging the kindling and looked up at Shylo who was holding out two sticks, "Here are your fire starters."

Chuckling, Boston said, "What, is everybody a comedian out here?" Shylo then handed the book of matches to Boston. "I'm sorry I didn't call you when you asked me to," Boston said apologetically.

"When did I ask you to call me?" Shylo asked with a quizzical expression.

"When I was stacking wood at your grandmother's house. You called there. She later told me you wanted me to call." responded Boston.

A big grin spread across Shylo's face, "No, I told her to tell you I said hello."

"Whew! That's a relief. I thought you might be mad when I didn't call, so I still have a chance to make an impression," Boston said with a smile.

With a smile came a quick reply, "Maybe? But I think you had better throw some more wood on the fire if you want enough heat to cook with."

Boston turned his attention to the fire and laid a couple of logs on the fire. A pickup truck came down the drive just as Boston finished placing the logs on the fire. Ike had arrived and stopped the truck at the lean-to. Walking toward the fire he hollered out "What's for supper?"

"Whatever it is it's going to be hot!" Boston said sarcastically. Ike headed into the house and Boston sat down opposite from where Shylo was sitting. Shylo was poking at the fire with a long skinny stick when Boston said, "Tell me about Shylo Meadow."

CHAPTER TWENTY

"What do you want to know?" Shylo responded.

Boston paused, then said "Just how did you come to know Jo and Ike?"

Shylo stared into the fire momentarily, then spoke, "My folks lived in another town and were traveling back here to pick me up. I had spent a couple of weeks with my grandparents. They wrecked coming up the mountain and both were killed, so I just stayed living with my grandparents. I first met Jo at the General Store, she worked there I guess, and she and grandma always talked." Before she was able to continue, Jo came out with some ice tea.

"What are you two doing?" She inquired.

Boston quickly replied, "Shylo was telling me how she met you and Ike."

Jo handed out the glasses and then sitting down she said, "Let me explain something about this relationship between Ike, Shylo and me." Jo continued, "When my folks first came here, your grandparents helped my mother and father feel at home. They helped my folks purchase things for the store, equipment or merchandise, by loaning them money or sometimes just giving them money. Years later my folks carried your grandmother when it became difficult for her. We helped each other through those tough times. I have never forgotten their kindness. Another thing, my folks died in an automobile accident on the same stretch of road where your parents died Shylo. So it was natural for me to know how you were feeling. Your grandmother and I talked often about you as you grew up. I just wanted to help your grandmother in any way I could." While Jo took a drink of tea, Shylo began, "I remember Jo coming over to the house and giving me piano and guitar lessons. You always asked how I was doing in school. When I got that scholarship to the junior college. You paid my books and tuition for those two years." Shylo walked over to Jo and giving her a hug said, "You have been like a parent to me after mine died."

"I feel the same closeness to your grandmother."

About this time, Ike came out and said, "Now do we sing Kumbaya?"

The two ladies just shook their heads and sat back down as Boston just listened. Taking this opportunity Boston inquired, "Ike, when did you and Jo meet?"

"I knew her since we were little kids. Her folks and my folks were good friends. The two families came to Wages within a few weeks of each other after World War II. Shylo's grandparents lived a few miles from this place so we saw and worked with them often." Ike responded as he joined them by the fire. Jo had gotten up to go inside for a glass of ice tea for Ike. When she returned, she continued the story, "Your grandfather helped Ike's dad get a handle on how to run a ranch, and of course your grandmother and Ike's mother were very close. When Ike's folks came to town we would play together at first. Of course as he got older, being a boy, his interests were different than mine. I didn't see him as much because he was doing more things around the ranch. But at sporting events or school activities we saw each other. I always liked him. When I was a sophomore, he asked me to the Junior Senior Prom. Wow, I was thrilled. But…"

Ike interrupted her, "You can stop now!"

Pausing, then giving a sweet smile to Ike, she went on, "He got a little fresh and I had to put him in line. The first slap wasn't very hard and didn't seem to get his attention. But the second one landed square. He didn't look or even speak to me for weeks, unless we ran into each other with our folks. I was crushed, because I knew I only wanted him, but he went his own way."

Taking advantage of the pause Boston asked, "So you have known Ike your whole life?" "Yes, except for the years he was

170

in the U. S. Marine Corps and a couple years afterwards." Jo acknowledged.

Turning his attention to Ike he asked, "How long were you in the U. S. Marine Corps?"

"I'm starved. Let's get those steaks and start this shindig!" Ike exclaimed, then continued, "Maybe after we eat we can visit more. Boston, help me with this little portable cook stove."

He and Boston walked over next to the house and carried back to the fire a small rectangular box with a metal grate on top. "We just place this in the hot coals and we have got ourselves a grill to cook with." Ike stated. The ladies went back into the house and returned shortly with a pan of mixed vegetables, some potatoes wrapped in tin foil to bake and a plate with four nice steaks. While the steaks were cooking, Ike replied to Boston's last question. "I enlisted in the U.S. Marine Corps in 1965 and was discharged in 1968."

Boston then asked Jo, "So you saw him again in 1968?"

They sat eating their supper while Jo carried on with the story, "Not exactly. I saw him at his mother's funeral in 1966. He really looked handsome in his uniform. He didn't say anything to me at the funeral home or at the gravesite. I just remember how he stood so still looking at the coffin next to his dad. We walked past to give our condolences and he just stared at me with those piercing eyes. I couldn't believe he didn't like me, but he had changed in some way. A few days later his dad came into the store and when I asked about Ike he said, "Ike helped me at the ranch for a few days then just left." He didn't come into town once while he was home. Fourteen months later his dad died and we all were expecting him to come home from the war for the funeral. He didn't show up. I remember staying after the service at the cemetery, thinking if he was detained, somebody would still be there. I left at dusk but Ike never showed up."

"Well, when did you see him again?" Shylo asked impatiently.

"Well," Jo grabbed Ike's hand and continued, "it wasn't so much seeing him, but hearing him. It was near the end of 1968. My folks and your grandmother would come out to this ranch and clean and tidy things up. Ivan, Ike's father, took the loss of his wife pretty hard, having lost all interest in the ranch. One day I came out by myself and saw smoke coming from the chimney. I was afraid someone broke in and was temporarily living there, especially since I didn't see any vehicles. I stood at the bottom of those stairs, pointing towards the house, and yelled who was in the house. It was late afternoon and the shadows were beginning to stretch over the house, which didn't allow me to see into the house very well. I slowly went into the porch walking slowly to the door. I opened the screen door and was about to step into the kitchen, when a voice I didn't recognize stopped me with these words, 'Far enough!' 'Ike, is that you?' I asked. 'Don't move. Stay there!' the voice commanded again. I began assaulting the voice with questions. 'Are your OK? Why didn't you come home for your dad's funeral? When did you get back?' No answers came back, only silence. Thinking the person left, I started to move forward. 'Stop!' the voice boomed and then in a softer voice said, 'Come back tomorrow and maybe we can talk.' I backed out of the kitchen doorway and walked across the porch and left. I was excited that he was home but at the same time disappointed that I couldn't see him. I knew my feelings for him but I also knew at that time he didn't have any feelings for me. I hurried back to the store and told my folks all about the encounter. Since I wasn't absolutely sure it was Ike, my mother decided to come back with me the next day."

"It was another cool day and when we arrived there wasn't any smoke rising from the chimney. We both got out of the car and walked to the stairs where I hollered his name but there was no reply. We walked into the porch and proceeded to the kitchen. There was no voice this time. My mother noticed a note on the table asking for some supplies along with a hundred dollar bill.

Most were just staples anyone would ask for, except he asked for two quarts of whiskey to be brought every three days. There was a P.S. on the note which requested my dad to bring out the supplies and when this money was gone not to come out anymore. That stung me more than it did my mother."

Interrupting, Boston asked, "So you never saw him then?"

Jo smiled and then continued, "Not then, it was almost six months later when a scraggly, dirty, whiskey smelling man came into the store to buy supplies. I tried not to look at him as I rang up his order. When he handed me his money and I saw his face I gasped. He said hello and then pocketed his change and went out the door. My mouth was open in disbelief. I went to the window and watched him as he put supplies in panniers and then struggled to get on the horse. I knew those eyes and they were Ike's but the sparkle was gone. As I continued to watch, he rode over to the liquor store, and then rode out of town."

"That's it?" exclaimed Boston, looking at the two of them sitting together smiling. "There's got to be more. He's here and you married him!"

Jo looked back at Boston, "Well, I guess Ike will have to tell you the rest of the story. But tomorrow is another big day."

Ike, who had been sitting quietly, spoke up, "Boston you and I will be heading to the camp tomorrow early. Do the chores and then saddle. We'll get a biscuit and bacon for breakfast. Now get some water to douse this fire."

"Yes sir." Boston responded. Walking over to the hydrant he heard Shylo's voice say "Good night!" Boston returned her goodbye with a wave. He finished dousing the fire, then walked to the bunkhouse with his mind in overdrive. He was thinking that this is all good book material, but he sensed he was getting closer to knowing why Ike went to prison.

CHAPTER TWENTY-ONE

Boston arose early, with a refreshing cold shower and change of clean clothes, he headed to the barn. He saddled his horse and then went about cleaning the barn. He was in the middle of that chore when Ike came to the corral. "Here's breakfast Boston," handing him a biscuit with a couple of strips of bacon sandwiched in the middle. As Boston was enjoying his breakfast Ike saddled his horse. By the time the corral was cleaned Ike had both horses out of the corral. They mounted up and started up the trail in the dark, with Ike in the lead.

When they arrived in camp, Jiggs had just finished breakfast, but offered them coffee. Boston hadn't had anything to wash down his breakfast biscuit so was glad to accept. As they sat around drinking coffee, they awaited Ike's instructions for the day. Ike wanted Jiggs and Boston to ride to the Goolsby's headquarter in New Mexico and assist them in stripping the calves and sorting the young cows from the old.

He further explained, "Mr. Goolsby usually lets high school boys get a chance at working on the ranch, but this year they ran late and school has already started, so he is asking if you two will assist. Besides Boston, this will give you some valuable experience in helping us in a few weeks when we do the same thing. You won't need your bedrolls, they have room for you in their bunkhouse. We'll need to clean up the camp some before Jo gets up here." Ike concluded.

Boston immediately went into action, he picked up the empty can of water and went to the stream. Upon his return, he started chopping wood for the fire. He even took an old rope and rode out to find a log he could drag in. While he was busy doing all this, Jiggs and Ike went to check the herd. Boston had finished chopping the latest pine tree he had found as Jiggs and Ike returned to camp.

"Grab what gear you need Boston and we'll lit out of here." Jiggs said.

Boston quickly glanced at the back of Jiggs' saddle where he saw a blanket wrapped with a rain slicker. Boston tied his sleeping bag on behind his saddle and slipped on his jacket. "I'm good to go." Boston replied.

"If we want to get there by supper we'll need to ride." Jiggs exclaimed.

They headed to the high pasture and then out through the small gate. About an hour later they were on the valley floor just past Nesbitt trap. The sun was almost straight overhead and they started into a trot with Boston about a half length behind Jiggs. They kept that pace up for a good thirty minutes before slowing to a walk.

"How far is this Goolsby's headquarters?" Boston wanted to know.

"It's about twenty miles, near Crowther Cow Camp," Jiggs replied as he looked straight ahead.

Jiggs coaxed his horse back into a trot with Boston following. The long shadows of the riders cast across the ground which Boston admired, thinking of those movies he used to watch. As if the two of them were chasing or being chased by someone. He smiled as he rode along, observing Jiggs with his wild rag flapping in the wind, his braided hair dangling below his hat, the ease he showed in the saddle or how easy he stood in his stirrups. He dreamed this must be what it was like a hundred years ago. He could easily see the birds, animals, flowers and feel the wind. This pace seemed to allow him to engage with all of it. Maybe this pace has been underrated since the automobile, Boston mentally concluded. Jiggs now stepped his horse into a lope. Boston followed, although a little puzzled, he said, "What's our hurry?"

Before Jiggs responded, he brought his horse down to a walk, as did Boston. "There's this place I thought you might want to see, it's the closest thing to what an old time saloon used to look like. Maybe you could write about it sometime. We can't spend much time there as I feel a storm coming. When we leave that place, we'll need to be at a high trot." Jiggs explained.

"Does this place got a name?" inquired Boston.

"Rosita" Jiggs said without looking towards Boston. Jiggs continued, "It's a couple miles out of our way but we can still make it to Goolsby by evening. We could wet our whistles and then go on."

Smiling Boston replied, "I could go for that."

As they came over a rise, there below stood a few broken down building which once was a town. The town sat in a small valley ringed by gently rising hills on every side. A two track road came in from the East and exited the valley on the South as they approached the town from the North. The place looked like a movie set. In front of one of the building were two horses tied to a hitching post along with a couple of older cars. "This place looks like a ghost town." Exclaimed Boston.

"Except for a couple of building it is. A few people come here but not the kind you find in other places." Jiggs said.

Boston wasn't sure what Jiggs meant by that comment and kept riding. They reined up alongside a building whose roof was only five or six feet off the ground. Jiggs took a set of hobbles out of his saddle bags and put them on his horse. He then reached in the other side of the saddle bag and brought out a braided cotton rope about three feet long. Boston watched as Jiggs twisted the rope around his horses fetlocks making a set of hobbles.

They walked to the front of the building. Jiggs turned toward Boston stating, "One beer and then we're out of here."

Boston's quick replied signaled compliance, "OK."

Jiggs pushed the front door open and immediately the two were engulfed by the odor of smoke, stale beer, sweat and musty air. The pungent air hit Boston's nose like a fist. The place was illuminated by the yellowish glow from kerosene lamps. Along one side was a short bar with an overweight Mexican or Indian man standing behind it resting his forearms on the top. Sitting at a table next to the dirty smoked up window were three men playing cards with two women standing alongside two of the men. Jiggs and Boston walked to the second table past the card players and across from the bar, being careful not to hit their hats on the lanterns hanging from the ceiling. After they sat down the man at the bar yelled out, "What are you drinking?"

Jiggs replied in a loud but strong voice, "Dos cervezas."

Boston watched him as he reached below the bar and brought out two beer bottles dripping with water. The two women left the card game and walked to the bar. One picked up the two beers and set them on the table, one in front of each man. She then looked at Boston and said, "Buy the ladies tequila!" It was more of a statement and not a question.

"Sure," Boston said without looking or checking with Jiggs. Without looking back at the bar, the second woman came to the table with two shot glasses of tequila. The women appeared to be in their mid-forties, wearing heavy makeup and dresses that were a size or two too small. The dim light and the heavy makeup concealed most of their features. Boston took a sip of beer, more warm than cool. As he was setting the bottle back on the table, one of the ladies sat on his lap. She picked up her shot glass and said, "Saludos" and she and the other woman downed their drinks. Boston, not fully recovered from the weight of the woman on his lap, took another sip looking past the bottle to Jiggs. Jiggs took a small sip as the second woman who was standing next to him lowered her empty shot glass to her side. Boston had just set his bottle back on the table from his second drink when the fat man came alongside the table and set down two more beers and two more shot glasses of tequila. "Twenty dollars," the fat man exclaimed.

"I didn't order those." Boston words shot back.

By now the fat man was standing over Boston when again he said, "Twenty dollars for drinks."

Boston pushed at the woman sitting on his lap and said, "We only ordered two beers and two tequilas."

"Twenty dollars," as he grabbed Boston's arm and began lifting him from his chair. The chair fell over backwards as Boston was trying to regain his balance. He had no more than regained his balance when the table they were at was tipped over by Jiggs.

"We are not going to be cheated. Here is five dollars and we're out of here." Jiggs yelled. The women hurried over next to the bar as the big man moved towards Jiggs still holding onto Boston's arm. Boston glanced over towards the card table hoping someone from that table would back them up. Sure enough, one cowboy was moving toward them, but the other two were heading towards the door. Boston's attention quickly went back to Jiggs as the fat man took another step. Quick as a cat, Jiggs kicked the fat man in the front of one of his knees, causing him to release Boston and slump forward. Jiggs then threw a jab into the fat man's nose while yelling at Boston, "Get the horses, pronto!"

Boston pulled away from the fat man and turned, only to run directly into the chest of the oncoming cowboy. The two of them fell into a tangle of kicking legs and pushing arms. Boston quickly scrambled to his feet and ran to the door as Jiggs yelled "Go!" Before the door closed, Boston heard a chair smash, as screams came from the women. He hurried to the horses and with shaking hands unbuckled Jiggs hobbles and then freed the legs of his horse. Through the walls of the building he could hear the scuffle, the yelling, screaming, and shrill cries coming from inside the building. Quickly stuffing the hobbles back into Jiggs' saddle bags, he brought the horse to the front door. Jiggs burst out the door in a stagger, grabbing his reins from Boston and mounted. Boston quickly followed. The two of them loped their horse away from

Rosita. They were over the hill before Boston noticed that Jiggs' shirt sleeve showed a lot of blood.

"Let me tie my wild rag around that wound." Boston offered. Jiggs reined up to allow Boston to lean over and tie his wild rag around Jiggs' forearm.

"We need to go back to Ike's place." Jiggs said emphatically.

"What about Goolsby?" Boston asked in a questioning voice.

"That will wait! I need Ike to sew me up. It will be dark soon, there's no time to lose, we must ride."

Before Boston could reply or ask a question, Jiggs had kicked his horse into a lope. Boston followed, wondering if they would be able to find the way in the dark. But then Jiggs had probably ridden this many times before.

Jiggs slowed his horse to a trot but only briefly, then to a walk. Boston noticed as he came alongside that Jiggs was slumping forward in his saddle. He looked over at Jiggs who was looking straight ahead as they continued on without a word. The next time Boston went to glance over at Jiggs, his horse was now a half stride behind Boston's horse. They walked for some time and now Jiggs had fallen behind. Boston circled back as Jiggs sat in the saddle with his horse standing still. As Boston reined up he said "You OK?"

Without looking at Boston, Jiggs said, "Help me down."

Boston quickly dismounted and stood alongside of Jiggs who was slumped now against his horses neck. Tucking the rein of his horse under his chaps, he reached up and put one hand on Jiggs' shoulder and placed his other hand on his back. Boston's hand had accidentally slipped between Jiggs' shirt and vest, this hand was met with a warm sticky fabric. Jiggs had kicked his feet free of the stirrups and as Boston gently pulled him off his horse, Jiggs slid to the ground. In the light of dusk Boston could tell there was blood on his hand. Standing next to his horse Jiggs was holding onto the horn to keep himself upright. Boston quickly untied his sleeping bag, spreading it out on the ground, he helped Jiggs lay down on it. Jiggs was still holding onto his horses reins as he lay on the ground. Boston next untied Jiggs' blanket and slicker from behind his saddle and used those to cover Jiggs, tucking them underneath him. The sky had darkened faster with the oncoming storm. In the distance lightning flashed as thunder rumbled.

"You got to get to Ike," Jiggs commanded.

"I'm not sure I can find the way," Boston said ashamedly.

"You will, just go with what you know. Hurry," Jiggs implored.

Boston remounted, and then glanced down at Jiggs who just nodded. Boston kicked his horse into a trot in the direction they had previously headed. He glanced back over his shoulder to see Jiggs' horse standing by what looked like a yellow cocoon, hoping in his mind to get back to this place. As he rode on he thought to himself what is it that I know. He wished he had paid more attention to the surroundings when the rode this way earlier. The outlines of a few mountains were all that Boston could see in the faint light. Just as the light was dimming his memory was beginning to dawn. He remembered a pasture with cholla, a dry wash and an arroyo with old junk in the bottom. He was walking his horse being able to see only a little ways in front of him. He strained his mind to remember anything that he saw on the ride to Goolsby's. By now the storm had caught him, with a little rain and lots of lightening, thunder and wind. He sat there unable to see anything except twenty feet in front. "What do I know?" he said out loud as he sat on his horse, pivoting around trying to see anything from this afternoon. As the lightning flash and outlined the mountains around him, so did the flash in Boston's mind illuminate what he knew. The shapes of some of the mountain peaks or points. He looked at them before to figure out which way he needed to go when looking for the cow camp. He had stopped his horse in the direction he and Jiggs last traveled.

With the next flash, he took a bearing on a peak to his front and started in that direction at a trot, adjusting with each lightning flash. Always looking ahead to make sure he was on the proper bearing. Stopping to orientate himself, the next flashed showed him Spires Point. He thought for a few seconds then changed direction toward Spires Point. It seemed like it had been hours since he left Jiggs and he, still in his mind, wasn't any closer to headquarters. The storm was passing, the lightning was further off now, he was left with darkness and nothing for a bearing. He sat waiting for the next bolt of lightning to illuminate the outlines of the mountains. He felt like he had done all he could but was lost. It was that thought which brought to mind his conversation with Adeline. There wasn't anything he was going to do to get home or to heaven. Without another thought he said out loud, "God I'm lost, I need to know the way, just show it to me." Boston didn't know why he prayed, but it seemed to give him comfort. A lightning bolt off to his left flashed, and in it's illumination outlined Gunsight Mountain. He turned and trotted in that direction at a steady pace. In a few minutes he cut into the county road, with excitement kicked his horse into a lope knowing exactly where he was. Jiggs' words echo into his mind, "Go with what you know." Riding towards the ranch more recognizable objects came to his view, he felt a little relief, but still needed to get to Ike.

Riding down the ranch drive way, he remembered seeing a rifle hanging above the kitchen door just inside the house. Figuring to use the rifle to signal Ike, he surely would come hearing rifle shots. He just hoped the rifle was loaded. While he was waiting for Ike he could saddle another horse and be ready to ride back.

Riding up to the corral he put the horse inside and would unsaddle him after alerting Ike. He then ran to the house and reached up over the kitchen door and brought down the rifle. It had a lever action similar to what he saw in movies, it was heavier than the 22 rifle he fired at his grandfather's farm. Going outside to the base of the stairs and aiming uphill hoping that would help carry the sound toward the cow camp he pulled the trigger. Nothing. His mind raced. Was the rifle loaded, was it broken, where's the safety? He went back inside and turned on the lights, and studied the rifle. There it was just below the hammer. He pushed the button and stepped back outside. Again aiming uphill he pulled the trigger causing the rifle to bark. The recoil took him by surprise and knocked him off balance. He jacked the lever and aimed and fired, being more prepared for the recoil he quickly jacked the lever ejecting the spent round and inserting another. He repeated this process five times before all the cartridges were spent. He hoped they would realize the rifle reports meant trouble and to come quickly. Replacing the rifle, he headed to the corral to begin stripping one horse and then saddling another.

Turning on the barn lights to signify where he was at, along with providing light to the corral he realized there were no other horses. He stripped his horse and put out a couple flakes of hay. He ran down to the bunkhouse and gathered a couple of his tee shirts to use as bandages and then quickly ran back to the barn. He paced along the outside of the corral and racked his brain trying to think what else he should bring to help Jiggs. Where is Ike, why is it taking so long? The minutes passed by like days and with each second added to his concern about help for Jiggs. What else should he do? Did they hear the gun fire? He should not have taken the saddle off his horse! He was mentally beating himself up when he heard the hoof beats of a horse.

CHAPTER TWENTY-TWO

Boston was standing by the corral anxiously waiting as Ike rode up bareback, "We heard the gunfire. What's the matter?" Ike asked in a serious manner than added, "Where's Jiggs?"

Blurting out words faster than he ever had Boston replied, "Ike, Jiggs is hurt bad. He said he needs you to sew him up. I feel terrible for causing all of this."

"Show me where he is quickly!" Ike demanded.

Anxiously replying Boston said, "I don't really know. It seems like I have been riding half the night just to get here. I will try to take us back to him. I got some of my tee shirts we can use for bandages, he's really bleeding bad. We need to leave right now!"

Ike's voice sounded authoritatively barking commands, "Put this horse in the corral, clean off the back of the pick up and make sure it has plenty of gas. Throw a bale of hay on the back, and bring the truck to the house."

He turned towards the house running and disappeared inside. Boston was driving over to the house as Jo came riding in on Peaches. The three met just as Boston was getting out of the truck,

"What going on?" Jo blurted as she dismounted.

"Boston put her horse in the corral. We'll meet you with the truck." Turning to Jo Ike continued, "Boston will fill us in on the way."

When Boston closed the corral gate, he headed toward the pickup where Ike and Jo were waiting. Boston quickly got in,

"Which way?" Ike asked.

"I came up the county road from the direction of town."

Ike tore down the road as Boston continued, "I cut the county road from some valley that was pretty flat."

"Yeah, OK, I know where that is," Ike responded as the truck speed down the road.

Boston began again after Ike turned off the county road into a pasture, "It seemed like I rode for a long time. I had to stop a number of times to get my bearing."

Ike, listening as he drove, asked, "Were you trotting, loping or walking?"

"Well, it was mostly walking. It was pretty dark and I had to wait for lightning flashes to light up the mountains." Boston explained.

Still with his gaze straight ahead, Ike asked "Tell me what you used for your bearings." They now seemed to be driving back into the storm as Boston continued explaining. "The first mountain I recognized was Spires Point which I rode towards for a distance, but as I got closer, I waited for the lightning to show me something else. That's when I saw Gunsight Mountain. Then I changed my direction and rode for it until intersecting the county road." Boston could almost see Ike's mind mapping out the area from what he was hearing.

The three gazed intently out the window when Ike asked "From the time you saw the lightning flash until you heard the thunder, how much time elapsed?"

Boston paused, "I never heard any thunder."

Ike continued asking questions, "What direction from your position was the lightning that flashed?"

Boston pointed in the direction he saw the lightning as Ike continued questioning him, "So the lightning was kind of off your left shoulder and behind you?"

"Yes," replied Boston as Ike stopped the truck and got out to look around. Boston continued, "Oh, I feel so terrible that anything like this could have happened."

In a non-emotional voice Jo asked, "What happened?"

A flash of lightning lit up the surroundings as Ike got back behind the wheel.

"We need to get to Jiggs, he's bleeding bad, worse than I thought at first." Boston said anxiously.

Ike turned the truck slightly as they drove off, "What else do you remember, Boston?" Ike questioned.

"I remember seeing a pasture with a lot of cholla, a big wide wash and an arroyo that had junked cars or metal, then past that somewhere is Jiggs. I couldn't tell you how far."

Ike looked at Boston, "Where were you two going? I don't recall any arroyo with junked cars on the way to Goolsby's."

With a sigh Boston began, "Sometime back I told Jiggs I was gathering information for a book on western places. He remembered me saying that and thought I should see this ghost town of Rosita. He said it was a few miles out of the way but we could still make Goolsby's if we hurried."

Quietly but emphatically Ike said, "We'll talk about this later."

The three stared out into the night as rain drops began pelting the windshield. Ike then instructed, "Jo give Boston the flashlight! Boston sweep the light to either side of the headlights, but do it slowly so we can see more area."

Boston excitedly interjected, "I saw Jiggs tie his horse to his side, and I covered him with his slicker."

"That's good!" Ike said hopefully.

Boston leaned out the window and slowly swept the flash light beam from one side of the truck light to the other. All eyes stared out into the lighted area hoping to get a glimpse of Jiggs or his horse.

Suddenly Ike blurted, "Bring that light back this way!" as he stopped the truck.

By now the sprinkles had turned into a cold rain, as Boston opened the door and leaning against it, slowly moved his light towards Ike's side of the truck. There in the distance stood a horse, "Get In" barked Ike. He swung the truck toward the horse's direction. As the image grew closer they could see next to it a small silhouette. Ike parked far enough back and turned off the lights. Boston turned his flashlight off and got out with Ike. As the two of them approached in the dark Ike instructed Boston, "Take his horse and tie it to the back of the truck, while I check over Jiggs. Once you get the horse tied, tell Jo to turn on the lights."

Boston reached down to pull the reins out from Jiggs chaps, but there was no movement from Jiggs. Slowly leading the horse to the truck, Jo ran past the two of them carrying a bag. The horse buggered some but Boston held onto him walking to the truck. Reaching into the saddle bags Boston took out the hobbles Jiggs used on his horse. Once secure he pulled out a couple of handfuls of hay dropping them in front of the horse. Reaching inside the truck he pulled the light switch on. In the beam of light was a scene which seared into Boston's mind. The rain was coming down steady, as Ike was kneeling, with his head bent down next to Jiggs as if listening. Jo was kneeling just past the two of them her face uplifted toward the sky with her hands folded beneath her chin. He couldn't hear the words but he knew she was praying aloud. Jiggs lay stretched out on the ground. His form seemed so small against the wide open prairie and the dark spacious sky, barely visible to the surrounding. Grabbing the flashlight, he ran to the physical scene although he knew that mental picture would not dissolve. He turned the light on and shined it down on Jiggs' chest. His face was white, he was talking to Ike in a soft voice.

Ike had one arm across Jiggs' chest with a grip on his shoulder. His other arm lay bent with his hand supporting Jiggs' head. Ike was talking into Jiggs' ear and Ike's ear was level with Jiggs mouth. Boston stood there numb to the elements around him, his rain soaked clothes hung on him as he looked, seeing but not believing what was unfolding before his eyes. His mind seemed to focus on this man Jiggs, who he admired from the first glimpse. This man who Boston accepted anything from, who always told him the truth, now lay motionless in front of him. Ike moved his ear even closer to Jiggs' mouth and nose, then raising slowly with his face directly over Jiggs' face reached his hand up and closed his eye lids. Ike paused momentarily on his knees, as Jo now knelt down next to him on the other side sobbing. Boston stood there holding the light with tears streaming down his face shaking from sobs or the cold he didn't know.

Softly Ike spoke, "Boston, help me wrap Jiggs in his blanket."

Ike spread Jiggs' slicker next to his body, then laid his blanket on top of it. "Help me roll him onto his blanket."

Boston knelt down next to Jo and together they rolled him onto his blanket. It was then he saw how much blood he had lost, his vest was soaked along with the sleeping bag. They continued to roll him as Ike smoothed out the blanket. When they had finished, Jiggs lay wrapped in his blanket which was wrapped by his slicker. Ike and Boston gently picked him up and carried him to the pickup. In a little time they had Jiggs resting on the back of the truck, with his feet toward the back of the truck. Ike took the hobbles off his horse and using the tie down rope was about to tie him to the truck.

"I'd like to ride back here with Jiggs" Boston quietly stated.

Ike just handed him the tie down rope and got inside the truck with Jo. The truck slowly made a wide turn headed back to the ranch. The rain had quit as a partial moon darted between the fast moving clouds.

CHAPTER TWENTY-THREE

It was almost grey light when the slow moving pickup truck came down the ranch drive. No words were spoken, the truck stopped, Ike and Jo got out and walked to the house. Boston took Jiggs' horse to the corral. There he stripped it along with Jo's horse, putting the saddle, pads and blankets on the top rail. He began brushing Jiggs' horse, retracing the times they spent together and recalling all the things Jiggs had told him about horses and cattle. Boston must have been brushing the horse for over an hour when his thoughts were disrupted by an approaching vehicle. The car coming down the drive had the word sheriff written across the door. He just stood there looking over the corral rails as the sheriff got out and walked towards the house. Ike met him before he got to the steps, a few words were exchanged and the two headed in Boston's direction.

Boston came out of the corral, and had just secured the gate when the two arrived. Ike began the introductions, "Boston, this is sheriff Raymond Tallas, he needs to ask you some questions. Ray this is Boston, I mean, what are your initials again?"

"Sheriff my name is H. B. Sullivan, at Jiggs' suggestion they decided to call me Boston." Boston somberly explained.

"Do you have some identification?" the Sheriff asked.

"Yes sir, but it is at the bunkhouse." Boston responded but continued, "I can run and get it for you." Boston then ran down to the bunkhouse to get his wallet. When he returned, the sheriff and Ike were standing at the pickup, as the Sheriff said, "I'll need to see his wounds and take some pictures."

By now Boston was standing with them as Ike said, "Sure Ray, if we can do that now I would appreciate it."

Holding out his driver's license, Boston said, "Sheriff, here is my identification."

The sheriff responded "I'll just hold onto this for a minute. Why don't you help us lift the body off the truck so I can take some photos?"

The three men then lifted Jiggs' body onto the ground, allowing Boston and Ike to unroll the blanket and slicker. Ike began to unbutton Jiggs' shirt as the Sheriff went to his car to retrieve his camera. When he returned, Ike had lifted the shirt and vest over Jiggs' head and rolled up each sleeve. Boston had never been this close to any dead person, or even touch a corpse. Now he was striping clothes from the body of a friend, holding arms and fingers for photographs. Chills went through him as he held or moved Jiggs' arms or hands. Experiencing the coldness of human skin after death, the white pallor of the skin, the black and bluish of the cuts and bruising was something he never thought he would experience. The blood had dried and there was swelling around the puncture wound in his back, his knuckles were bruised.

The sheriff was busy taking pictures said out loud, "It looks like someone cut his forearm and then stabbed him with a large knife."

"Where is his knife? His sheath is empty!" Ike asked, "What do you think Ray?"

The sheriff responded, "I think I need to have a long talk with Mr. Sullivan, before I make any statements about what I think."

Before he could finish what he was going to say, another truck was coming down the drive. It was Shylo's truck pulling a horse trailer with Adeline riding on the passenger side. Ike directed them to park closer to the house, away from the corral and barn. Ike assisted Adeline inside as Shylo followed. The sheriff and Boston tried to hide the body from their view. The sheriff went through all of Jiggs pockets, emptying them into a big brown envelope, including the neatly wrapped paper with the poem he read and his spurs.

When the Sheriff had completed taking his pictures and collecting evidence, Boston and Ike again rolled Jiggs in his blanket and lifted him back onto the pickup. While in this process, another pickup followed by a truck pulling a trailer came down the drive. They parked near the barn. It was Mr. Goolsby, Maylon, Naught and Sears. They walked over to where Ike and Boston were. Mr. Goolsby removed his hat as did the others. Ike backed away and then pulled Boston back. They stood there in silence for what seemed like minutes, until Mr. Goolsby put his hat on followed by the others. Walking over to Ike he said, "Since you're shorthanded, I thought Naught and the kid Sears might help you out for a couple of days until you get back from taking Jiggs home."

Ike looked intently at Mr. Goolsby, saying, "I could use a couple of hands for 2 or 3 days. But what about your plans? You were going to sort and move."

Maylon interjected, "A couple of extra days grazing in the big pasture won't hurt us."

Ike quickly replied, "Give me a minute to get a horse saddled and Shylo and I will take you to the camp."

Boston, either not wanting to be left behind, or possibly not wanting Sears to have a chance to talk with Shylo replied," What about me?"

Ike called out for Shylo. Then looking at Boston replied, "I believe you have some business with the Sheriff."

Boston turned his attention to Mr. Goolsby, "Maylon, I'm sorry for letting you down." He walked back to the sheriff as they stood together watching Sears and Naught get their saddled horses from the trailer. Shylo had taken her paint horse, which she saddled earlier, from her trailer. By now Ike had saddled a horse and led them up the mountain to the camp. The sheriff and Boston turned and went into the barn.

It seemed to Boston he was in the barn answering the sheriff's questions until early afternoon. He would ask the same questions over and over. Still Boston had the same answers, or didn't know. Finally, as the sheriff was walking out of the barn towards his vehicle he said, "You can tell Ike he will be able to pick up Jiggs' possessions the day after tomorrow." Boston just shook his head yes, as he watched the sheriff get into his car and drive away. Boston walked to the pickup slowly, staring at the form in the blanket which twelve hours ago was a breathing person. The tightness in his stomach was still there, like a knot twisted in a rope. The numbness wasn't abated by the memories. He walked to the side of the truck and reached out touching the form on the shoulder. "Jiggs, I'm so sorry!" he said aloud. He was startled by someone calling his name as he quickly pulled his arm back.

Jo was looking at him from the stairs asking, "Would you like a sandwich?"

Pausing, he then said, "No, thank you. I just don't feel hungry." Boston turned back to looking at the form on the truck, the rolled up blanket with booted feet sticking out. Before his thoughts could congeal, he heard hoof beats coming. He turned seeing Ike bringing two horses with Shylo leading another one.

Boston put the three horses in the corral and removed their lead ropes. Shylo was attempting to turn her rig around and Boston assisted by providing directions. Once she got it pointed toward the drive she stepped out saying, "Ike is going to use my trailer to take Jiggs' horse to his family. Would you help me unhitch it?"

"Sure, I think I can manage that," Boston said, without smiling.

Shylo got back into the vehicle and with an "OK" from Boston she pulled the truck forward. She walked past Boston without saying a word. Ike had started the ranch truck and was backing it to Shylo's trailer with Boston giving directions. This time Boston attached the trailer to Ike's truck. "Boston, get Jiggs' horse into the trailer and bring his tack along to stack on the back of the truck.

I'll get us some coffee and food. We'll be heading out shortly, bring what you think you need." Ike instructed.

Boston caught the horse and walked him to the rear of the trailer, Shylo stood there holding the door open.

"Just lead him to the back. I'm sure he knows what to do, keep to the side or you'll get knocked over." Shylo suggested.

He did just as Shylo instructed and the horse stepped into the trailer. "Let go of the rope," Shylo said.

Shylo eased the door shut as Boston said softly, "Thanks."

Looking at him she asked, "Are you O.K.?"

"I feel so ashamed. If I knew this would have happened, I uh, uh, I just wish it hadn't happened. I thought the world of Jiggs, I can't even find words to express how I feel." Boston said quietly.

She reached out, taking one hand and holding it with both of hers she said, "I pray the Lord will give you some comfort."

Boston was saying "Thank you" as Ike came down the stairs giving the instructions, "Let's go Boston."

The two got into the truck as Jo, Adeline and Shylo waved good bye. They drove out the drive slowly.

CHAPTER TWENTY-FOUR

It had been thirty minutes of silence since they left the ranch headquarters, when Boston spoke, "Where is Jiggs' home?"

Looking straight ahead Ike responded, "What is left of his family is on the Jicarilla Apache Indian Reservation, somewhere north of Ojito, New Mexico. I wanted you to come along because they will want to know what happened. We may need to wait a spell before anyone shows up."

Boston quickly responded, "Didn't you call and tell them what happened?"

Ike replied, "They are too poor to have a phone, I doubt if anyone on the reservation has one."

The comment caused Boston to remember, "The sheriff said after he catalogues Jiggs' possessions we can pick them up." Boston paused and then went on, "What's going to happen now?"

Replying Ike said, "I suppose the sheriff will contact the sheriff in the New Mexico County and they will go to Rosita to investigate and ask questions. They want to make sure your story is correct."

Boston said, "I told him the truth, I didn't lie."

Ike turned to look at Boston and said, "I'm not going to ask you anything, but I will listen first to what you tell Jiggs' family. Then I will ask questions if I have any."

"Ike," Boston stated, "what I meant was, what is going to happen about me working for you?"

"What about it?" Ike quipped.

Boston replied hesitantly, "Well, being as there was trouble and that Jiggs is dead…" Boston stopped mid-sentence.

"Look Boston, you signed up for the six months work. As far as I'm concerned I hope you're going to honor it. In my way of thinking this doesn't change anything between me and you." Ike replied.

"Thanks, I do plan to honor my commitment, I just wasn't sure what you were thinking." Boston said with a relief.

"Good! Now break out those sandwiches and anything else Jo packed for us. My stomach has been gnawing on my backbone since early this morning."

He then reached under the seat and pulled out an old brown speckled cup. "When you get done sorting the chuck, pour each of us a cup of coffee. You can use the cup on the Thermos."

Boston picked through and set out sandwiches, cookies and apples, handing Ike's portion to him. Ike put his apple back into the sack saying, "I think I'll save this for later." Boston paused thinking about how hungry he was but then a thought came to him that maybe Ike knows something he doesn't. He followed and placed his apple back in the sack. The two sat quietly eating their sandwiches and cookie, washing them down with hot coffee. They continued along the dirt road driving slowly. It was approximately an hour and half later when Ike pulled in front of a building with a sign reading Trading Post. Ike got out and went inside to get directions, he returned shortly and they drove off. "Just a few more miles ahead" he said as they left the Trading Post. The land was more cholla than anything, grass was very sparse. As Ike turned onto another road, the sun now shone on Ike's side of the truck. Coming to a cross road, he turned the truck left which put the sun low and shining in the front windshield. They kept driving very slowly until Ike saw a trail heading off to the right of the road. He turned the vehicle, keeping to the side of the trail as he reduced his speed even more. In front of them the ground began to slope gently downhill and there at the bottom was a structure. It wasn't a house or a shack, it was called a Hogan, with a corral to one side with a lean to away from the house.

"We are here." Ike stated. At the bottom of the slope they both got out as Ike hollered, "Hello inside," with no response. Boston asked, "What do we do now?"

Ike responded, "Wait."

The sun was almost touching the horizon in the West when a two wheel cart appeared in the distance. It stopped on the ridge line, followed by three single riders all lining up along the ridge. On the ridge line to the East appeared two additional riders. Ike did not seem nervous which put Boston's mind at ease. "Family or friend," Ike said softly, as he stepped away from the truck followed by Boston, "they are cautious people," came the soft words from Ike. All the riders came in slowly and stopped a couple hundred feet from the truck. They dismounted and stood next to the horses. No words were spoken, they just looked towards the truck. The wagon with the two people came slowly down the slope, then it stopped with the rest of them. Ike spoke softly, "Stay here," he then walked to the trailer and unloaded Jiggs' horse. The two people in the wagon walked up very slowly.

Ike introduced Boston and himself to the elderly woman and much younger man. The lady said she was Jiggs' mother's sister and the young man was her son, a cousin to Jiggs. They all walked back over to the rear of the truck. Ike gently removed the slicker laying over Jiggs' body, then waited. "Bring him into the house." the woman commanded. Boston and Ike carried Jiggs through the narrow door and laid him on the floor. "Outside now!" commanded the woman again. As soon as Ike and Boston got back to the truck, the remaining people waiting entered into the house. In a couple of minutes the old woman and young man came back outside. They walked to the fire pit at the side of the house and the young man commenced to build a fire. The old woman motioned with her hand for Ike and Boston to join them near the fire.

By now the sun had set and the evening was turning cool. As the flames built up, so did the warmth in their bodies. They

195

sat quietly staring into the fire when the old woman spoke in a matter-of-fact tone, "Tell us how this happened!" Boston looked into the woman's eyes as he began relaying the events of that day. He told them all he remembered that took place that day beginning with the morning they left the cow camp, the ride to Rosita and the events there and afterwards as he rode for help, and continued until all of them, Ike, Jo, Boston and Jiggs, returned to headquarters. Boston paused, then continued, "My heart is so heavy right now, I want to talk with Jiggs. I miss his company, his voice, his form, his presence. I enjoyed being with him, he was a straight talker with me, he read me like a brand. Even when he was saying things to correct me, I could sense the compassion and understanding in him. I feel ashamed, if I had known what was going to happen, I would have stayed. Instead I did what he told me to do. Please forgive me, I am deeply sorry."

The woman stared back into the fire momentarily, then lifted her face and looked at Boston. "Now is not the time nor will there ever be a time to place guilt. You did as you were told, I have no doubt that if you knew what was going to happen, you would have stayed and stood with your friend. But the outcome may not have been any different, maybe worse. Now is not the time to focus on our feelings or guilt. That sadness stems from self. Now is the time to focus on the good Jiggs did. The joy he brought and the time we spent enjoying each other's company. Now let us celebrate in our hearts and voices the time we spent with Jiggs and all the good he brought to our lives. Tomorrow after daybreak we will send him on his way. We thank you for bringing him home to us. Good bye."

"I'll bring his personal belongs when the sheriff releases them to me." Ike said.

The old woman quickly responded, "You keep."

Ike and Boston got up and walked slowly to the truck, as she and her son went back into the house. By the time they got to the truck the chanting and songs from the house could be heard.

They both looked back at the house as Ike was turning the truck around, seeing Jiggs naked body through the open door. Boston kept staring at the house as they drove away until it was out of sight.

Ike again stopped at the Trading Post, before getting out he said, "I need to get a mailing address for that woman. I'll send her Jiggs' pay."

Boston chimed in, "Yeah, and I think they can really appreciate having an extra horse."

Ike paused and then looking at Boston said, "The horse is part of the burial ceremony. They believe they need to kill Jiggs' horse so he will have something to ride in their hereafter."

Boston felt another wave of emotion and guilt wash over him. Returning to the truck, Ike drove off in a different direction from when they first drove in.

"Taking a different way home?" Boston asked.

"Sort of, we're going to the town down this road to get a meal. I think we both need some coffee and hot food." Ike explained.

In fifteen minutes they were pulling into the parking lot of a café. They had placed their order and were sipping their coffee while waiting for their food.

Ike spoke up, "Looks like you and me are going to be spending more time together."

"Yes sir" agreed Boston.

"You're probably wondering how Jiggs and I met." Ike stated.

"Well yeah, but didn't think I should ask." responded Boston.

Ike continued "Well you're right about that. It was about ten years ago, sometime in 1970, I was serving time in Canon City, Colorado state prison."

Boston interrupted, "Excuse me, you were in prison? What for?"

Ike continued in a quiet voice, "Yup! I was serving a ten year stretch for armed robbery. That's how and where Jiggs and I met."

Boston turning in his chair exclaimed, "Yeah I wanted to know, but that statement raises all sorts of questions."

Again in a soft voice Ike continued, "Jiggs was sentenced to five years for assault and battery. I had just arrived and was unpacking my few belongs when the block commander sent Jiggs over as my cell partner. The next day the warden called for the both of us. Normally going to the warden's office isn't so good, so both of us were apprehensive. The warden informed us that the prison was starting a new program which involved breaking wild horses. Since the two of us had experience with horses we were the first two selected to be in that program. A senior guard with ranching background was put in charge. He was the person we would report to and work for at the prison farm."

"From the beginning we set up the place to receive the horses, board and feed them, provide a pasture for them to rest and eat in, as well as round pens, traps and arena to show them. It was Jiggs and that kind of work at first which helped me make it through my time. Jiggs, I soon realized was much more of a horse trainer, he had a natural way with horses, the likes I had never seen before nor think I ever will again. He taught me so much. We received our first twenty horses about two weeks after being transferred to the farm. Needless to say we didn't have hardly anything built except the round pen. We were told fifteen of them had to be ready for the sale in thirty days. We rode a lot of knot heads in a short time and had the best ready for the sale day. At that time Jiggs and I were the only ones who could bust, I mean train, them so we did a lot of training that first year. Sometimes a real gem would show up and learned quick and was smart, those made our jobs worthwhile knowing that some of the horse were pretty smart, but they all were tough. There were a couple of other fella who knew how to ride and they helped show the horses in the arena. By the start of the next year a couple other fellas were capable of breaking those mustangs. Sometimes we would experiment with different techniques, once we built a large pond about four feet deep to break the horse in. It wasn't an original idea but one Jiggs said the Indians used. We had only marginal success doing that and besides it wasn't fast enough, but we did enjoy it on hot days."

"By the end of each day, arriving back at the cell we were dogged tired. The routine was the same every day of the week except if you got sick or hurt." Ike continued talking about all that he and Jiggs experienced through supper and as they started their drive home. "When Jiggs was released, my happy days seemed to end. It seemed we clicked together so well. So when I got out, I searched for him for a month. I found him working at the Waugh Ranch in Cotopaxi, Colorado. I told him I was starting up my ranch and wanted him with me. I said I would double his wages if he'd sign on. He told me he wasn't going to leave Waugh shorthanded and he would see me after the fall work was done. We shook hands and he has been with us ever since. He stayed there in the bunkhouse in the winter and the two of us built fences and worked cattle and horse the rest of the year." By now they were pulling into the ranch headquarters. "Let's call it a day, and we'll talk at breakfast." Ike suggested. Each got out and headed in opposite directions, Boston stopped and turned around to say, "Good night Ike," just as he arrived at the steps to the house.

"Good night Boston," came the reply. Walking to the bunkhouse, his mind was spinning with questions and reviewing the last day, or was it two? He fell asleep before he figured out that answer.

CHAPTER TWENTY-FIVE

Out of habit, his body stirred before early light. It was almost October and dawn arrived later but Boston's body clock was still awaking early. He lit the lantern and walked to the shower and wash stand. The cold water at first shocked his system, then quickly brought him to being fully awake. As he was shaving, his mind re-wound the last thirty six hours. So much had happened, he still felt the hollowness, a void knowing Jiggs was gone. He seemed listless just going through the motions. Jiggs voice was still echoing in his ears as he rewound and replayed the sounds and events of those past hours.

He dressed in layers ending up with his jacket as the outer layer. Sometimes he would be undressing before noon and then again adding layers by late afternoon. Leaving the bunkhouse he went to the barn beginning his cleaning and feeding chores. Having completed these he walked to the house, coming to the base of the stairs he hollered, "hello in the house."

A quick reply from Jo came back, "Get in here and have some coffee."

As he opened the kitchen door Jo was setting a cup of coffee on the table where Ike was already sitting. After setting the cup down, she came along side of Boston, reaching one arm around his shoulders and squeezed him saying, "We just want you to know, we're glad you are alright and we know you did all you could to help Jiggs."

Giving a halfhearted smile he said "Thanks," and walked to his chair.

Lying on the table in front of Ike was a Bible. "Am I interrupting?" Boston asked.

"No! I said come in didn't I? Besides breakfast isn't ready yet." Jo replied caringly.

The three of them sat at the table drinking their coffee. This time it was Boston who spoke first, "Jiggs told me he thought the world of the two of you and that you had hearts of gold. I believe that from what I have seen of the two of you. Ike, thanks for letting me know a little about you and Jiggs. But how, and when, did you and Jo get married if you were in prison? As a guest it may not be any of my business but as a kind of employee it would be nice to know."

There was a pause as Ike and Jo searched each other's face. The pause was so long Boston thought about apologizing for being rude. Finally Ike spoke up, "You're right Boston. We need to be honest with you. We know you have been honest with Jiggs and we need to be honest with you." Again he paused, then went on, "I'll pick up from when I came home from Nam. You will need to hear this in order so you can make sense of some other things. The unit I was with in late 1967, was at Phu Bai, we had been kicked around some. When I lost my buddy who I enlisted and grew up with, it made the war a personal thing. By early 1968 I received notice that my dad had died, but I was not going to leave my buddies, especially when I wanted revenge. The notice had misspelled his last name. It was at the same time the city of Hue was under siege. My unit was ordered to go in and re-take the city. Here was my chance for revenge and I wasn't going to miss out. Besides I wasn't going to leave my brothers in a fight."

"I told my Commanding Officer that the notice of my parent passing wasn't my father, his name was spelled different. He accepted my explanation and told me to board the truck. If we had thought the previous months were bad, we soon found out what bad looked like. The arrival at the Military Assistance Command Vietnam (MACV) compound wasn't bad but then we crossed the river to take the fight to them. We accomplished the crossing, but it cost us a third of the company to complete it. Every day was tough. Each yard we gained we paid a price in blood. Next we were ordered to take the school and church. The Viet Cong and North Vietnamese Army had snipers everywhere.

"We were going along the church wall, I was on point. I heard something metallic hit the ground right behind me. Thinking something fell off my gear, I turned and saw a grenade. I started to yell but the explosion silenced me. When I awoke I saw a couple of guys yelling at me but I could not hear them even though they were in my face. They started to pick me up and I told them I was OK as I stood on my feet. I could feel warm liquid on my face and neck, a corpsman came up and sat me down. He bandaged my head and sent me back across the bridge to an aide station at the MACV with one of my squad members."

"The chief checked me out and said there is shrapnel of some sort in my head and they will have to operate in order to remove it. I was to be medevaced out, but choppers couldn't fly because of the weather, so I went by boat. Sometime later I arrived at the hospital ship anchored off the coast. There I was operated on and sent to Japan. All this took place in a two week period. In addition to losing part of my ear," (he pointed to his ear) "they cut open my skull to remove the fragments from my brain, stapling and stitching me back together. It took a long time to heal. I was sent back to the states and was discharged."

"By the time I got back to the ranch it was late September, I could tell the place had been cleaned up. My dad was not much on cleaning house, he had trouble with running the ranch after mom passed. I knew the family friends had been taking care of the place. I was really feeling down on myself and, in general, miserable. I lost my best friend, damn near killed, called a baby killer by the first civilian I ran into. The only clothes I had were my uniform, so wherever I went I was shunned as if I had a contagious disease. I had started drinking heavily and found comfort in that and memories of my Marine buddies."

"One day Jo surprised me when she showed up. I hid in the shadows of the bedroom, I didn't want her to see me, but a part of me wanted desperately to see someone I knew. The face was rather puffy and ugly and the scars were still fresh and deep. I asked her to bring some provisions and I would leave money when she brought them back. That went on a few weeks I guess until I forgot and went to a number of dives, drinking to console myself, not really knowing about what any more. I hated people in general, they didn't care about anything about those guys fighting for them and in particular they didn't care about me."

"By now the ranch was even more in a shambles except for the house. I had spent what money I saved while overseas and was having trouble staying current with the mortgage payments. The ranch didn't generate any income and my disability check was going for booze and some food. I wanted to get back at the people and I wanted to get some money."

"Somewhere I managed to obtain two horses, I went to town and bought some provisions. One item was a sack of flour at the General Store. In my fogged up thinking I had planned to rob the train that passed between Chama, New Mexico and Antonito, Colorado." As Jo put breakfast on the table Ike continued, "It was a tourist train and all the rich folks from Denver or Albuquerque ride it in the fall to see the colors. They advertised it as a chance to step back in history and experience the West. During one weekend they even put on extra cars to accommodate these people. My plan was to board the train dressed like an old time outlaw and asks for their money or valuables. If they asked questions, I would say they will be given back at the other end of the car. I laid in ambush with the two horses hidden in the trees out of sight. My ambush site was a location where the train slowed down to make a curve and I could step onto the back platform. I had gone out the night before and laid out so that nobody would see me ride anywhere near the train. I brought a little bracer for the chilly night air since I didn't start a fire. By mid-morning the train was coming whistle blowing and I was just arousing from sleep. I hurriedly got myself hidden at the curve, as the last car on the train came by I jumped onto the back platform just as I planned. I took out the flour sack from the long black duster I wore and quickly pulled it over my head. I took out a pillow case and a revolver and stepped into the train. I yelled at the top of my lungs 'This is a stick up' but nobody paid any attention. I held open the pillow case telling everyone to put their valuable into it. I would tell them when I got to the other end of the car I would give them back. Some people actually believed me and did just as I asked." Ike stopped and looked at Jo who was beginning to pick up the dishes and taking them to the sink to be wash. "Beauty, why don't you pick it up from here, I'll clear the dishes and scour the pots."

Jo turned and looking at Ike said, "Are you sure?"

Boston finally stated emphatically, "You can't leave the story hanging like this. I got to know what happened."

Jo wiped her hands on a towel and bringing a cup of coffee picked up the story. "Each fall I would take a ride with my folks to see the colors change. This particular year they stayed with the store and let me go by myself. I had heard about the new train and thought it would be a lot of fun to ride and enjoy the fall leaves without the driving. I booked the ride and was enjoying the scenery like everyone else when I heard commotion towards the back of the train car. Yeah, a few people were doing what Ike asked, his face was hidden by the flour sack. I was sitting at the opposite end from where he entered, he had been thrusting his pillow case at various people as he made his way forward. When he thrust it in my direction his head was turned to the side. I was looking at the flour sack and saw one of my dad's marks. You see my family marked each flour sack so if the family brought it back to the store he would give them fifty cent off the next purchase. I didn't know who this actor was playing a road agent but I knew the flour sack. Then he turned his head to face me. Through the holes in the sack I saw those eyes, eyes I have looked at most of my life, eyes I had hoped to see up close, but not wearing a flour sack. In a quizzical voice I said 'Ike.' He paused as if to focus and then quickly stepped through the door exiting the train. When they saw him through the windows jump off the train with the pillow case, they knew this was not a game or part of the promotional package. Most kept staring at him as he was running into the woods. By the time someone got the conductor, the train had gone around another curve and the man in the black duster with the pillow case had disappeared. The train ground to a halt and the engineer and fireman came back there was a lot of commotion. They had been communicating with walkie talkies so everyone could hear their conversations and soon the whole train heard about the robbery. The train crew decided to proceed to Midway ranch and there call the authorities. The people in the car where the robbery took place were to remain in the car until they had been questions by authorities. After arriving at Midway Ranch the crew uncoupled the car and the rest of the train proceed to it's destination. The car would be picked up by the second train in the afternoon to complete the ride. A New Mexico deputy was the first law officer on the scene. He went to each person asking what was taken and anything unusual about the robber. They all said the same thing, long back coat, flour sack, pillow case and a six gun. When they got to me I told them I recognized the flour sack and I think I know who the bandit was. The deputy quickly took me off the train and set me in his squad car until his supervisor arrived. Within thirty minutes the Sheriff arrived and was led over to me. I told him what I knew and he said I needed to wait until the FBI arrived. He went on to say because this train runs between two states this is considered a federal crime and they would have jurisdiction. I was offered a sandwich and coffee as I waited in the squad car. The FBI man showed up after the train car I was riding in was attached to the second train. I told him what I knew, told him my name and where I lived and how I knew Ike. I told him he had just got back from Vietnam and he had been drinking heavily."

"The FBI man radioed the Sheriff in Wages and the FBI office in Colorado to alert them. He then told me I was free to go. When I said I had no ride the last train had left, he brought me back to the deputy who first took me off the train, telling him to give me a ride home."

"He was arrested the next day at the ranch while he was sleeping and taken to jail. They had a trial and I testified to everything I saw and what I knew about him. It was a very difficult thing to do. They found him guilty and sentenced him to ten years at the Colorado State Penitentiary in Canon City, Colorado."

Boston interrupted the story, "Didn't you love him then?"

"Sure!" Jo said as she continued, "I knew he needed help and this was God's way of getting it for him. I believed that the LORD was going to make everything come out alright. I just had to trust Him and let Him work on Ike. I know at the time he was very very angry with me, because I tried to visit him right after he was incarcerated and he didn't want to see me."

"Within a month after Ike went to prison, I lost my parents in a car accident. Now I had lost most of those who I really cared about, my folks, Ike, and his folks. I was crushed. Adeline would come by once in a while and try to cheer me up. We would read the Bible and pray. Three months later, I received a letter from my father's father or his counselor. I was informed that my grandfather had also died, and it requested my presence in Torino, Italy. When my father moved to the United States he had little to do with his family and rarely spoke of them. My grandfather's will left me a piece of real estate and a dowry. Returning to the United States I was a wealthier woman but just as lonely as when I left. The wealth meant nothing to me. The only comfort I got was reading the Bible and studying what God was saying. Morning and evening I would read and pray and work at the store in-between. I enjoyed living in Wages, it was my home, I didn't want to go anywhere, I wanted to stay and grow old here with Ike if it would be God's will."

"I did charitable things without anyone knowing. I would donate food to families, and in so doing I felt joy, something I hadn't felt in a while. Then one day I saw in the paper that Ike's ranch, where he grew up and that his father put together was going to be sold at a sheriff's auction. I called my attorney in Albuquerque and asked him to inquire what it would take to buy the ranch before it went to auction, but not to divulge who was making the inquiry. He called me back and we discussed what I wanted to offer. He said that my offer was more than what was necessary. I told him to put my offer in as a sealed bid to be opened at the auction listing him as the representative of the buyer. Then when he received the deeds, he was to prepare the necessary paper work to transfer it back into Ike's name. My offer was to pay all back taxes and bring all taxes current, in addition I was paying more than what the bank had as a lien against the property. I did not want to miss this opportunity."

"In the meantime almost two years had elapsed since Ike went to prison. I would write him, talking about all that was going on in town without telling him anything about what I was doing. He didn't even know at that time that my folks had died."

Again Boston interrupted, "Wait, wait. You bought the ranch and gave it back to him, even though you knew that Ike didn't want anything to do with you?"

"I'll answer that in a little while." Jo responded continuing with the story, "I would send letters and let him know there are people here who still care about him and are praying for him. I asked if it would be possible if I could visit, but I won't come unless you invite me."

"Finally, after many months had past, I received a note card. It was from the man in charge of the prison farm. He wrote that Ike was in the hospital and your visit would be welcomed. I took that as my invitation to come to see him. On the very next Saturday, I went to see him. He was trussed up like a calf, I figured he couldn't get up to leave. I did all the talking or the majority anyway. I told him how I had always cared about him and how I knew I loved him. I told him I did what I knew was right, and hoped he would realize this was best for him. I said I would be back next Saturday.

then on I went every Saturday afternoon, and
could on any special day. The chill between us slowly
ng replaced by more conversation. I would stay as long
on each visit, as he told me all about the farm operation
and what he and his friend Jiggs had done. I even went to a few
horse auctions, just so I could see more of Ike. He would point
out Jiggs each time I went. When Jiggs was released it was hard
on Ike, he didn't seem to have the same excitement or enjoy the
farm and horse operations as much. They were a team and they
enjoyed working with each other, he did not get close to any of
the other prisoners at the farm."

"I continued to come every Saturday and special days, years
went by and we had talked about everything, I filled him in on
the death of my parents but did not tell him about what my
grandparents had done. I told him how through reading the Bible
and prayers I was able to get past my emptiness and loneliness. I
eventually brought my Bible and we would read passages to help
Ike, but I was the one receiving encouragement and seeing God's
Holy Spirit working. Ike accepted Jesus as his Lord and Savior
and was beginning to understand what Jesus taught. Ike's anger
seemed to dissolve, he was more patient, he was at peace with
where he was at and his life, this was where God wanted him for
now. His attitude improved and he found the good in each day
and was thankful in all he accomplished. One weekend he asked
me if I would marry him when he got out. I said I would but
asked him why we had to wait. In a couple of weeks the prison
Chaplin married us with Adeline in attendance."

"After eight years and nine months, Ike was released. I waited
outside the gate to meet him. On our drive back to Wages, I told
him how his dad's ranch had gone up for sale. I went on to tell
him I had purchased it for him, and then explained why. While
reading the Bible, especially the Gospels, I would think about
what Jesus said and what He did. In Matthew 7:24, Jesus said,
'Therefore everyone who hears these words of mine and puts
them into practice is like a wise man who builds his house on a

rock.' Then in John 15: 14, 'You are my friends if you do what I have instructed you.' I knew that Jesus died for me and saved me even when I didn't care about Him. Jesus purchased me with His blood and it is through Him that I can live. I knew I loved Ike and I wanted to purchase the ranch back for him and give him a new start, even if it meant that he wanted nothing to do with me. That is basically what Jesus did for all people. Just like Ike's heart had softened and he came to love me, so to our hearts need to soften and accept the gift, eternal life, God offers us through His son Jesus. Again Jesus says in John 14:6, 'I am the way the truth and the life, No one comes to the God except through me.' If we don't accept God's gift we are lost. Jesus example was to love his enemies, those who hated Him, rejected Him, and murdered Him. But He still gave them His gift, if they would accept Him."

"I loved Ike and I wanted him to have this gift of his father's ranch. I was willing to give him the gift even if he didn't love me. I am thankful that God has brought us together."

Ike continued, "We are all partners in this ranch, God, Jo and I. Boston, you now know the story of the IO Ranch, and why it is so special to us.

Boston responded, "That's truly an amazing story. I saw an old paper in the wash house which had a paragraph in Point of the Past section, about you being arrested for robbery. Since then my mind has been conjuring up different scenarios of what might have taken place. Thank you both for trusting me enough to open your lives to me to experience this wonderful life you have on this ranch. Now that I know the rest of the story, it makes it even more of a special place."

"Hey, you and I," Ike said pointing at Boston, "need to see the sheriff. He called while we were gone."

The two excused themselves and headed to the truck. As they approached, the two seemed to focus on Boston's sleeping bag, which laid on the back of the truck soaked in blood. Ike picked it up and brought it over to the fire pit. He instructed Boston to bring a can of gas from the lean two. When Boston had returned, Ike had already dropped the sleeping bag in the fire pit. He took the can of gas and poured it over the sleeping bag. Taking a match from his pocket, he struck it and pitched it onto the sleeping bag. The bag ignited with a "whooph." They stood there in silence watching as the bag melted, then burned. Before the bag burned completely down, the two turned away and went to the truck. Ike backed the truck up, then turned down the drive heading for town.

Without looking at Ike, Boston asked, "What was the last thing Jiggs said?"

Ike looked over at Boston then returned to stare at the road pausing before he spoke, "He was very weak, he knew his time had come. He first told me, 'Pard, I think this is the last showdown!'

Softly, I said yes.

He said, 'I should have had more sense than to go to Rosita. Don't blame Boston for any of this mess.'

I tried to hold him on his side so he could breathe easier and wouldn't drown in his own blood.

He spoke again, 'I'm not afraid of death nor do I fear it, but I fear without this Jesus Jo talks about, I dare not die. I can't squander any more opportunities to turn to Jesus.'

I then told him he can ask forgiveness for his mistakes and ask Jesus to restore his relationship with Him.

Quickly Jiggs whispered, 'Won't He be insulted coming to Him so late?'

I whispered in his ear, 'NO! Jesus has been waiting for you.' By now, Jiggs' voice was very, very soft, even with my ear next to his mouth, I could hardly make out what he was saying. Suddenly in a clear voice I heard him say, 'That's one fine specimen of a horse you got there.' After that his body went limp, I continued to hold him, I guess more for me than out of necessity." Ike quit talking and Boston could see his eyes glisten with tears. The two finished the ride to town in silence.

CHAPTER TWENTY-SIX

The sheriff had instructed Boston to either let Ike or the sheriff know where he would be at all times when leaving the ranch. The two were leaving the building with Ike carrying Jiggs' possessions. They had turned the truck around heading back to the ranch when Ike spoke, "We need to get back to this cow business!"

Boston responded, "What about Mr. Goolsby? Do we still go there to help him?"

"No!" came a quick reply from Ike. "He knows we can't leave our herd unattended. He'll manage. Besides we need to cut his two hands loose from our camp, remember? When we get back, you get your clothes for a week's stay and I'll meet you at the barn. I'll get some provisions and have Jo call Maylon to bring a trailer over for his boys."

Arriving at the ranch they each went their own ways to pack and gather provisions for the trek up the mountain. Shylo had brought back Boston's laundry bag which held his clothes he had at camp. In addition to his normal clothes, he repacked a sweatshirt, long underwear and extra socks. The calendar was showing October, by now the nights were much cooler. The morning air was frosty sometime there were flurries in the air. Having warm clothes and lots of layers was necessary. He made a mental note that he needed to replace his straw hat with a felt one which didn't allow the air to flow across the top of his head. The aspens leaves had turned from green to a bright golden and many had already fallen to the ground.

He was in the barn saddling his horse when Ike returned holding out his hand he said, "Here, I'm sure Jiggs would have wanted you to have these!" Boston stared at Ike's outstretched hand, there in his palm was Jiggs' spurs with those small silver bells he had admired the very first night. Ike continued, "Here are some clean sheets, I'm sure Jiggs would have wanted you to have his bed roll."

Boston kept staring at the spurs in Ike's hand when he said, "Ya know I have always admired these and the beautiful sounds they make."

Ike laid them in Boston's hand and said, "He made those in the prison, they have 7 points, some prison rowels have 11, but he choose 7. Jiggs thought a lot of you, he said with some guidance that you could make a pretty good hand, but then again you might turn out to be some big shot writer."

Boston shot Ike a look when he responded, "So you knew about that also?"

"Yup," Ike replied leading his horse from the corral. Boston quickly buckled on the spurs and gathered up his horse.

They slowly climbed the trail accompanied by music of wind rustling the aspen leaves. Passing through the pines the music changed to a hum and whistle, along rock outcroppings the sound changed to a moan as the wind glanced from rock to rock. The air now had a bite but just enough to make it exhilarating.

Ike called out to the camp as they approached, but there was no reply. They unloaded the pack horse and loosened the cinches while putting the saddle horses in the corral. Immediately Boston checked the wood supply and water. Both were in order. He then busied himself stowing his gear and making a fresh pot of coffee. Before the coffee had boiled, two riders came in from the upper pasture. Both Ike and Boston watched them come in. There is just something about watching riders coming into camp.

Naught gave his report to Ike concerning the cattle and anything else he noticed that might be of importance. Naught and Sears gathered their belonging and packed their horses. Ike mentioned, "I called Maylon and told him to bring a trailer for ya, so I'm pretty sure the two of you will have time for a cup of coffee."

The four sat around the fire and reflected on Jiggs and asked Boston exactly what happened. Boston relived the experience at

Rosita, again adding that he would have stayed, but he did what Jiggs told him to do. They were about done with coffee when Sears spoke, "This high country cowboying is different then down below. The works kinda the same, just done differently. Like learning a new knot, start with basics but done with a different twist."

"Couldn't have said it better myself." Ike responded.

Sears continued, "Mr. O'Bryn, if you need a hand come Spring, I would like to ride for you and work some of this beautiful country."

Ike responded politely, "We have to think about what our plans are, but I'll keep your offer in mind."

Finishing their coffee, Naught and Sears said their good byes, mounted up and rode out of camp. While Boston and Ike stood there, Boston asked Ike, "Do you have that poem Jiggs kept in a waxed wrapper?"

Ike turned and looked at Boston, "Yup."

Boston continued, "Without being disrespectful, and if it's not something you want, would it be OK if I could keep it?"

"I think that would be fine. Jo still has it in the envelope, she'll give it to you." Turning back to the fire Ike continued, "Let's sit a spell and I will lay out for you what we will need to do within the next few weeks or sooner depending on the weather."

Quickly Boston responded, "I'm ready, tell me what you want me to do! Would you hire Sears?"

"Like I said, it's too early to make that decision." Ike replied then continued, "But I know I'll need to do something by January or February. Anyway, let's talk about what is in front of us from now until you leave in November."

The thought about leaving had been the farthest thing from Boston's mind, yet Ike made him come back to reality.

Ike began laying out his plan, "The herd will need to be moved to Meadow's pasture, but I will need to line up some help for that, plus I will need to check the winter pasture fences and make sure everything in those pastures is right. You will need to be up here by yourself for possibly a week. Are you OK with that?"

Confidently Boston said, "Sure!"

Ike continued, "Once the herd is down off the mountain, I will need to do a count, then we'll work the cattle. First taking the bulls off, then separating the cows from the calves and sex them. The heifers will go one way, the steers another and finally cull out the dry stock. The dry stock and old stock will go to the sales barn. The bulls will come to the headquarters, cows to one pasture and heifers to another. I had stacked hay in each of these pastures to feed through the winter. Now, check over the camp and make sure you have enough provisions to take you through for a week. If I'm later than that, you'll fend for yourself. I'll take the rifle out and a box of ammo. The bears and mountain lions roam about quite freely this time of year. If it's a mountain lion near camp, kill it because you are going to be his meal. A bear, just shooting over his head will possibly scare it off." Boston had never thought about wildlife before, he had heard the wolves, coyotes and elk but had not felt threatened.

Ike continued, "Use up as much of the water, so when I come up to strike the camp, I won't be dealing with a bunch of Ice, or frozen Lyster bag. Make sure you keep your fire going or have a big bank of coals. You never know when a snow storm will blow in here. The fire can mean your life or death. I'm not trying to scare you but there are things which you need to be aware of. This time of year brings new dangers." All this time Ike was walking around the camp checking things over for himself, with Boston following. When they got to the corral, Ike turned and asked tentatively, "Are you sure you are up to this?"

Boston replied confidently, "Rest assured. I and the cattle will be alright."

They walked into the corral as Ike continued, "I'll leave you with two horses. Help me get the others ready to go."

The two then put halters and lead ropes on and tied them head to tail. Ike mounted and leading the string of horses rode out of camp.

There was plenty of day light left to check the camp again, move the rifle over to the log where he was to sleep and gather more wood for the wood pile. As the sun touched the peaks, he began preparing his meal of steak and potato. While cooking his supper he enjoyed a hot cup of coffee.

Finishing his supper he cleaned and put his dishes away, added a few logs to the fire and sat back thinking about the last couple of days. So much had happened so fast, all of it unexpected. Many of the conversations over these two days were meaningful and enlightening to Boston. He thought about the conversation he and Adeline had when she asked if he was going to heaven. Or the last conversation Jiggs and Ike had while Jiggs was dying. Boston realized that conversation was worth more than all the conversations he had with Jiggs. He sat in the light of the fire thinking about those conversations and what Jo had said earlier today. There was no sound except for the wind and the crackling of the fire. He turned his back to the fire to warm it, while staring off towards the night clouds and stars.

By now the wind was blowing pretty hard, he felt a chill even with his coat on. He walked over to retrieve his laundry bag in order to get his long under wear. He laid Jiggs bed roll on the upwind side of the fire, then removing his boots, chaps and britches, he pulled on his long underwear and jeans. Unrolling Jiggs' bed roll, he took off the existing sheets and put on the fresh ones Ike had given him. He walked back to his laundry bag and stuffed the dirty sheets into it. He carefully put his hat, chaps and boots under the rain fly and slid between the canvas covered sheets and blanket. Immediately he realized this bed was far more comfortable than his sleeping bag, as a big smile spread across his face. In his thoughts he thanked Jiggs for the bed roll. Tucked below the big log and out of the wind he could look up at the night sky. He laid there watching the grey clouds skim across the sky propelled by the wind as the stars flashed between them. He laid there warmer than he had felt in a long time smiling as the power of sleep subdued him.

The next few days were filled with camp chores including a trip to the creek to set his hooks hoping to catch a trout. The cattle moved about more, looking for protection from the wind and better grass. He was concerned they would test the fence trying to get to better grazing. He rode to the fence to make sure everything was tight. One morning he awoke to a dusting of snow. With the coming of colder weather brought changes to the sounds he heard, the creak of the leather as he rode, now combined with a gentle tinkle sporadically from Jiggs' spurs. He consumed more coffee and it took longer for him to get into his chaps and boots due to the extra layer of clothes.

By the end of the third day, while making the last trip up the hill with a freshly caught trout, he realized he was talking out loud to himself and had been talking to his horse most of the day. While fixing supper it dawned on him that this was the first time in his life that he was actually alone. He wasn't afraid of the loneliness but just felt like he needed to talk. This got him to thinking how quiet Jiggs was most of the time. Boston concluded that Jiggs wasn't lonely but that he just enjoyed solitude and still enjoyed the company of those who were like minded.

After supper was done and everything was stowed away, he again sat there staring into the fire with a cup of coffee. He still missed Jiggs and the knot in his stomach hadn't left, he would recall those conversations of Adeline, Jo and Ike. He realized that life is only as long as the breath you are taking. Nobody knows when or where the last breath will be drawn, we don't have a crystal ball. Mankind goes about his tasks without giving it a thought, but when we do, what is there besides this? Thinking about his time at the IO Ranch he realized how hazardous this work is especially if you are here by yourself. He looked up into the night sky at the countless stars covering him like a blanket. He took off his hat and right there talked with God, about what he's done wrong, about not wanting to know about Him or His son Jesus. Boston asked God to forgive him and told God he would promise to learn more about what and how Jesus tells us to live. He thanked Him for sparing his life and for allowing him to work with people like Jo and Ike who have a relationship with Jesus. He then stood up and got ready to slip into his bed roll.

Again staring up at the night sky he wondered how many people are doing the same thing. He wondered when he again would get a room like this one, with such a magnificent view morning and night. He let his eyes close in sleep.

Boston was up at whatever felt like normal, but the sun was coming up later, so he played the coffee pot longer. Today Boston hoped Ike would be coming back, the provisions consisted of baloney, bread and a can of peaches. He would fry the baloney and have it on bread, skip dinner and save the peaches for supper just in case Ike didn't make it today. The day broke to clear and cold skies, the camp fire felt especially warm this morning. Boston had banished his fried baloney sandwich and had cleaned up the pan when he heard a familiar voice in the distance, "Hello in camp," Ike's call echoed. In the distance were three riders coming. Boston quickly threw another log onto the fire and made sure there was coffee for everyone.

The four sat around the fire talking about the fall in temperature and the need to move the cattle. Ike began lining out what he wanted each person to do mentioning, "I'm really counting on the older mama cows to lead the others off this mountain." Jo was going to take point leading the spare horse as she went, Shylo and Boston would work the flanks and Ike would bring up the drag. While the rest finished their coffee, Boston saddled his horse and put a lead rope and halter on the other horse.

They all mounted their horses as Boston handed the lead rope to Jo, and slowly the gather began. The cows had been staying close to the pasture and water lately so the drive started easily and once the cows figured out where they were to go everything seemed to line out. They all kept their distance from the cows as the herd moved slowly along towards the upper pasture and the far west gate. Once the herd made it to the Meadow pasture, they would be allowed to rest letting the cows and calves come together before working them. So far the herd was moving according to Ike's plan, and were most of the way off the mountain, Jo already was in the Meadow pasture heading toward the pens. A couple of calves squirted out and headed into the evergreens, Boston pressed his horse into a trot in an attempt to cut them off and turn them back towards the herd. He was holding the reins in his left hand while keeping his right forearm in front of his face to prevent branches from smacking his face directly. His horse was responding and he hadn't lost sight of the calves, he was approximately fifty feet from the calves. Suddenly, he felt a sharp stabbing pain in his inner thigh. The pressure from this stabbing cause him to rotate in the saddle which removed his left leg from the stirrup, pushing him out of the saddle. In an instant he was off his horse. Just before he went off, he glanced down to see what caused this. In that glance, he saw a dead tree branch sticking into his leg, as he and his horse passed the tree, forcing him off his horse, the branch broke from the tree. He landed on his back still holding onto his reins, the jolt from hitting the ground didn't replace the pain he was feeling in his leg. He sat up and stared at a half inch diameter dead tree branch sticking into his leg like an arrow. He reached out intending on pulling it out, and then gave that a second thought, what if it hit the artery? He got himself up and attempted to mount his horse but was not able to lift and bend his leg. He sat back down, he could feel blood on his leg but nothing was showing on his chaps. In the distance he could hear the herd, but the denseness of the trees prevented him from seeing anything. He propped himself up against a tree and decided to rest. Waiting there for help reminded him of Jiggs and how he waited for Boston to get help, It wasn't a pleasant memory. A thought struck him that he should keep his leg elevated higher than his heart and that was supposed to slow the blood flow to the area. He lay back down on the ground with his legs uphill from his head. He lay still staring up at his horse, it was not the normal perspective a person would view a horse, but they still look powerful and beautiful. Every once in a while, the horse would look down at Boston as if to say why are you laying there, we need to be going.

It seemed like hours had gone by when he heard Ike call his name. "Over here Ike, I can't get back on my horse." Boston yelled.

Within a few minutes, Ike was peering between the pine trees at Boston. "Seems like you have been gathering firewood." Ike said sarcastically.

"Very funny" Boston quipped, "I didn't think I should take it out, it might have hit an artery."

Ike said with a firm response, "That was good thinking."

"Do you think it's bad?" asked Boston.

Ike paused than said, "Your heritage is intact and it appears to be a long way from the heart."

"That's really comforting to know," Boston shot back.

"I thought it was!" Ike countered. The two just laughed. Ike ducked back away from the pine trees. Boston listened to his horse's hoofs fade into the distance.

Again Boston lay there in silence thinking about what must have been going through Jiggs mind while Boston was trying to get help. Gradually he could hear hoof beats walking closer to where he lay. "Hello" Boston hollered out.

"Boston?" came the reply.

"Shylo, I'm over here laying on the ground." Boston responded. He tried to look back over the top of his head or lift his head to peek past his feet, to see where she was. Then, in front of his feet, stood Shylo with studied look on her face as if examining patients and said, "What did you do?"

Boston taking his cue from Ike said, "I thought I would gather some firewood…"

But before he finished, Shylo said "Oh shut up! You have been hanging around cowboys to long."

Boston just smiled.

"You should just lay there and not move a muscle, Ike went to get his medical bag." Shylo commanded.

Boston just smiled.

"What are you grinning about?" Shylo asked.

"Oh, nothing. I'm going to take you up on your offer to go to church. It seems that is the only way we can spend time together." Boston stated.

Shylo quickly replied, "That's not a very good reason to go to church."

"I know, replied Boston, then continued, "I got thinking about things Adeline, Jo and Ike had said. They have some kind of assurance. I want to find it or find out about it. Actually, I had a talk with Jesus last night. I really want to know more."

A big smile spread across Shylo's face, "I'm very happy for you. I'll be thrilled to go with you to church. Maybe both of us can learn about the kind of love Jesus has for us."

"Yeah, just like Jo showed the kind of love Jesus has for her to Ike. I didn't know we could experience these things first hand." Boston said.

Their conversation was interrupted by Ike cutting a path through the trees to the fire break where they moved the cattle. As Ike came along side of them he stated, "Now that will allow us

221

to get you out of here." He then sat a satchel down next to Boston and took out a bottle of whiskey, handing it to Boston, "Here take a pull on this!"

Boston took the bottle, after taking a sip he was about to hand it back when Ike said "You need to take three or four gulps not sips." Boston brought the bottle back to his lips and took a few big swallows. He quickly pulled the bottle away from his mouth and coughed. Ike instinctively held the leg with the stick, so it wouldn't move. "Take another but try not to cough." Ike commanded. Bringing the bottle back to his mouth he took another big swallow, then held the bottle out at arm's length. "Shylo, grab that bottle and hold onto it." Ike stated in a commanding voice.

Ike unzipped the legs of the chaps, cut the leather thong in front and removed one leg of the chaps, leaving the other leg which was pinned to him by the branch. With one hand holding the stick he then lifted the other chap leg up the shaft of the stick until it was freed, exposing the blood stain on his jeans. While Ike examined the wound at the base of the stick, he told Boston, "Take a couple more swallows." Shylo quickly handed him the bottle. Those two swallows seemed to go down with less of a reaction. Shylo reached out taking the bottle back. "Looks like I need to cut it!" Ike said matter-of-factly.

"Can't you just pull it out?" Boston said with panic in his voice.

"I'm talking about your britches." Ike responded.

"Always the comedian." Boston said with relief.

Ike took his sharp pocket knife and cut out a large patch of jean around the stick. Now Ike could see the discolored skin and some blood coming from the wound. He studied the wound for almost a minute, then got up and went to Boston's saddle. He untied one of the leather conchos and untied a long strip of latigo. When he was finished he had approximately twenty inches of a leather half inch in width. Returning to Boston he slipped it under his leg and positioned it between the wound and his groin.

"Give him another shot of that hooch," Ike commanded. Shylo handed the bottle to Boston who took a long sip and handed it back.

Ike then tied a square knot around a small fat stick, and began slowly tightening it against Boston's leg by twisting in a circular manner. He watched the blood that was dripping out of the wound stop. "Shylo, I want you over here," pointing to the other side of Boston, "When I pull this out I want you to pour a good amount of whiskey into the wound, but not all of it." Ike commanded. He reached into his bag and pulled out a sealed package of gauze and a roll of tape.

"Yeah ready?" Ike asked looking at Boston and Shylo, as they both nodded. Ike took one final look around the base of the stick, "Shylo hold the tourniquet!" Ike's voice commanded and she immediately complied. Ike then held Boston's leg down with one hand and taking a firm grip on the stick quickly pulled it straight out. There was only a quick inhale of breath from Boston. Shylo poured alcohol into the wound stopping at Ike's "Enough!" order. Removing the fresh gauze from the package he placed it over the wound, ordering Shylo "Wrap this around Boston's leg when I get it elevated." Ike lifted his leg off the ground as Shylo quickly and neatly wrapped the tape over the gauze pad thereby securing it in place.

Shylo and Ike helped Boston to his feet and Ike took him to the off side of the horse and assisted him in mounting so he could use his good leg to lift himself into the saddle, while Shylo held the horse steady. All the while Boston was holding the tourniquet tight. Ike took a lead rope and halter from his saddle placing it on Boston's horse, then handing it to Shylo who had mounted her horse. Ike quickly mounted and the three of them slowly proceeded down to Meadow's pasture. On the opposite end of the pasture Jo was waiting with the pickup truck. Shylo and Ike helped Boston dismount and get into the truck.

"Keep that tourniquet tight Boston!" Ike barked, as he closed the door allowing Jo to drive off.

That evening after the sun had set behind the peaks, the truck with Jo and Boston returned to the ranch. Ike had been organizing the gear in the barn and Shylo had started something for supper. Boston stepped out and hopped to the back to retrieve his crutches. After greeting Jo, Ike asked, "What did the doc say?"

"We can talk about this in the house," Jo interjected, "Shylo and I will get supper on." They all went inside, and while the table was being laid, Boston explained, "The doctor said I nicked the artery so he localized the area and put a couple of stitches in, but the puncture needs to heal from the inside out. I need to keep it clean and clean the wound at least once a day and re-dress with fresh bandages. I need to go back to see the doctor in a week."

Jo continued by saying, "We stopped at the pharmacy before coming home and picked up what bandages and cleaning supplies Boston would need. They are still in the truck."

Boston continued assuredly, "I can help with the cattle just as soon as I finish my morning chores. I'll just make sure I have enough bandages to protect the wound and keep it clean."

"OK," Ike began, "I'll sew a new piece of leather over that hole and that should provide you with additional protection. But working cattle is a dirty business and you will need to make sure you clean the wound morning and night."

Jo asked Boston, "Shouldn't we call your folks?"

Boston quickly replied, "Oh no! This wasn't that big of a deal. I'll tell them all about it when I get back. Thanksgiving is almost here anyway."

Shylo responded, "Don't you want to let them know when you will be home?"

"I want to surprise them," Boston replied confidently. Besides I told them I would be home by Thanksgiving."

They sat down for supper as Ike planed out the next day's activities, which was the last day Shylo was available to help. After supper Boston was limping out the door as Jo brought bedding for Shylo to use on the couch. Picking up the pharmacy supplies from the truck Boston continued toward the bunkhouse. By now his leg began hurting from the pain and swelling.

The November evenings were much cooler, almost demanding a fire to keep the bunkhouse warm. He set a kettle, which Jo had provided, on the stove to heat water which he could use to clean out his wound. Once the water was warm, he unwrapped the bandages observing how the nurse had wrapped it. He laid his leg straight out on the bunk and he got his first good look at this wound. His leg showed various colors depending on the proximity to the wound, black, purple, blue and yellowish. He wiped the area around the wound and then poured some hydrogen Peroxide into the wound. He watched it foam and bubble, then taking gauze he dipped it into the wound to absorb the fluid. He would then put a small patch of gauze over it at night. In the morning it would be more important to protect the wound from dirt. Once this process was complete, he took a pain pill, placed another log in the stove and went to sleep.

The morning began with a fresh two inches of snow. He organized himself and applied a fresh bandage and headed up towards the barn to begin his chores.

After finishing his chores, he limped towards the house, leaving his crutches at the bunkhouse. Before he reached the stairs, Shylo stuck her head out saying, "It's a beautiful day! Good Morning! Come in and have breakfast."

He replied with a cheery "Good Morning to you!" and limped up the stairs.

While enjoying a hearty breakfast, once again Ike laid out the days plans. The snow had eliminated any dust problems but made the footing for those working on the ground more treacherous. Jo and Boston would stay mounted and push the cattle into the pens. Shylo would work the gate while Ike would do the sorting. They all cleared the table and did dishes while Boston went to the barn to saddle the horses. While riding out to the Meadow Pasture, Ike explained how they would ride past the heard to the far side then pressure the cattle back toward the pens and alleyways.

For most of the morning Boston sat his horse and only walked his horse short distances. By mid-morning he asked Ike if he could swap with Shylo so he could move his leg. Ike agreed to his request. Ike came over and explained to Boston how the gate system worked. When he hollered, "In" he was to open this particular gate. When Ike hollered "By" he was to open the other gate and allow the cow to enter that particular trap. Boston, understanding said, "Yes sir!" By the time the sun was behind the mountains they had sorted those they would ship and the ones they would feed through the winter.

The cattle trucks or "pods" were coming in the morning to haul the cattle to the sales barn. Normally Ike and Jo would go to the sale, thus allowing them to pick up a check the day the cattle were sold. But since being shorthanded, they would wait to get the check in the mail. When the cattle were loaded and trucks left, Ike, Jo and Boston began sorting the calves from the mothers. This sorting went much quicker but the noise level was louder than the previous day. Leaving a pen full of calves, they re-mounted and began moving the remaining cattle down the county road to the first winter pasture Ike had rented. Arriving at this pasture, Boston saw that Ike had fenced off a portion where he stacked the hay used to feed them through the winter. By now the day was almost spent. Just needing to bring some hay to the calves and evening chores were all that was left to do. The following day they moved the calves down the county road to another rented pasture which was between the headquarters and the pasture where the cows were dropped off. The remaining week and half was spent with Ike feeding bulls in the headquarter pasture, loading hay and feeding it to the cows and then going to the calves and do the same thing in that pasture, always checking the water supply.

Jo and Ike planned a farewell dinner at the café in town for Boston. They invited Adeline and Shylo to attend. Everyone got dressed up and headed for town, making their first stop at the feed store. As they unpiled from the truck and entered the feed store, the sheriff was about ready to exit.

"Howdy folks, I was planning on heading out to your place tomorrow to talk with you Mr. Sullivan." Looking much surprised Boston replied, "Hi sheriff Tallas."

Ike smiled and said "Hello Ray. Can we talk now outside?"

The sheriff turned toward Jo saying, "Would you excuse us for a moment? Thank you!" The three men now stepped back outside.

"I won't take much of your time, but I will fill you in a little on the investigation progress." Explaining, he continued on, "We still need to interview some folks but we could tell there was a terrible fight in there. Lots of blood, didn't recover Jiggs' knife, we are still analyzing the blood to determine the different types. So far, haven't been able to locate any witnesses but we have some leads."

Ike explained, "We're in town for Boston's farewell dinner. Do you need anything else from him?"

The sheriff looked over at Boston, "No, I know where to find him. Have a safe trip! Goodbye." He then turned and headed to his vehicle. Ike and Boston turned and re-entered the store, walking to the back counter. Jo was standing next to the counter with a large box setting on the counter. On the side of the box was the word Resistol Hat Company. Looking at Boston she said, "This is our gift to you. Thank you, Boston for all your hard work. Open it!"

Ike grinned and said, "You wore a straw hat later in the year than anyone I know." Boston smiled and opened the box taking out a new black felt hat that was a perfect fit. "Thank you, this is great! Can this guy shape this hat to look like Jiggs'?"

Ike replied, "I'm sure he can."

They stood there and watched the man shape and crease the hat just like the one Jiggs wore. Boston, wearing his new hat, walked outside with Jo and Ike, where Boston stated, "I would like to wear this for a spell. Do you mind if I walk to the café?"

Jo smiling replied, "We'll meet you there."

Entering the café, he hung his hat on the peg next to Ike's, then joined the others at the table. Ike asked questions about how he felt in his new head gear, as westerners call it.

The evening was full of good times, as well as good food. Of course there were lots of jokes about Boston's driving ability and other early day adventures. After the meal and as it quieted, Boston took his water glass and stood up, "I propose a toast, to good friends here and those gone. For those who are here, their shows of genuine care and concern. For those who have gone, the wonderful memories we have and lesson told." They all stood up and raised their glasses and in unison said, "Amen." Before anyone could say anything or regain composure Boston said, "Adeline, you once asked me if I knew where I was going. I now can tell you, I do! I am following a new trail, the one that Jesus laid out. I may not know much about it now, but by reading the Bible, I'll be able to see his tracks." Boston had shocked himself with his use of western words as he continued turning toward Jo and Ike. "Ike and Jo you have treated me so very kind and when I heard your story, I realized the two of you are the definition of joy, peace and hope. I can't say I have seen it all displayed by anyone anywhere. Shylo, I admire you for staying true to your heart, your most desired possession is to obey your LORD. Your focus is admirable. I honestly and truly have never met anyone like all of you. I can only say thank you for how you live your lives and treat others. If these are the things you learned from Jesus than I want to be able to have those qualities also. God opened my eyes to glimpse all He has done, all He has allowed and all this He has controlled." They thanked him for his sentiments and offered to help guide him along anytime. He just needed to ask them. The dessert arrived, changing the conversation to ohh's and ahh's, followed by coffee. Boston asked, "Would you excuse Shylo and me?"

Shylo looked at Boston, as Jo smiled and said, "Just for a few minutes."

The two of them stepped outside the café and went just around the corner, so they couldn't be seen from inside. Boston began, "Shylo, I probably won't see you again but I would like to kiss you good bye if its OK with you." In a soft voice Shylo replied, "Sure, that would be OK." Boston stepped up close and gave her a short kiss on the lips, then backed away.

"That's a good bye kiss?" Shylo said in a strong voice as she continued, "I get those kinds of kisses from my nieces and nephews. Here is what I had in mind." She stepped up close to Boston, put her arms around his neck and rested her lips on his for quite a spell. Boston responded by placing his arms around her. When she finally broke away she said, "That's a good-bye kiss!"

"I'll say so!" Boston quickly replied, "One I won't soon forget." Boston exclaimed. As they walked back into the café, Boston couldn't stop smiling. "My somebody's happy." Ike chortled.

"Just quit" came a snappy reply from Jo.

They said their farewells as Jo, Ike and Boston piled into the truck for the trip back to the ranch. It was a moon lit night as they drove along in silence. Jo finally spoke, "We'll need to leave by seven in the morning to get you to the airport for your flight." Ike interjected, "Don't worry about doing chores Just bring your bags up when you come for breakfast."

The truck was coming down the drive as Boston responded, "Yes sir."

Getting out Boston again thanked them for the hat and all they had done for him. Then walked to the bunkhouse in the moon light. He hastily laid out a clean pair of jeans and a shirt. Boston retrieved his ticket from the suitcase under the bed. He then threw his old, torn and dirty clothes in his suitcase.

Unrolling his bed roll, he laid on it his clean underwear and any other clothes that he was taking along. He then rolled it up as tight as he could, stacking it in the corner and placing his hat, coat and airline ticket on top of it. He grabbed his shaving kit and headed to the shower.

He slept restlessly, not wanting to over sleep. He looked at his wrist watch, something he hadn't done in months. It was five o'clock, so he lit the lantern deciding to get this day started. Returning to the bunkhouse, he began cleaning and re-bandaging his wound. Leaving the remaining bandages in the bunkhouse, he took one last look around the bunkhouse. He put his coat and hat on, blew out the lantern, picked up his bedroll and suitcase and walked up the path to the barn.

Lights were on in the kitchen when Boston hollered out his "Good morning." Ike returned his greeting with the invitation, "Come on in and eat." They had steak and eggs with little table talk. Ike got up to do chores but before leaving he said, "Write us let us know how you're doing. Take care. Vaya con Dios!"

He then shook his hand with that iron grasp. Jo followed up by saying, "Put your things in the trunk of the car. We'll need to be leaving soon."

Boston got up and went outside where he had left his bedroll and suitcase. He opened the trunk and dropped his bedroll inside, placing the suitcase next to the door of the garage.

After the two got into the car, Boston said, "I want to leave those few clothes behind. If Adeline can sell them, fine otherwise use them for rags. Maybe Adeline can sell the suitcase. I just put everything into my bedroll."

Jo smiled and then handing Boston an envelope she said, "Here is you second payment you gave us. We decided that you needed something for all the work you did. Besides, we are more than content with the first payment we received." Boston didn't know what to say except "Thank you."

CHAPTER TWENTY-SEVEN

On the drive to the airport Jo encouraged Boston to buy a good Bible, New American Standard or updated King James Version. Then attend a Bible believing church and get into a Bible study group. Jo said, "Adeline once told me you not only need to get into the word but let the word get into you."

Boston asked, "What does that mean?"

Jo responded, "Study, meditate and memorize." Jo continued to explain, "Eastern religions stress emptying your mind to meditate. Jesus tells us to fill our minds with all He instructs us to do. Boston being a Christian isn't a religion, it's a relationship with Jesus. In order to have a good relationship you need to spend time with Him. The same as having a good marriage. The two need to spend time together and discuss. Anytime you want to talk or have questions just call me or Adeline."

Boston paused and stated, "I don't even know your number or Adeline's."

They both laughed. "I'll give it to you when I drop you at the airport," Jo responded.

They had been so deep in conversation, the trip seemed short. Jo quickly jotted down their telephone number and then got out. Boston was already at the trunk removing his bedroll. Standing at the back of her car, she handed two things to Boston saying," Here is our phone numbers and the poem of Jiggs' you asked about. I've got to get back to the ranch. Sorry to leave you at the curb like this." Boston nodding his head said, "I totally understand." Shaking her hand he continued, "Thanks for giving me the chance of a life time." She turned and got back into the car and drove off. Boston stood there watching her drive out of sight.

Lifting his bedroll onto his shoulder, he limped into the terminal. His first stop was at the gift shop, where he purchased a plain thank you card and a blank card with a pen. He then headed to the gate where he would catch his plane to Denver. After checking in at the gate, he dropped his bedroll so he could rest his leg on it as he leaned against the wall. He began writing a few lines to Ike and Jo, thanking them for opening a whole new world to him. Allowing a greenhorn to stay on when a more experienced hand was needed. He signed it and sealed the envelope, addressing it to Jo and Ike O'Bryn Wages Colorado. He paused briefly staring out the window and then began writing in the blank card. Not seeing a mail drop he decided to post it at the Denver airport.

They announced that his flight was boarding, so he picked up his bedroll and limped to the boarding ramp. They told him his bedroll was too big to put in the overhead bins, but he could put it in the front coat closet. However, he would need to be the last one off otherwise he would be blocking the exit. Having found his seat, he barely had time to think or get situated for the flight and they had announced they were landing in Denver. Boston waited for everyone to get off the plane before he went to retrieve his bedroll. One of the stewardess suggested he should take a cart to the next gate since it was going to be a long distance from where they landed to where he was taking off again.

He limped from the gate area into the corridor where he saw an empty cart and a driver. Boston inquired, "Could I get a ride to Concourse C gate 32? That's where my plane leaves from."

The sky cap looked at Boston and said, "Sure, you're kind of disabled. Put your bag on back and sit down."

"Thanks," said Boston, "Do we go by a mail drop, so I can post these letters?"

The sky cap paused and with a quick turn of the cart he said, "It's right on our way."

Boston was still recovering from that sharp turn and was surprised that his bedroll had stayed in place. Shortly the cart stopped in front of a window with a slot marked U.S. MAIL.

233

He dropped his envelopes into the slot and the driver sped off. Boston was thinking it would have been a long walk, had he not taken the advice of that stewardess. His leg didn't hurt so much from pain as stiffness in the muscle. Boston watch as the driver slipped through the flow of people going in both directions and sometimes cross ways. He thought how it resembled cattle moving in an alleyway. The driver stopped at gate 32 as he announced, "Concourse C gate 32. Watch your step!"

Boston gently stepped off the cart asking, "What do I owe you?"

"Nothing, the privilege to drive a real cowboy around doesn't happen often." the sky cap bragged.

"Look here you don't work for free." Boston exclaimed, "What if I give you five bucks? Would you feel cheated?"

"No sir." the sky cap replied.

"OK, and I wouldn't feel like a free loader."

They both smiled as they departed different ways. He checked in at the gate and again he found a nice spot next to a wall where he could prop his leg up on his bedroll. He sat there observing the people around him and the level of noise and activity. Pretty soon a ticket agent came over and said he could board early due to his difficulty walking. But when he reached for his bedroll the agent informed him he would need to check it. "Might I stow it in the coat closet?" came a quick reply from Boston.

"I guess if they have room. I'll find out." The ticket agent responded.

By now Boston had limped to the loading ramp when the ticket agent came back from the airplane. "Sure we can put it there. Please fill out this identification tag and attach it to your bag please."

With a grateful smile Boston said "Thanks."

The stewardess put his bedroll into the closet as he limped to his seat on the plane. A stewardess came by and asked, "Would you like to put your hat in the luggage bin?"

Boston courteously replied, "No ma'am, I like it to sit where it is."

Being close to Thanksgiving the plane was filling up with families and students. Boston felt fortunate that he had a window seat. The other seats in his row were occupied by an elderly couple. He turned his attention to the stewardess as she announced all about emergencies and what everyone was supposed to do. As the plane taxied for takeoff he just stared out the window. When the plane left the ground so did his thoughts, retracing the past six months which seemed like six weeks. He had completed his assignment for *The Saturday Evening Post*. When he returned he would write up his article and recommend responding to one of these ads only if they are not afraid of hard physical work. His personal goal was to gain a sense of the West, to experience their life styles and to see the best it contained. He figured he had accomplished all that and then some. He had experienced what only a few people get an opportunity to do. True he had enough material to write the article and possibly a book if he desired. He thought about that as he relived the past six months and all that took place. Writing about what he experienced for the past six months was something that would excite him. He was still doing this self-evaluation as they announced the approach to Chicago.

After the passengers destined for Chicago had deplaned, Boston stretched his legs by walking to the front of the plane which also allowed him to check on his bedroll. It was still standing there in the closet, wrapped tight with the leather belts, showing all its stains and dirt. Boston just smiled and returned to his seat. He stared out the window not really focusing on anything. His thoughts soon returned to this personal dilemma of what to do with this experience he just went through.

He ate the meal the airlines served and drank coffee for the rest of the flight. He had just finished his third cup when the announcement for landing preparations for Hartford, Connecticut came over the intercom. Arriving at the terminal gate, he waiting until everyone else had gotten off. He noticed how they all seemed to be in such a hurry to get going.

By the local time it was evening and darkness had fallen sometime during the flight. Limping down the corridor carrying his bedroll on his shoulder, he became aware that people were watching him. He tried not to pay any attention to them and continued his slow long walk, trying to remember when, in the last six months, he had walked so much. Echoing off the walls was a soft faint bell like sound. At first he hadn't heard it but now his mind was trying to identify what it was. He stopped and sat down to rest his leg, dropping his bedroll in front of the chair to use as a leg rest. It was there he realized he had not taken off Jiggs' spurs, and that faint bell sound was coming from his own boots. He had become accustomed to wearing and walking with them not thinking about removing them. Just the thought of Jiggs brought back a smile and he decided to wear them until he got home.

It seemed to take him hours before he reached the parking area for limo's. The limo driver was standing alongside his automobile and waving, beckoning Boston to his vehicle. Approaching the front of his vehicle Boston heard him say, "Is the rodeo in town?"

Boston remember how Jiggs and Ike played off each other responded, "Yup! This is New York, right?"

With a strange look on his face the driver responded, "Cowboy, you got on the wrong plane, because this is Hartford, Connecticut."

Now Boston took on a puzzled look before responding, "Awe shucks. Well, I guess I'll go visit some folks out here first. Do you think you could find 11 Washburn Road in Canton, Connecticut?"

With confidence in his voice the driver said, "Cowboy, I can take you anywhere you want to go! Climb in, I'll put your bag in back."

Boston put his bedroll down and climbed into the spacious

back seat. The driver had slammed the truck lid and gotten behind the wheel, "Sit back and relax!" Boston replied, "I think I will take you up on that."

Tipping his hat so it covered his eyes and part of his face, he closed his eyes and listened to the sounds of the traffic and city noises.

The driver woke him up when they came into the town of Canton. Boston gave him directions but asked the driver to leave him off on the street and not go up the driveway. Shortly the driver stopped his limo in front of Boston's parents' house. The driver had already gotten out and was removing the bedroll from the trunk before Boston had gotten out of the vehicle. He paid the driver and thanked him for such a smooth ride wishing him well in his business. Boston stood there in the dark street watching the limo drive off.

Boston gazed skyward, at the few stars shining through the dark sky. Mixed emotions passed through his mind. He wanted to see his folks but at the same time did not want the western experience to end. Picking up the bedroll, he limped up the driveway to the front door. Ringing the doorbell he waited to see who would open the door. The outside light came on, as the door opened. He stood there face to face with his sister, "Hi sis!" Boston said in a calm voice.

She shrieked and said, "Why didn't you call and tell us when you were coming home?"

Boston quickly responded, "Then what kind of surprise would that be? Quietly tell Mom and Dad I'm here, I need to use the bathroom and drop my gear. I will meet you all in the kitchen."

Eagerly she turned back towards the kitchen, while Boston took off his boots and took the bedroll upstairs to his room. In a few minutes, he came back downstairs heading toward the sound of voices in the kitchen. Stopping in the doorway Boston said, "Hello." The three of them came over and hugged him with kisses from his mom. "It looks like you lost fifteen pounds. Didn't they feed you?" his mother said.

"Looks like you got lots of sun!" his dad mentioned.

"Yes we ate pretty regularly. I guess the work just causes you to burn up all the calories. I spent the majority the last six months outside night and day," Boston responded.

"Well you sure looked like a cowboy standing in the doorway earlier," his sister responded heading toward the dining room.

"You can tell us all about it, we are just now sitting down to dinner." His dad stated as he also turned for the dining room.

Boston started to follow when his mother's concerned voice asked, "What's the matter with you? What happened?"

The sound of her voice and the questions caught the attention of the others turning them back to the kitchen.

"I'm fine." responded Boston as he limped past them to the dining room, "I'll tell you over supper."

The rest of the family came into the dining room with his mother carrying a large bowl of spaghetti. They sat down as the spaghetti was dished up. Boston took his napkin and while placing it on his lap silently gave thanks. When his father, in a demanding tone said, "Now tell us what happened to your leg. Did you break it? Do they have insurance?"

Boston slowly lifted his head up and said "Ike and Jo O'Bryn are wonderful people. I feel fortunate that I was able to spend time with them and I have learned so much. I can truly call them my friends. No, I didn't break my leg, if there is any blame or fingers to be pointed they would be pointed at me. Twice those two saved my life, in the first few days of my stay, by killing a rattlesnake and then a few weeks back by making sure I didn't bleed to death." The table went silent and more questions assaulted him. "Let me get some of this supper down and I will explain," as he turned his attention to the food. He was sitting drinking coffee while the others were still eating.

"You shouldn't eat so fast, it will make you sick." His mother said.

"Oh I'm fine, ate like that for the past six months and I feel great." Boston replied confidently.

Everyone else was eating or drinking wine when Boston began, "Remember, this all started with me researching those ad for the magazine, so I could write an article or story, well it has done just that. As a matter of fact, I have the whole thing in my head right now. Dad, I would like to use your reel to reel tape recorder to put down all my thoughts, then have somebody type up what's on the tape. I think I have enough for a whole book."

"What's the title?" his sister asked.

"I'll tell you that after I get it all down on tape."

His mother interjected, "So, this adventure was a good thing, you're on your way." Calmly replying Boston said, "In more ways than I can tell you right now." Rising from the table he asked, "I'm getting coffee, does anybody need anything, water, wine?"

With no response he poured himself another cup of coffee and returned to the table.

"Now about this leg," Boston began, "We were moving the cattle from the mountain pasture to the Meadow in the valley. I was on a flank, the cow boss was at the drag. He had instructed us that any calf or cow that quit the herd would either come in on their own or we could do a re-ride and bring them down. We were making our way down the fire break, when two calves quit. I thought I could press them back, so I went into the trees after them. My horse was covering ground faster than I should have allowed. I was trying to protect my face and eyes, from the branches slapping in my face, by holding up my right forearm across my face. Suddenly I felt a sharp pain hit my leg with such force that it spun me in the saddle and unseated me from my horse. It happened in the blink of an eye. I landed on my back still holding on to one of the reins. I picked up my head to see what hit my leg. Sticking out

239

like an arrow was a branch, planted into my thigh. At first I was going to pull it out but something told me not to. Ike came back and found me when he realized I hadn't got back to my position with the herd. He assessed what happened and went for help telling me not to move. He came back with his doctor bag and Shylo. She was a girl who was also helping move the cattle. He instructed Jo to get the pick up so I could be transported to town after I was brought to the valley. He put a tourniquet on and pressure bandage after he removed the stick. They helped me onto my horse and led me to the pickup for a ride to the clinic. I just need to clean it out a couple times a day to prevent infection. The puncture needs to heal from the inside out which will take most of a month. This reminds me, I need to clean it, so if you would excuse me it is my bedtime. Tomorrow would one of you give me a ride to the emergency room to have it check to make sure it's OK. The clinic doctor told me to have it checked when I return." Boston then got out of his chair and limped upstairs.

He unrolled his bedroll on the floor, taking out his extra clothes, he took off his britches and removed the bandages from the wound. All the walking did seem to irritate it some in addition to tiring him out. He then applied clean gauze over the wound, securing it with band aids from the bathroom. After opening his window,he crawled into the bedroll and soon fell asleep as the cool night air washed over him.

Thirty minutes later, his dad went to check on him, when there was no response to his knock he peeked into the room. Seeing the figure lying on the floor startled him somewhat, but he remembered the comment about being outside even at night. So he must have slept on the ground and a bed was probably too soft. He slowly closed the door and returned downstairs, explaining that he was sleeping on the floor because the bed was too soft.

CHAPTER TWENTY-EIGHT

It was a Friday morning, twelve days after Boston had arrived. He had been to the office of *The Saturday Evening Post* most every day since his return. He had finished writing the articles for the magazine. Now, while sitting at the breakfast counter, he said, "I know you all are still wondering and have lots of questions about my experience over the past six months. I have purposely not said much in way of answering your questions. I took this ranch job hoping I would get some flavor of western life style and maybe have something I could put into an article. After writing about some of the experiences for the magazine articles. I believe the complete experience can be book material."

His mother interjected, "It sounds very serious!"

Boston continued, "It is! for me a life changing event in so many ways. I have learned so many things but only scratched at those things I want to know more about and pattern my life after. This Saturday, I would like you all to sit down and listen to the tape I made. Would the two of you help me to find somebody who can type from the tape so I can have it on paper?"

"You want someone who takes dictation." said his dad as he interrupted, "I think I can find you someone."

Boston continued, "Yup. Thanks Dad. I hope this won't interfere with any of your plans."

After a quick breakfast, his folks left for work leaving Boston and is sister at home.

Saturday morning arrived with the aroma of fresh brewed coffee and biscuits filling the air in the Sullivan home. They found Boston's note next to the coffee pot stating that he was not going to be home until 4:30 p.m., thus allowing them plenty of time to listen to the tape completely before asking him any questions. The family spent a leisurely early morning reading the paper and preparing snacks to take into the office while listening to Boston's tape.

Boston had taken his car and drove to a nearby riding stable, because he wanted to smell the horses and listen to their sounds. Since it was early winter with business being slow, the owner let him hang around and even feed and brush a few horses. Later in the day, he headed downtown to the Bible bookstore. He was browsing around in the Bible section when a clerk came up asking, "Do you need any help?"

Boston said, "I'm looking for a New American Standard Bible or a New King James Bible, I haven't read it before, and I was told to ask for one of those."

The clerk nodded as she reached a Bible off the shelf, "This is the New American Standard translation, it is very easy to read and understand, it has lots of notes which provide additional insight from a commentary perspective."

Boston took it in his hands looking at no particular page. Momentarily taking the Bible from Boston, the clerk turned to the book of Ephesians, chapter 2. She pointed to verses 8 and 9 while she read,

"For by grace you have been saved through faith; and that not of yourselves, it is the gift of God; not as a result of works, that no one should boast." Handing the Bible back to Boston, "See how smoothly it reads?" she stated.

Boston was looking at the Bible when he said, "That's what Adeline said! I'll take it!"

"May I show you one other passage before we go?" the clerk asked politely. "Sure!" Boston quickly stated.

Taking the Bible back in her hands, the clerk turned to John Chapter 3 and pointing to verse 16 she began reading, "For God so loved the world, that He gave His only begotten Son, that whoever believes in Him should not perish, but have eternal life." That's what is called the good news in a nut shell. Let's go up front and I will ring this up for you. This book will increase your wisdom and knowledge about what is important in life."

For some strange reason Boston felt at peace saying, "That's what I want to know!"

He decided to park the car in the drive way and walk to the house. Going in the back door he could hear his voice on the recorder, He quietly poured himself a cup of coffee and slipped out the back door. He sat there staring into space being a little anxious about what he would face once the tape ended. He didn't have to wait long, his dad's voice came from the back door, "Well hello Boston!" he exclaimed. Boston turned and entered the house where he was greeted by the voices of his mom and sister. At first they were talking over each other, he stood there, taking a sip of coffee before saying, "I can only answer your questions one at a time."

His mother spoke first, it was more of a statement than a question, "If we had known what kind of people you were getting involved with."

Boston quickly interrupted her, "You are only focusing on what they used to be, I saw what they became." Boston's calm response seemed to have an effect.

His dad had two questions, "Did all of this happen or is this your imagination for a book? If this actually happened where do you stand with the authorities regarding Jiggs' murder?"

The kitchen went quiet immediately waiting for the response. Boston's response was slow and deliberate, "I did lose my friend that evening. A person I thought highly of and respected and wanted to emulate. It is an ongoing investigation, the sheriff knows where I am at and how to get in touch with me should he need to. If they find the men, and if there is a trial, I will testify for my friend who no longer can speak for himself. I have learned many lessons these past six months, life lessons. I try not to take anything for granted, and enjoy each day God gives us as a gift which it is."

His sister spoke next, "Whether this is true or not, you have written and experienced the dangers of ranching and ranch work. I think this would make good reading material, and you say it is true, so I want to know more about this girl you named Shylo and who really is Jo?"

Boston smiled as he responded, "Jo is the glue that seems to hold it all together, I know where she gets her strength and from that source she can and does strengthen others, so does the lady Adeline. They have developed a strong relationship with the Lord Jesus basing all she does on that. In addition she is a wonderful cook. Ike's not a bad cook either, sorry mom."

His dad quickly interjected, "A train robber in this day and age? That's hard to believe!"

Boston shook his head up and down, "Yeah I couldn't figure that either. He evidently was so far into the bottle he wasn't thinking straight. Especially attempting something like that almost literally in his backyard. It never occurred to him that somebody he knew or knew him would be on that train. The booze had clouded all reason and logic. Foolishly thinking there would be enough money to assist in anything except buying more booze. Even though he knew the back country well, he still went home to sleep, and that's where they arrested him. It's probably the last train robbery in Colorado."

His line of conversation was interrupted by his sister, "Wait a minute! You didn't answer my question concerning this Shylo character. Is there something more between you and her?"

The whole family was silent as Boston responded, "Well, ah, I think she is someone special, I do like her very much and admire her. She works full time and helps her grandmother, neighbors and even strangers like me, before herself. I was not able to spend much time with her to know more about her, but I would like to."

His mother suggested we carry this conversation on at a restaurant celebrating his book and the beginning of a new career as an author. They all began moving about except Boston who stopped them when he said, "I sent a letter to Ike and Jo the day I arrived back in Hartford, asking for a job on their ranch."

His dad interrupted him almost mid-sentence, "You're not serious about that? What kind of a life is that? What kind of a future will you have? You've got a good job. Have you lost your senses?

Boston, turned and looked him straight in the eyes and quietly replied, "I spent a lot of time by myself and that gives one a chance to think. The clear air, natural beauty and the slowness of pace seems to clean your mind out of the non-essential things. I found myself enjoying being outdoors, experiencing life with animals both wild and domestic enduring the elements whatever came. At first it was a little scary, but then the beauty and solitude gave me serenity. As for the future, I don't know anything about it but then again do any of us know what the future will bring? I enjoyed each day as it came hard or easy. The money wasn't what drove me, remember I paid them, and for what I got, I feel like I still owe them. I found something I liked, even though I don't know everything, I have a desire to know and learn all I can. It's the kind of learning that can only be passed on by experienced people, "hands" as they call themselves. I want to learn from those top hands, and strive to become one. That can only happen by learning from others and experience. No, I haven't lost my senses, I found them. Sorry if this seems to disappoint you but I always thought you wanted me to find my nitch. These people in unnoticed places doing ordinary deeds have influenced me more than any professor in lofty halls of academia. In simple lives I saw how life is to be lived. Working with others, seeing their needs, giving aide when not asked for, listening and praying. The two of you have provided me with more than most children have received and I am grateful. Now I am launching out on my own."

His mother spoke first, "When does this job start?"

Boston paused and reaching into his pocket he said, "I don't know, I haven't opened the letter that arrived today."

THE END